PENGUI

Ribbons
of Grace

© Alan Dove

Maxine Alterio grew up in Invercargill and currently
lives in Dunedin, where she works as a tertiary educator.
She has a BA and a MA (with distinction in Education)
from the University of Otago, and also holds a Diploma
in Teaching (Tertiary). Her first collection, *Live News
and Other Stories*, was published in 2005 by Steele
Roberts Ltd. Several short stories have appeared in
anthologies such as *Penguin 25 New Fiction* (Penguin
Books (NZ), 1998); *Best New Zealand Fiction Volume
3* (Random House, 2006), and *Myth of the 21st
Century* (Reed, 2006), and others have been broadcast
on Radio New Zealand National. She is also co-author
of *Learning through Storytelling in Higher Education:
Using Reflection and Experience to Improve Learning*,
published by Dunmore Press in 2002 and Kogan Page/
RoutledgeFalmer in 2003.

Ribbons of Grace

Maxine Alterio

PENGUIN BOOKS

PENGUIN BOOKS

Published by the Penguin Group

Penguin Group (NZ), 67 Apollo Drive, Rosedale

North Shore 0632, New Zealand (a division of Pearson New Zealand Ltd)

Penguin Group (USA) Inc., 375 Hudson Street,

New York, New York 10014, USA

Penguin Group (Canada), 90 Eglinton Avenue East, Suite 700, Toronto,

Ontario, M4P 2Y3, Canada (a division of Pearson Penguin Canada Inc.)

Penguin Books Ltd, 80 Strand, London, WC2R 0RL, England

Penguin Ireland, 25 St Stephen's Green,

Dublin 2, Ireland (a division of Penguin Books Ltd)

Penguin Group (Australia), 250 Camberwell Road, Camberwell,

Victoria 3124, Australia (a division of Pearson Australia Group Pty Ltd)

Penguin Books India Pvt Ltd, 11, Community Centre,

Panchsheel Park, New Delhi – 110 017, India

Penguin Books (South Africa) (Pty) Ltd, 24 Sturdee Avenue,

Rosebank, Johannesburg 2196, South Africa

Penguin Books Ltd, Registered Offices: 80 Strand, London, WC2R 0RL, England

First published by Penguin Group (NZ), 2007
This edition published 2008

1 3 5 7 9 10 8 6 4 2

Copyright © Maxine Alterio, 2007

The right of Maxine Alterio to be identified as the author of this work in terms of
section 96 of the Copyright Act 1994 is hereby asserted.

Designed by Mary Egan
Typeset by Egan Reid
Printed in Australia by McPherson's Printing Group

ISBN: 978 0 14 300930 6

A catalogue record for this book is available
from the National Library of New Zealand.

www.penguin.co.nz

For Verona

CONTENTS

Water, first creature of the gods.
It dances in many masks.
GEORGE MACKAY BROWN

There is no calamity greater than lavish desires,
no greater guilt than discontentment,
and no greater disaster than greed.
LAO-TZU

Prologue

I come with a heavy heart to my daughter's fung mu in Arrowtown, where she lies in her father's arms. My fingers run across the tombstone that bears both their names: Fang Yin and Conran. Each character is chiselled with love – even 'r', which I cannot pronounce clearly, so he is always Con-Lan to me. For fifteen years I have come to this place. Now MaMa calls me home. Her voice travels across the sea and mountains and years.

Some people say, forget old life when go to new. But the past enlightens us. It cannot be left behind. Today, like the wind, it circles around the illustrious mountains that overlook this well-positioned site on a small hill facing the gorge through which the Arrow River flows, its gold once mined by industrious hands like mine. Sometimes my memories of those years feel heavier than a load of wood on tired shoulders. Other times, light as air. Such variations concern me. I do not want any aspect of my sojourn to fade when I return to China. So I am here today at Fang Yin and

Con-Lan's fung mu to tell my story until it feels part of my skin. But it will not travel in straight lines because I do not want demons to steal my words. And I will speak of shadow times, as well as happy ones, for stories, like people, have many sides. We must study them in different ways before we learn what they have to teach us.

Early this morning the sun rose round as an orange and hot as the fires of love, warming the already dust-dry ground outside Con-Lan's schist cottage, while inside the whitewashed walls gleamed like skin on a pail of milk. These walls are thick, so the cottage stays cool in summer and warm in winter. There are two rooms: one for cooking and the other to sleep in. Con-Lan built a fireplace in each room and positioned a window in the bedroom. But our daughter, Fang Yin, did not see the stars through this glass pane. She was only at our friend Ida's home.

In the gorge the ice-heavy river resembles a mass of broken glass. On either side poppy seeds, dropped from the soles of boots worn by miners from California, germinate in pockets of dirt and shingle. Soon they will flower again and hang like coloured lanterns from the cliffs. Fang Yin never saw them either. Her eyes closed too soon.

Con-Lan and I loved among these poppies. We filled the space between the river and mountains and sky, flattened the tussock grass and warmed the schist. And, in a hut, high on the side of a mountain, we burrowed deep into each other's hearts. Happiness lived within us until our secret flew out the door, tumbled down the gorge and rushed into town on the wind. Dark times followed.

You see, Chinese sojourners were not welcome in this small mining town in the South Island of New Zealand. The British miners resented us reworking their abandoned claims and finding gold they had missed. Their women feared us because we looked different, with our hair in queues and our shoulder poles. Local merchants complained because we bought supplies from our own shopkeepers and hawkers. Bankers did not like us sending money back to China. But family always comes first, not Arrow settlers who do not understand a sojourner's duty. So I closed my ears to their angry words and lowered my head when they stared with eyes the colour of water. Cold eyes, I thought, until I grew to love Con-Lan's.

We wondered whose eyes Fang Yin would have. Black like mine – held in still, white moons, or big and wide and blue like ribbons of Orkney sky.

Each Thursday my British friend, Ida, walks with me to Fang Yin and Con-Lan's fung mu. On the way we discuss what poultices and potions Ida has recorded in her nursing scrapbook, and who has asked me to write a letter or read one received from China. But today I am alone, for reasons already explained.

My story will travel through the years: fifteen in China, where BaBa ferried opium up a river larger than this valley; the other twenty-four spent here in Arrowtown among the mountains and gullies of inland Otago, where I mined with Soo Tie, worked as an interpreter for Su Sing and later washed hospital linen. Then Con-Lan will take up the story, returning from time to time to Orkney, a land north of Scotland, surrounded by wild seas. After he shares his memories, Ida will give her version of events.

We will talk in English, for it was Con-Lan's language and would have been Fang Yin's. I speak it without thinking now, although on frosty nights when stars fill the sky and I walk in the hills until my bones feel like dust, I dream in Chinese. Then I travel back to a time when the only words I knew were those of my ancestors. They speak to me today, filling my head with images of Pong Woo village, where MaMa traded gossip along with goods, her tales, colourful as kites, flying between the market stalls. And in the fields, among cabbages and beans, Second Brother Fu Ling showed me how to draw Chinese characters in the dirt. He also taught me English words sojourners brought back from New Gold Hills. He shared others, too – learned from missionaries as they passed through our village, talking about their god and showing pictures of a man with straggly hair wearing a long white tunic. All the while our bellies rumbled with hunger, although we farmed every scrap of earth BaBa leased from our landlord, Chang Huan.

In Arrowtown land is more plentiful than people. But farmers, such as Ida's husband Alfred, plant fewer crops than Second Brother Fu Ling did in Pong Woo. And children play under trees that do not bear fruit or nuts but have pleasing shapes, and leaves that change colour with the seasons.

When I first arrived in this goldfield town I dreamed of China, where banyan and kumquat grow; and crows and grackle, sometimes plover, nest near the water-pine and tallow trees. In these dreams MaMa pleaded with BaBa. Her voice sounded like a strange wind that had lost its way in the cane field; his rasped back and forth until she was silent. Then her eyes drank in a thousand sorrows as BaBa put on his Tsung Fa river clothes.

During my childhood I often asked why they argued. My questions exploded around them like firecrackers. On one such occasion my meddling caused BaBa to strike me and MaMa to say, 'Ming Yuet, "Moon who burns too bright" – I should have given you a timid name.' Rivers of sadness ran down her face, so I blew her cheeks dry as she helped me up. 'My Little Wind,' she called me, and held me tight.

These days I have different dreams. Now MaMa pulls me back to China with a rope made from yellow and blue headscarves, but it sags like Grandmother and Great-auntie's old nan, which resemble wizened pears, making it impossible for me to hold on. I wake with empty arms, aware that MaMa's life contains more than my memories. But we have not talked as women yet, so I do not know her stories. I was a young girl full of selfish thoughts when I left China.

'Journey' was the first big English word I learned. Second Brother taught it to me as he prepared for his own sojourn. 'Landscape', was another, heard for the first time as I travelled with Chinese companions through inland Otago to Arrowtown. A British man with hair the colour of preserved lemons, walking ahead with two pale-skinned miners, said, 'What a landscape!' as we entered the Arrow valley, which in 1871 had few crops. Instead, stacks of grey rock littered the fields. The yellow-haired miner took a pad and pencil from his swag and drew pictures as the sky curdled in the heat, changing from saffron to amber to cerise. Then it wept. 'A sun-shower,' said this same man, giving me another English word.

Minutes later the sky grew dark and shadows formed on the mountains. I stood beneath them and thought of my family: Second Brother Fu Ling, a wise stone showing me a new path; First Sister Li Mei, sliding down a schist face so fast she breaks into a million pebbles; First Brother, a shadow crouched in fissures BaBa carves with shame; Second Sister Nuo, a silk cocoon, floating across the purple-bruised sky; MaMa, a bush of sweet thyme, hiding me from danger, while on the ground Grandmother and Great-auntie rest in skins the colour of dried leaves, and Day-Day, my youngest brother, along with First Sister's river baby, who does not have a name, turn to dust beneath my feet.

Arrowtown chilled my bones that first winter, although it was already late August when we arrived. Our words froze in the air, making them easy for demons to steal and turn into lies. Only way to discover truth is to tell many-sided stories. They transport us across the bridge of time and knowing, which is why I am here today. Once our stories have been told and pressed like flowers onto my skin, Fang Yin and Con-Lan will rest peacefully in the next world.

PART ONE

Ming Yuet

ONE

Dragon Fire Steals MaMa's Heart

I will draw a map in the dirt to show where I lived, on the tip of the Pearl River delta in Kwangtung province. Then I will place myself like a shadow on the wall of my childhood. First, I make Upper Panyu almost square. North is Hua county, and east, the White Cloud Hills. South is Canton. See Tsung Fa, which MaMa calls 'River of Shame'. Lorchas and junks, some with bamboo-matting roofs, use this waterway. All ride low, weighed down with animals and belongings. Entire lives are lived on these boats. People with what Ida calls 'serious afflictions' cannot leave unless family members carry them to land on their backs.

Now come away from the river and follow the path to Pong Woo, a large village with an ancestral hall for each clan. Inside the halls are tablets that describe every ancestor back to the founders. Other villages on the delta are smaller. But each has a market where goods such as fish, pigs and baskets are sold. You can also buy bamboo hats that shade all parts of the face from the sun.

I often accompanied MaMa to the market to sell duck eggs. On the way she would tell me stories about her ancestors, who came from a different village. 'They could write many characters, Ming Yuet. Their inscriptions were highly prized. To have one hanging on your door was considered lucky. If my father had not died when I was young, or if he'd had sons, I would not have been given to a man who could not write characters. Illustrious ancestors are important. They remind us of better times.'

Temples are also significant. When there is a drought and the earth dries up and rice cannot grow, the men in our village go to the temple and pray for rain. Second Brother went with BaBa once. He told me later that three men placed an idol in a sling, which they hung over a bamboo pole, rocking it back and forth. A favourable turn to the right meant a promise of rain. If the idol did not swing in this direction they had to dig deep pits and tread water-wheels night and day, for they could not afford to lose one grain of rice.

Fields in stubble signify the quiet time before spring planting. Sweet potatoes and water caltrop will have been harvested. Also ginger root, arrowroot, melon and taro. Land is well used. Rice is planted three times a year. Nothing is wasted; hungry people live in this village.

Walk back through the years with me. See the girls with heavy baskets hanging from their shoulder poles? Hear them giggle as Second Brother walks by.

'They all want you as their husband. Who will you choose?'

'I am not interested in their foolish games, Ming Yuet. Find me a good drawing stick.'

Look, there's our village pond, stocked with frogs and fish: some caught in the paddyfields, others bought at the market. Pond water also has other uses. When flames leap like dragons into the air, villagers form two lines. People in one line pass buckets of water towards the fire, while those in the other send the empty ones back to be refilled, toiling until only sodden ash remains.

There is my childhood home. Unlike Con-Lan's cottage it has no windows. Just sun-dried bricks bound with sand, clay and lime. Pong Woo bricks do not sparkle in the sun like Arrow schist, but they make sound dwellings. See that two-storey house on the left? It was built with money sent back by a sojourner. 'Dutiful son in New Gold Hills,' said the family as the house rose, symbolising their new wealth and prosperity. Sometimes a sojourner's money bought more than a new house and good food. One man paid for a well so his mother, and other women, such as MaMa, did not have to walk great distances to fetch clean water.

There's MaMa standing in the doorway with me by her side. I am ten years old, so it must be 1866.

'Fu Ling,' MaMa calls, 'Take Ming Yuet to gather firewood.'

I run towards Second Brother, eager to leave behind the smell of Grandmother and Great-auntie, who sit in the corner of our hut rubbing their cramped feet. Today I am hungry and have bad thoughts. I want these two old women to go away so there is more food for me. First Sister Li Mei is hungry too. She needs food to make milk for her new baby. He cries, so I pick him up. He sucks at my tunic. First Sister watches but does not smile. She did not cry when her other baby died. Not once.

I ask Second Brother about First Sister.

'Why did she get a new baby?'

'A river pirate gave him to her, Ming Yuet.'

'But she does not like him.'

'Sometimes we get things we do not want.'

'Like boils and toothache?'

He shakes his head and smiles. 'You are funny, Ming Yuet.'

I follow Second Brother along the strips of turf that divide the fields. He shows me how to measure their width. Every day he teaches me something new, sometimes in Chinese, other times in English.

'Now it's your turn.'

I measure as he asks. 'Between six and eight inches,' I say.

He laughs and says, 'Always you give wide answers. Never narrow ones.'

We follow the path that takes us to the pines, where we gather twigs for MaMa's fire. Once we have an adequate bundle, we sit in the shade and watch the crows peck at small cones to dislodge insects.

'I wish I was a bird.'

Second Brother Fu Ling writes the characters for bird in the dirt for me to learn. 'Where would you fly?'

'Far away, and I would take you and MaMa on my wings. We would cross Tsung Fa, maybe go to the mountains.'

'Bandits roam the hills. Better to stay near water where it is easier to escape.'

Second Brother makes a shape in the dirt.

'What is that?'

'Pearl River delta,' he says.

Next he draws a river with waves, as though a storm has blown in, one that could toss lorchas and junks around like tea-leaves. BaBa and First Brother do not go on the river in such weather. Instead they fill their pipes, lie on the bed and smoke. MaMa makes me and Second Sister Nuo sit in the darkest corner of the house with our faces to the wall, bent over like Grandmother and Great-auntie. Then she cleans and sweeps and curses until the river men come for First Sister. When they take her away, her baby cries. Only BaBa is happy. A dreamy smile floats across his sallow bony face.

BaBa's need for opium still saddens me. Other disturbing memories have also returned. Like the river pirate with greedy eyes who came for First Sister and poked me with a stick as he passed, saying, 'Fresh meat tastes good.' My stomach heaved with fear. Would he take me next time instead of First Sister? I wanted to float away like BaBa, so after the river man left I said, 'Can I smoke Dragon Fire?' MaMa's face hardened. Her eyes turned cold. She picked up a stick and hit me until I was wet with blood. 'Never,' she said. 'You understand?'

Second Brother fetched the water bucket. I cried like First Sister's river baby as he washed me. My bright red blood did not make me think of happiness. I was happy, though, when Second Brother took me outside, away from MaMa's black mood.

'Can you keep a secret, Ming Yuet?'

Honoured that Second Brother trusted me, I nodded and sat at his feet.

'I plan to go to a distant land.'

'How many days' walk is it from Pong Woo?'

'It is further than you think. I must sail across an ocean wider than China.'

At first I could not imagine anything that large, but I thought again. 'Is this ocean bigger than the sky?'

Second Brother ruffled my hair and grinned. 'The sky is greater.'

'Does it cover Canton?'

He laughed again. 'Yes, all people live under the same sky.'

'Even those in distant lands?'

Second Brother nodded.

'You might get lonely in this place.'

'Men from Upper Panyu are there already. Do not look troubled, Ming Yuet. I will be safe.'

'How did you learn about it?'

'Men talk of nothing else in the village square. They say gold is as plentiful as animal droppings.'

'Can anyone find this gold?'

'Yes, industrious miners can earn a good living and send plenty of money home,' Second Brother said.

'If you send BaBa extra taels will the river men stop taking First Sister?'

'I cannot help Li Mei. She is too damaged. But soon I will send money home to keep you safe, Ming Yuet.'

'BaBa should not let them take her. I hate opium. BaBa should find a new way to pay Chang Huan. He owns our fields – he does not own us. Are there greedy men in every village?'

'Yes, there are, little hot-head.'

I did get angry but never around BaBa because he might have given me away too.

'Does BaBa want to travel to this new land?'

'No, he only wants opium. So does First Brother.'

'Why?'

'They smoke to dull their pain.'

But the pirates hurt First Sister, not Baba and First Brother. 'I don't understand. What pain do they feel?'

'You ask too many questions, Ming Yuet. Let's take MaMa's wood back.'

She was waiting silently in the doorway, her body still, but her eyes flicked over me to check whether I was still in one piece. Her hand stroked my hair as we entered the hut. I helped Great-auntie hobble outside to relieve herself in a pit overrun with rats and flies and other vile pests.

Great-auntie and Grandmother had Golden Lilies: tiny feet shaped like lotus pods. They could not walk without an arm or a stick to lean on. Cramp-footed women considered it an honour, not a hardship, to have Golden Lilies. Grandmother and Great-auntie told me their stories one afternoon as I washed their feet.

'I was seven years old,' began Grandmother. 'My mother made me eat red bean dumplings for weeks. Then one day she took me outside and put my feet in a basin of hot water. While they soaked, she threw grain to the rooster. When the rooster pecked at it, my mother reached down, grabbed his neck and twisted, snapping it like a twig. But instead of pulling out the feathers and cooking him, she sliced open his chest with a sharp knife. To my horror, she then took my feet out of the basin and plunged them straight into the carcass. His blood was hot and smelly. I screamed and screamed.

But she took no notice. Later she rubbed my feet hard, all the time bending them back and forth. I will never forget the pain. Soon all the toes on my right foot, except the biggest, were folded against my sole. Then she bound one foot with strips of cotton, pressing my four smaller toes down and in towards the heel. She bound both feet this way. I suffered greatly. That night I took the bindings off. Next morning my mother was very angry. She said, 'You will not get a husband without beautiful feet,' and bound them again, sewing the cloth firmly so I could not loosen a single stitch.'

While Grandmother talked, her sister nodded and made noises. 'Eeeeee! Agghhhh!' Great-auntie's face was wrinkly as a pickled walnut. She was smaller than Grandmother and her hands resembled bird claws, but she made the best dumplings.

'Was it the same for you, Great-auntie?'

She smiled and clicked her tongue, which meant she was ready to talk and I had better listen because she would not tell me twice.

'There were no dumplings or roosters because our mother wanted to speed up the process but, like Grandmother, I experienced terrible pain. My mother bent each foot back, then wound strips of rough cloth around them, saying, 'Quicker feet die, sooner find husband.' To help them die, she put a chip of porcelain between two toes. You cannot imagine the pain. My feet rotted slowly, like two starving animals trapped in a cave. All my life I have this misery for a husband who thrashed me.'

I decided to give her an extra spoon of jook at supper to make up for her hurt.

'How old were you, Great-auntie?'

'Same age as my mother when she had her feet bound – five, maybe six years old.'

'Why hasn't MaMa got Golden Lilies?'

'She said her mother tried, but she kept undoing the bindings,' said Grandmother. 'Even when they were sewed tightly she found a way to loosen them.'

'Perhaps she did not want a husband,' I said.

'Everyone wants a husband, Ming Yuet, even you,' said Grandmother. 'And it pays to remember that Cantonese men look for good-natured young women with thrifty habits.'

'I want love, not a husband.'

Great-auntie's wrinkles deepened into furrows. Her two front teeth – the only ones left – wobbled. Afraid they would fall out, I reached up and pushed them back down into her gums. Great-auntie slapped her hands together and laughed. Grandmother joined in. Soon our little house rocked with happiness.

Two days later I asked MaMa if she remembered undoing her bindings. She looked surprised, as though I had unlocked an aspect of her past with a key she did not know I had.

'My mother thought she was doing a good thing, Ming Yuet. Never think otherwise.'

I could not comment, for I never met that grandmother. She died a long time ago. Only BaBa's mother and auntie lived with us.

'Is BaBa ever sorry after the pirates take Li Mei away?'

MaMa's face clouded over. I thought she was angry because I had forgotten to address Li Mei as First Sister, which I must do because she is older and therefore deserves such respect. But she said, 'Hush, Ming Yuet, or bad things will happen to you as well.'

Her reply annoyed and frightened me. I wanted answers, not threats. She was full of secrets. No wonder Second Brother wanted to go away. MaMa would miss him, though, since he was kind and stood up to BaBa and worked hard in the fields. A sliver of fear entered my heart. It ached like the porcelain chip Great-auntie's mother had put between her toes. If Second Brother left, what would happen to me? Would I starve and rot and die like Golden Lilies? Or would the river men give me babies? I lay beside First Sister. Her swollen nan felt hard as two rocks. I closed my eyes and tried to remember what she had been like before the river men turned her to stone. Had she talked about her dreams while she helped First Brother collect twigs for MaMa?

What I saw was something I did not understand. Fire and smoke in our village, people running. Me wrapped in a cloth sling tied to Second Brother's back. He was maybe eight years old. My feet banged against the backs of his knees. MaMa whispered, 'Quick, Fu Ling, go to the pines and hide.' I bounced up and down. Behind me, men with knives went into our home. Screams erupted – so long and loud I thought the whole world was crying.

There are other memories, too. MaMa's dead baby, buried far away from the bones of our ancestors, and First Brother's blood seeping through the bed. First Sister Li Mei so quiet, and Second Sister Nuo sprawled on the floor like a young bird fallen from its nest. She never spoke again.

A week later, BaBa took Second Sister away. The night before, MaMa prepared extra food. After supper she took Second Sister outside, where she talked to her in low whispers. They came back with bowed heads, patting each other. Something had changed. Benevolence surrounded them.

Instead of going to the fields early next morning as MaMa had instructed, Second Brother and I hid behind a stone wall. Grandmother and Great-auntie wailed when BaBa and Second Sister emerged carrying blue cotton bags. I do not know what was inside them. Second Brother drew sad faces in the dirt but I stomped on his pictures. Then I cried. 'Do not worry, Ming Yuet,' Second Brother said. 'I will keep you safe.'

Five moons later BaBa returned without Second Sister. After he lit his pipe I said, 'Where is she now?'

He did not answer, only stared at me with dull, empty eyes. MaMa sent me her do-not-ask-any-more-questions face, so I slid onto Grandmother's lap, and she whispered, 'Nuo is at the silk factory.'

'Why? What will she do? She will miss us.'

'Nuo will turn cocoons into silk. She might be happy.'

I did not think so because she would not be with me or MaMa or anyone else in our family. 'When I am older I will fetch her home.'

'Hush, child. There's nothing more to say or do.'

Soon afterwards BaBa worked longer hours on the river and First Brother joined him. Sometimes they disappeared for weeks, occasionally arriving home with gifts. Once BaBa gave MaMa a beautiful bowl decorated with green birds and blue flowers. The next time the river men came for First Sister, MaMa picked it up and threw it at BaBa, saying, 'Dragon Fire has stolen my heart.' The bowl flew over his head and landed with a loud thunk on the ground, where it broke into small pieces. Maybe MaMa's heart shattered, too, but I did not hear it, although her eyes glinted like shards of porcelain. She ran outside; her samfu, tunic and trousers, flapped around her like an angry rooster. BaBa sighed and lit his spirit lamp. He joined First Brother on the bed and put a pea-size ball of brown opium paste on the end of his long, blunt needle. Then he held it over the flame of the lamp until it bubbled and swelled and turned golden. After he had cooked the paste three times, he rolled it back into a round shape and pushed it into a hole in the bowl of his pipe. He held the bowl close to the lamp so the flame could hit the opium ball, then he and First Brother took several hard sucks on the pipe. The air became heavy with a creamy sweetness, and another smell, like peanuts roasting.

That night I thought of MaMa's life, and First Sister's, too. Because I did not know whether Second Sister was happy in the silk factory, I thought about her as well. I wanted a different life, away from river men and opium and danger; maybe in a country where gold was plentiful. A warm haze tucked itself around me. I would ask Second Brother to take me with him, like he did on the Day of Fire and Knives.

TWO

Moon Lights Fu Ling's Path to New Gold Hills

The day after Second Brother told MaMa he was leaving our village, a great mist hung over the fields, hiding us from BaBa. Second Brother drew a map in the dirt: China large as a melon and New Gold Hills smaller than a grain of rice.

'How will you get to this place?'

'A boat will take me, Ming Yuet. I will find gold and send money home to build our family a fine house. Then you will be safe. Not long – maybe four years.'

'I could come with you. Clean your house. Cook, too.'

'Girls are not allowed to leave China,' Second Brother said, as spears of white and yellow light flashed across the darkening sky.

Maybe the whole world was angry about this silly rule. 'It's not fair. I want to go.'

'MaMa will look after you, Ming Yuet,' Second Brother continued.

'She can't do anything. Look at First Sister Li Mei.'

What had MaMa wanted at my age? Did she have a muhng, a dream tucked into her heart like a sleeping bird? One she hoped would open its wings and carry her back to the village where she had illustrious ancestors? I tried to imagine her as a young woman living in a grand house with her father, but could only see a tired face gazing across the delta and worn hands cooking and cleaning for BaBa in Pong Woo. Sadness came over me like a late afternoon shadow. I did not want such a life.

'How will you get to New Gold Hills, Second Brother?'

'Sail in a junk to Canton, then go on another boat to Hong Kong, where a ship called *Jean Sands* waits to take me across the ocean.'

'How long will your journey take?'

He opened his hands wide. 'See?'

I nodded solemnly, thinking it was too far for him to travel alone.

'We will sail for a long time, and see no land for many weeks.'

I could not imagine sailing that far. My hands trembled. I clasped them together, hoping to hide my distress. 'When will you leave?'

'After spring planting.'

'How much does such a journey cost?'

'Forty taels of silver, which I plan to get from Chang Huan.'

'Why will he give you money?'

'It's a loan, Ming Yuet. I must pay him back with interest.'

Boats have dark places, I thought. Perhaps I could turn myself into a black snake, slither aboard and hide. I smiled. Thinking I approved of his plan, Second Brother grinned back. But I did not want to stay in Pong Woo without him. Better to work hard, help MaMa, be kind to everyone, even First Sister's river baby, then pack my life into a bag and slip away.

From daybreak to dusk, Second Brother walked behind the water buffalo working the plough, while I followed, breaking stubborn clods with a stick until a fine red blanket covered the fields.

Day-Day trailed after us, making clucking noises like a foolish chicken. He helped plant cabbage seedlings in straight rows, along with sweet potatoes, arrowroot and water chestnut. None of which would fill my belly. I would leave the delta before they were harvested. Grasshoppers jumped in my stomach as I looked across the fields. I settled them by packing memories into my heart: mahogany-coloured earth, songs of delta birds and the smell of peach blossom. I also thought about New Gold Hills. Would anything remind me of Pong Woo? How soon before I could send money home to MaMa?

No one watched me shed my Pong Woo life. Or saw it lie discarded like an old snakeskin on the ground.

MaMa salted fish for Second Brother's journey. What could I take? My answer arrived when Chang Huan appeared at our door. His puffy cheeks and thick frog lips jumped up and down as he demanded his rent. A bad thought came to me. I tried to be honourable and push it away but it kept returning. Three times I went to Chang Huan's store at night, wriggling under the wall like a rat, and filled my sack with rice and tins of salted fish. Chang Huan wouldn't miss it. His belly hung over his trousers in big pillow rolls, giving the impression that it could fall to the dirt floor of his shop and roll out the door.

I also took seeds, along with BaBa's sharpest knife and a fish-hook First Brother made me a long time ago. While he sharpened the barb, I had plagued him with questions. 'Ming Yuet,' he yelled, 'if I see your tongue again I will pull it out with this hook.' I was too scared to sleep that night. What if my mouth fell open and First Brother carried out his threat?

This experience taught me the value of remaining silent. I hid my sack of supplies under a pile of stones stacked against the east wall of our home. Every time I walked by, a great happiness entered me, resting peacefully in my heart until I saw MaMa or First Sister, then it disappeared like a stone dropped in a fish pond.

On Second Brother's last day MaMa prepared a feast. That morning I washed Grandmother and Great-auntie's feet with care and brushed their scraggly white hair one hundred times. I would miss their stories and hugs. My heart filled with sadness and the grasshoppers in my stomach returned. I emptied my sickness, along with the contents of Great-auntie's night pot, into the pit outside.

'You're a helpful worker today, Ming Yuet,' MaMa said later as I spooned steaming noodles into her best dishes.

She looked proud, and also sad, for Second Brother was her most dutiful son.

'It is an honour to work beside you, MaMa.'

Her eyes rested on mine. Like water scooped from a well we drank each other's love.

Twenty-three people from our village came to say goodbye to Second Brother. Another family's Second Son was also going to New Gold Hills. Like Second Brother, he had promised to send money back to his family, so there was a big celebration. Four men got yám-jeui – so drunk they rolled in the dirt like pigs, which made Day-Day laugh.

'Well, Fu Ling, this is your last night in Pong Woo,' said a neighbour, patting him on the back.

'Four years and I will come home with many taels,' Second Brother said.

'You will live like an emperor, and have no trouble finding a good wife. I have a good-natured cousin . . .'

Second Brother smiled politely but I could tell he was not interested.

After everyone left, MaMa said, 'Fu Ling, I have made a special gift for you.' She reached into the box at the foot of her and BaBa's bed and handed Fu Ling a blue cotton shirt, which Great-auntie had folded earlier into a pleasing shape. The old woman beamed when Second Brother bowed to her as well. To Mama's joy, the shirt fitted perfectly. We laughed and bowed as Second Brother turned this way and that, before strutting outside and raising his long arms towards the cloudless night sky.

'Look, the moon lights Fu Ling's path to New Gold Hills,' MaMa said in a choked voice. Great-auntie ran her hand gently down MaMa's arm, a small kindness to aid a big sorrow. I wanted to hug everyone, even BaBa, who had graciously looked after our guests. Instead, I said to MaMa, 'I will say goodbye to Second Brother now and go to the fields at daybreak.'

'Yes, very well, Ming Yuet.'

MaMa walked over and brushed a strand of hair from my cheek. I still carry this touch. Skin remembers the feel of love.

Second Brother and I sat near my hidden sack and stared into the night.

'See those stones, Ming Yuet? Imagine each is a person.'

I nodded, even though my imagination was not as good as his.

'Every day this family carries their heavy burdens around with them. Nothing changes until a middle-sized stone wriggles out from under the pile and makes its way down a different path. The other stones have to move to fill the space, so something changes for them, too.' Second Brother's hands stroked the air like paintbrushes.

'That is a beautiful story,' I said.

'Always remember that one small movement can make a big difference.'

'You are a good son and brother,' I said, pressing my cheek against his skin.

Fu Ling's face felt soft as mulberries. Village girls smiled behind their hands whenever they saw him. But he never stopped to talk – always hurried by, eager to draw pictures, which is another way to tell a story.

Second Brother was like that middle-sized stone. He was never meant to be a farmer, but BaBa did not understand. Each time he caught Second Brother drawing and making characters he beat him.

'I've told you: work not draw.' Second Brother's response was always the same: 'My hands and heart are free things.'

'And you are a good sister, Ming Yuet,' Fu Ling said. 'Try not to worry. Soon I will send money.'

Yes, two lots, I thought. 'Who will take you to Canton?'

'Yee Loi. We leave early in the morning, before light, with men from Tong Pooi and Shui Lek.'

Yee Loi's junk was the biggest on the river. I could reach it quickly if I took the south path. 'Every day I will look at Tsung Fa and send you good wishes.'

'Look, but be careful. The river can be dangerous, like the mountains.'

I shuddered, imagining what it might contain. Second Brother put his arm around my shoulder. Together we had thirty-two years: fifteen for me, seventeen for him.

'We will always be under the same sky, Ming Yuet,' Second Brother said. 'Talk to it and I will hear you.'

'What will I say?'

'Tell me what you think and feel and learn. I will do the same.'

'Could you send pictures to me in the clouds?'

'Yes, I will do as you ask.'

We sat in silence for many minutes, looking across the delta, no doubt both hoping for a prosperous sojourn.

I did not sleep that night. Instead I listened to BaBa's smelly bottom noises, First Brother's dream cries and Great-grandmother's painful whimpers when her Golden Lilies hurt. These familiar sounds comforted me. Would I ever hear them again?

Long before daylight I dressed and crept outside. MaMa may have stirred and said, 'Goodbye, Ming Yuet,' but perhaps I dreamed it. After kissing the door of our house eight times, once for everyone inside, I wiped my wet face with the sleeve of my tunic and walked towards the south path, collecting my bag on the way. The grasshoppers in my stomach jumped as though they had landed on hot embers. I felt excited and sad and scared. Would I find Yee Loi's junk? Could I hide on it without being seen? What would Canton be like? Was the boat ready to sail to New Gold Hills? How would I get on board? These questions buzzed inside me.

My nightly visits to Chang Huan's store had prepared me for the ghostly shapes and sleeping village noises. I walked quickly, crossing the fields exactly as planned. My feet flew across the strips of turf. Soon I was on the path that would take me to the river. Shun, who lived near us, was taken by river men when she was twelve, and her cousin the year before. I imagined pirates everywhere. Each shadow made me jump.

My bag soon felt heavy, so I stepped off the path to rest. Darkness played tricks on me. Bushes turned into fearsome creatures. My mouth went dry and my heart thumped. Was I doing the right thing? Should I go back?

A noise interrupted my thoughts. Others were on the path too. They smelled sickly and sweet, like BaBa when he used his pipe. One relieved himself and sniffed the air. Another spat into a bush beside me. Fear squeezed my heart – thrump, thrump, thrump. I thought it would be heard but the pirates walked on. Benevolent spirits were with me that night.

I counted to one hundred before standing. Then I made my way down to the river, where the water slapped against the edge of the bank like a hungry cat licking an empty dish. My night eyes skimmed across the shadowy surface. I needed to find Yee Loi's junk quickly because I did not want to linger on the riverbank, where I might be seen. With my bag still slung over one shoulder, I slipped into the misty water and moved silently from one stern to another until I found the biggest junk. I was sure this was the one. My clothes felt heavy as I pulled myself onto the deck. Even my bones had filled with fear and sorrow. I slithered along the bottom of the junk like a snake, pushing my bag into the narrowest point before placing myself, as though a curved rib, against the skin of the bow. Loud breathing filled the space around me. I pressed one hand against my mouth, forcing my fear to slip back down my throat.

The junk smelled of fish. Any happiness I felt at leaving Pong Woo vanished. What would happen if Yee Loi found me? Would he let Second Brother take me home, or make me go by myself, not caring if I fell into the river pirates' hands?

I positioned Yee Loi's big fish baskets until they formed a row across the bow. I hoped they would hide me, even in daylight. I had just settled down behind the baskets when voices disturbed the night air. The junk rocked up and down as people climbed aboard. Coins passed from one hand to another. After each clink, Yee Loi said someone's name. After three clinks he said, 'Fu Ling,' and I relaxed.

We sailed for hours down Tsung Fa. No one talked. Maybe they were also saying silent goodbyes. Was Second Brother thinking about me? Or, now that it was light, was he taking in every tree and building and flower so he could draw them when he arrived in New Gold Hills?

People on the river and along the shore called to one another. 'Gédō chin' – how much? 'Joigin' – see you later. I heard other sounds, too, but could not see what had made them from behind the fish baskets. My body felt stiff. I longed to stretch; mostly I wanted to see Canton. Did it have great temples and paved streets? I closed my eyes and imagined arriving in this esteemed city.

Minutes later something hit the junk. I clung tightly to the bow, and blood rushed to my head. I went dizzy with fear. The junk rode up and down as angry voices yelled orders. I smelled river men again. One swore. Another threatened to kill everyone. I hoped Second Brother would not do anything foolish. Someone, maybe Yee Loi, said, 'Take my money, not my life!' My teeth rattled like Great-auntie's. Would I be found?

A loud commotion came from the stern. Second Brother said, 'We have food and tickets, but little money.' A rougher voice yelled,

'Hand everything over!' The junk rocked again. I peered through the weave of a basket. A large shape had fallen to the deck. I clung to a wooden rib, hoping the baskets would not move. My fingers ached as I tightened my grip, but I did not want to tumble from my hiding place and end up at the feet of a river man. The junk lurched again. Was Second Brother fighting? A shadow fell in front of the baskets, blocking my view. My skin burned. Then a long scream filled the air, followed by another, then one more. Bigger and bigger worries squeezed at my heart. The junk rocked violently and two large splashes followed. More shouts, accompanied by a noise that sounded like a sharp knife scraping fish bones. The junk rocked again as something knocked against its side. A final yell before the smell of river men faded. I counted silently to forty before peering between the baskets that had concealed me so well.

Imagine a group of young men, dressed in their best clothes, carrying the hopes of a village on their shoulders. Think of a blood-red stream running along the bottom of the junk. Place a man in it. See him turn crimson. Throw several men, including Yee Loi, into Tsung Fa. Scream silently, again and again and again, as you crawl from your hiding place.

The man lying in front of the fish baskets stared at the sky with unseeing eyes. Bloodied flesh hung in tatters around his neck, as though he wore an untidy scarf. On the deck beside him lay a severed hand. Maybe he had tried to hold on to his taels of silver. Tears scalded my eyeballs. With one hand over my mouth to contain my horror, I crawled and slithered across the slippery deck to the stern, where Second Brother lay, his head tucked into his chest like a sleeping mynah bird. His left leg was bent backwards, his right stretched out, as though he had been about to get up but for some reason had changed his mind. I crawled towards him, my trousers soaking up the blood that had pooled in the bottom of the junk. My stomach lurched into my mouth. It took great effort to swallow the bile that spilled across my tongue but I did not want

35

to make any sound – not even a spit, in case the pirates were still close by.

My heart leapt like a flying fish when Second Brother opened his eyes. He looked startled, then worried, and finally pleased.

'Youngest Sister, I am so happy to see you.'

'I'm going to New Gold Hills as well.'

He stared as though he could see right through me.

I squeezed his hand with mine to give him strength. With my other hand, I pressed MaMa's new shirt against his chest. Blood seeped through my fingers and ran down my arm. Second Brother's eyes filled with worry. I smiled to give him hope. When he next tried to speak, blood spurted from his mouth, which I wiped away with the sleeve of my tunic. His jaw swung loosely, like an old door coming away from its hinge.

'Don't speak,' I said. 'Rest for a while. I will sail Yee Loi's junk to Canton.'

In a mouse voice Second Brother said, 'Ming Yuet, the river men do bad things to girls. You must become a man. I hid my papers under that box before the pirates came on board. Take them.' His voice grew quieter as he pointed to a wicker container. I pressed my ear to his lips. 'Cut your hair like mine,' he whispered. 'Wear men's clothes. Talk like me. Take my life, and go to New Gold Hills.'

Such effort caused Second Brother to cough. Blood poured from his nose as well as his mouth. I squeezed his hand as his skin faded from chestnut brown to pearly white, eventually resembling the moon he had danced beneath the previous night. When his breaths slowed to small gasps, I blew puffs of love into him. 'Don't leave me.' His hand moved like a drawing stick across my cheeks, nose and eyes. Years later, I wondered if he had done this because he loved me and wanted to take the memory of my girl face to his next life, not the male one I wore for a long time afterwards.

'Leave nothing of me, Ming Yuet. It is the only way.'

I wrapped my arms around him, hoping he would speak again,

but he did not. Nor did he take another breath. Second Brother had started his journey to the next world.

I peered over the side of the junk. Bodies floated face down in the water. Everyone who had been on board, other than me, was dead. My only hope was to do as Second Brother wished. I pressed my face against his and whispered blessings before removing MaMa's shirt. Then I crawled to the middle of the junk, where the sides were lowest, and washed it in the river, squeezing the blue cotton until the water ran clear. Next I gathered up Second Brother's papers. I also went through the bag of the other man from Pong Woo, whose throat had been cut. Fortunately he was small and thin, like me. I took off my tunic and wrapped his red silk sash tightly around my chest so my little litchis would not show. After putting on his trousers, tunic and jacket, and hanging MaMa's shirt over a basket to dry, I used BaBa's knife to shave the front of my hair. I plaited the rest into a queue, checking my reflection on the bottom of a sardine tin. Once I had put on the other man's hat and clogs, my likeness to Second Brother was complete.

His last instruction was hard to obey but I tucked two taels, which I found on the deck, into his hand and filled his pockets with food from my sack. Then I tied a net with weights around him, until he looked more like a fish than a man. I fastened my girl clothes to the same net, so nothing of Ming Yuet would remain. A strange quietness had descended on the river. Just the occasional swoosh as boats passed by, with passengers pretending nothing untoward had happened, which was the best way to avoid trouble. I remained in a crouched position with my back to them while I tried to compose myself.

Although weighed down by great sorrow, I dragged Second Brother Fu Ling's body towards the middle of the junk. The net snagged on Yee Loi's belongings and I freed it with numb fingers. Tears slithered like snails down my face as I pulled Second Brother to the wooden rail. I joined my hands together in respect for him and the others who had died, having also equipped the unknown Pong Woo man for his final journey. After easing the skinny villager into the river, I positioned Second Brother's body against the side of the junk, but before I could tip him overboard he fell back against me. I wanted to hold him forever, but I also needed to carry out his final wish. Crying silently, I pushed and heaved until he was back in position. One last look and a single whispered 'Goodbye', then I pushed him over the side. He entered the water with barely a splash. I imagined him sliding into the belly of a silver fish and being carried far away to his next life.

THREE

Two Skins Travel as One

A black cloud hung over me after Second Brother died. Even now I cannot think about that time without sorrow tugging at me like a cold wind and tying knots in my heart. My first thought was to return to MaMa in Pong Woo. But I also had another need, a stronger one. So as Second Brother wished, I adjusted the sails on Yee Loi's junk, until the panels of matting, flattened by bamboo strips, caught the breeze. Tears, hard as sūkmáih, sweet-corn, stung my face as I steered past Yee Loi's floating corpse. My hands shook like fans. A fisherman shouted, 'Síusām a – watch out,' when I sailed too close to his lorcha. I crouched lower in the stern and worked the rudder with more care. But it was not until I imagined Second Brother telling me where to go that I was able to contain my sorrow and steer the junk well.

I stayed clear of other boats as much as possible, turning away when people waved or called out, as I did not want fishermen to ask after Yee Loi. Better to let them think he had a foolish new water-boy.

At dawn I sailed through The Bogue, a winding channel packed with small islands. Rows of grey roofs lined the shore, broken only by watchtowers. Imposing mountains and hill forts gave Canton an ominous appearance, although the harbour bustled with activity. Junks and lorchas, as well as boats I had not seen before, dipped and rocked on the grey water, which smelled of burnt cabbage. Other stinks hovered too, none pleasing.

People called to one another, using words I did not understand. How would I find the boat Second Brother said would take him to Hong Kong? What if someone saw through my new skin and reported me for taking Yee Loi's junk – or, worse, sold me to the river men? Just as despair joined hands with fear, a flash of silver appeared in the water – a sign from Second Brother. He led me to a wooden wharf, where I edged the junk between two smaller boats and threw the bowline over before jumping off and tying it to a pile. With the junk secured, I slung my bag over my shoulder and reminded myself to take confident man steps. Ignoring my dry mouth and prancing grasshoppers, I bowed my head and walked along the wharf.

Men pushed and shoved, so I did the same, not wanting to look out of place. I ploughed through the crowd, head down, elbows out, hoping to come across other sojourners, stopping only to buy rice noodles from a food stall where a young girl competed for custom alongside experienced hawkers. Her rounded shoulders and downcast face reminded me of First Sister after she had been shamed. A small child lay on rags beside the stall. Flies crawled around his yellow-crusted eyes.

I had just finished eating my noodles when I spotted a group of men standing close to a large boat. Their dialects were different to those I'd heard in Pong Woo, so it was hard to understand all their words, but one mentioned Hong Kong. I positioned myself close by, noting that his clothes were similar to mine – nankeen breeches, a loose tunic and warm jacket. His bag also bulged with supplies.

Once darkness descended I grew a little calmer, but I still did not feel safe in my new skin. Layers of misery hung in the night air, and a bitter wind blew across the harbour. With it came the stench of fire and hunger and dung. I pulled up my jacket collar and sat on the quay. All around me, men talked in whispers. One came from Shek Ma, a village near Pong Woo, another from Naam Tseun. Like Second Brother, they had borrowed their fares from moneylenders. 'Will I ever see my son again?' an older man asked the moon. I was the only person from Pong Woo. Second Brother's debt to Chang Huan was now mine. So was Second Brother's promise to send money back to MaMa. Beads of worry tightened around my throat.

We boarded at first light. Sorrowful thoughts accompanied me up the gangplank. A wave of what Ida told me later was called homesickness washed over me. I gripped the rail to steady myself. Two men close by wept openly but my girl tears stayed hidden. Was MaMa already out on the delta searching with her flick flick eyes, a hand running through the front of her hair until bits stood up like a cock's comb and would not lie flat until she wet and smoothed it down? MaMa's worry vane, First Sister called it.

I held on tightly to Second Brother's papers. When his name was called I answered in my new voice. Inside I was a young girl from Pong Woo, weighed down with sadness; outside, a young man hoping for a prosperous sojourn: two skins travelling as one.

Second Brother is still with me. He followed me across a rolling ocean to New Gold Hills. I saw him in Bush Creek and the Arrow River, which I got to know in all their seasons: playful in autumn, slow in winter, fast and high in spring. In summer the Arrow floods or roams, depending on the weather. I washed in this water, drank from it, nearly drowned in it. I also found gold. Water connects me to Second Brother; two faces look back.

What did BaBa and First Brother notice when they looked in Tsung Fa? Their reflections or something else: demons, maybe?

41

Memories live within me as though I am a house with many rooms. Some are good, like Con-Lan's love and Ida's friendship. Others sting like snake bites until I cry in pain. When these times visit, I sit outside the cottage Con-Lan built and think of a poem written about sojourners.

They have been washed by the rain and combed by the winds
They have wrapped themselves in the stars and worn the moon.

I am no longer a young woman with hope in her heart. Think of me as a forty-year-old fallen leaf returning to her first land. MaMa told me I was born in a hurry one hot summer afternoon. On the same day an abscess burst in Grandmother's ear. Great-auntie said my yells made Grandmother's ear go deaf. 'Never heard such a screamer,' she said, and later, 'Never heard such a talker.' Words still fascinate me. I need them the way BaBa and First Brother wanted Dragon Fire. Con-Lan loved words too. He taught me Orkney sayings and I drew Chinese characters for him. Sometimes we sang to each other, or took each other on word journeys, like the one I am taking you on now.

When our daughter, Fang Yin, opened her clear blue eyes at Ida's house, they stole the breath right out of my mouth, pulled me into an ocean where white-tipped waves sounded like music and a silver fish swam over golden stones. A moment of joy before Ida's hand rested on my shoulder. But it is too soon for that story. We must return to Canton.

Another hand helped me that day, pressing against my back when my girl feet stopped walking up the gangplank because I did not want to leave MaMa. Push, push, push, it went on my jacket. That wise hand belonged to Soo Tie, now a trusted friend. He was older than Fu Ling, and taller, with deep-set eyes and high cheekbones. A scar on the left side of his face and a splendid queue made him stand out, even in a large crowd.

Soo Tie guided me below deck to a dim corner in the hold, where we squatted like frogs. Two sojourners nearby prepared a meal. I couldn't imagine eating in an unfamiliar place among men from different clans. My stomach heaved and pitched like the sea, even though we had not yet left the quay. I pulled my knees up and rested my head on them. Images of Second Brother tied in a net swam into my mind. They were interrupted by the sound of ropes thudding on the deck and men calling instructions and heavy objects being dragged into place. I was a young girl about to sail across an ocean wider than my imagination. Terror engulfed me as the boat slipped its mooring.

Opium fumes soon filled the hold. For a moment I thought I was back with BaBa and First Brother. Then I realised that unhappy men everywhere smoked to deaden their burdens.

Soo Tie said later that I hardly spoke as we travelled from Canton to Hong Kong, where the *Jean Sands* waited. Nor did I prepare any food, as it did not seem right to cook Chang Huan's stolen rice. Perhaps Second Brother's death was a punishment. I was full of guilt and regret. But once aboard the *Jean Sands* I finally ate a bowl of rice gruel Soo Tie handed me, even though Chang Huan's puffy face still appeared in my dreams, along with the deformed feet of two old women.

I also stood behind a sack hung in one section of the hold and peed into a tin without lowering my trousers because my feet could be seen. It is hard for a girl to place her feet together, arch her back and pee like a man. Squatting is easier – I did that as well once a day.

Throughout the voyage I pretended to be shy and a little simple, hoping to be ignored, but sometimes I had to speak.

'You play fantan?' asked a man with rough, peeling skin and a right eye that did not open properly.

'Not well,' I said in my new deep voice and carried on eating my rice.

Fantan is played with copper coins. A large number are placed in a cup, then players bet on whether there is an even or odd number.

Soo Tie, who was standing nearby, said, 'I'll teach him later.'

I handed him a tin of Chang Huan's smoked fish to signify my appreciation.

By the time we passed through the Ombay passage I could play fantan as well as any man. I yelled each time I won. When I lost and wanted the ocean to curl its tongue through the porthole and swallow me, I did not pull the edges of my hat down further. Instead I used the spittoon and placed another bet. After a win, I slapped the closest loser on the back and wished him better luck next time. I learned how to be a man on the *Jean Sands*, sleeping beside Soo Tie, my teacher and protector.

Small green hills, not golden mountains, appeared one cold, windy day late in July. Soo Tie lost his hat when a gust caught him by surprise as we stood on deck. I held on to mine firmly. Small birds tumbled through the air like faded autumn leaves. Only those with wings as big as sails stayed on course. 'Albatrosses,' a deckhand yelled above the noise of the rigging, which creaked and strained as we passed through the 'Heads'. These giant birds terrified me with their loud calls and seemingly effortless swoops. So did the narrow channel and rough waters of Otago Harbour. And, although white houses dotted the shoreline, their fair-skinned inhabitants did not wave or extend any form of greeting to us, not even a bow. Loneliness encircled me like a bitter wind.

The ship creaked as it nudged into the wharf at Port Chalmers, near Dunedin, the nearest city to the inland Otago goldfields. I wondered if the two Customs men would notice my girl skin hidden under Second Brother's. One had bad breath, the other an incessant cough. Neither man welcomed us. We could have been a heap of rubbish. The cougher scribbled my name into a book while I silently practised an English word Second Brother thought could be used as an afternoon greeting. Thinking it was time to utter it out loud, I said, 'Guud haf-too-nuan,' and gave my best bow. But the Customs man did not greet me in return. Instead he pushed my chin up with a stick, then pulled his left eye back with two fingers until it became a small slit. I felt humiliated because he had not understood my greeting, and also dishonoured because he had ridiculed the shape of my eyes. One excellent thing, though: he had not seen any girl skin.

I walked down the gangplank with bendy legs. Soo Tie's also bounced about oddly. One leg buckled and the other waved in the wind like a flag. 'We walk like we have celebrated a fine New Year,' he said, gripping the rail.

Would I need to enjoy this special time like a man? Maybe drink and fall down yám-jeui?

Another lot of questions appeared. How soon could I repay Chang Huan? Which goldfield should I try? When could I send MaMa enough money for her new house? How could I tell her about Second Brother? His promise weighed heavier than ten buckets of water on a shoulder pole. I needed to find plenty gold. So did Soo Tie, for although his family had died long ago from river fever, he still had an obligation, which he did not tell me about it until later. How would I learn to go about finding this gold?

We walked along the muddy road to Dunedin, placing our feet carefully because the ground was littered with pot-holes. One man twisted his ankle. 'Any bigger and it could swallow a buffalo,' said his friend, helping him up. I struggled to keep my balance, which Ida says is a common complaint after a long sea journey. She works at the Arrow Hospital and knows about such things.

That afternoon, what had been a fresh wind changed into a fierce gale, flattening everything in its path, including us. Rain fell in great sheets, turning the road into a canal of rotting liquid and slippery clay.

'Bend into the wind – it's the only way to stay on your feet,' said Soo Tie, breaking off two sturdy flower-stalks to use as balancing poles. Even with these aids it was a tiring walk. Every hour we stopped to rest. On one occasion I sat on a clump of wet grass and looked at the dull countryside. No litchi or banyan. Or rice fields. Only a grey harbour to our left, and small hills perched like dumplings on either side of the churning water. Unfamiliar plants and trees covered the swampy ground. Later I learned their names from Con-Lan: flax, fern, cabbage trees and toi-toi. Overhead, white seabirds with red beaks squawked to one another. Did MaMa still call for me? Or had she decided I was lost to the river men? Maybe she covered Grandmother and Great-auntie's Golden Lilies with dust as she swept the floor in a despairing state.

My first impression of Dunedin was not favourable. The footpaths resembled mud-baths. We squelched and slipped, which made us appear clumsy. Decaying animal carcasses lay unattended on the roadside. Dung fermented in cesspools, and green slime formed unruly patterns over open drains that released a vile pong. Unfamiliar noises assaulted me from all sides. Men in wide-brimmed hats and wearing tight moleskin trousers and flannel shirts shouted and swore as they rode their horses down Princess Street.

An elderly man with a nose that resembled a wizened cucumber told us how to get to Stafford and Walker Streets, where we'd heard there were boarding houses. 'Devil's Half Acre,' he said, pointing to a small hill. My eyes followed his knotty hand. Untidy buildings lined the rise. Poorly arranged, I thought – they had the appearance of chipped crockery carelessly placed on a badly built shelf. These dwellings were made from rough planks of timber, not sun-dried bricks. Thankfully I had no time to dwell on bad judgements. I had to find lodgings.

'You want a bed, you pay,' said the man.

He took us to a boarding house that had a narrow passageway and small rooms leading off it. Mildew stained the walls. Other sojourners nodded or brought their hands together respectfully as we walked into a room thick with stale smoke. They would not have shown such respect had they known I was a girl. They would have ignored me, ordered me to cook for them, or forced themselves upon me. I sank deeper into Second Brother's skin.

Soo Tie and I found a space and settled down to eat a portion of cold rice. We did not speak, since we were tired. I thought about the young girls I'd seen with bright red lips and sad blue eyes in the doorways of houses along Stafford Street. Had I made a foolish decision? Would I regret coming to New Gold Hills? I glanced at Soo Tie, who was undoing his bootlaces. His hooded eyes flickered. What was he thinking about? I lay on the floor against a wall with my bag under my head. Soo Tie settled beside me.

By morning, ice had formed on the insides of the windows. My hands and face ached from the cold. Outside on the street, men called to one another. A few words sounded similar to the English ones Second Brother had taught me. Maybe I could understand and be understood after all. I raised my arms, hoping to revive my stiff limbs with a vigorous stretch, then remembered I should not draw attention to myself and dropped them.

'Come,' said Soo Tie. 'We'll cook some rice; warm bellies.'

Reluctant to stay alone in a room with strangers, even though I had travelled with 315 of them on the *Jean Sands*, I followed him outside.

'Find three sticks as long as my arm,' he said.

I searched through rubbish in the yard, gathering several of a similar size. I pushed them firmly into the ground to form a circle.

'Good. You have made a fine stand.'

Soo Tie bound the sticks together at the top with a piece of string he'd pulled from his pocket, and attached a metal hook. He hung a pot of water from it, under which we burned paper and smaller sticks.

I had wanted to light paper for Second Brother when he began his journey into the next world, but the river men might have seen the smoke and returned. Fear had kept me safe, but it had also stopped me performing an honourable custom.

Once the water boiled we put in a handful of rice, and later ate it with much pleasure, as it was our first hot meal since arriving in this strange land.

'It's easier to smile with a full belly,' said Soo Tie, attempting to lighten my despondent mood.

Help me, Second Brother, I thought. And he did. His goodness flowed through me like a warm ocean wave, enabling me to eat every grain of rice in my bowl. 'I feel much happier now, Soo Tie, thank you.'

We left the boarding house an hour later and made our way down the hill to buy supplies and a map, picking our way through mud and rubbish until we reached the flat, where each shop entrance had signs with Chinese characters, giving the cost of goods such as shovels, blankets, rice and ginger.

'Too much,' I said, as Soo Tie walked towards one store.

'Which has the best prices?' he said, looking confused.

I realised that, like BaBa, Soo Tie could not read. Perhaps I could help him. 'This one looks promising.' I pointed to a shop across the street.

'We must buy warm trousers and boots. This city is cold.'

'Don't forget to get a new hat!'

We selected our supplies carefully – we couldn't afford to make mistakes. A pale-faced man with stubble on his chin bought a canvas tent.

'Better to build a stone hut,' I whispered to Soo Tie.

'Maybe there are no stones.'

I wanted to make a shrine for Second Brother Fu Ling. 'There will be plenty of stones, and rich soil for vegetables.'

'But what will grow in this cold place?' said Soo Tie.

'Everything,' I said, hoping to be proven right.

Two days later, with sixteen companions, we left on foot to travel inland, weighed down with supplies but in a lighter mood. Other sojourners from the *Jean Sands* chose different routes to the goldfields, or decided to stay longer in Dunedin.

'This might be a lucky place,' Soo Tie said as we made our way through the centre of the city. 'It has eight sides.'

I nodded. 'Perhaps prosperous times lie ahead.'

Men with hung mo, red hair, passed us on wagons loaded with supplies. Each turn of the wheels flicked up mud. The bullocks that pulled the wagons rolled their tongues from side to side, sending lumpy strands of dribble in our direction.

We wound our way out of town like a mud-brown snake. Rain flattened our hats and soaked our boots. I longed for summer days in Pong Woo, when I had run to the fields with Second Brother, hoping to learn a new word or watch him draw a story in the dirt. My heels rubbed against the stiff leather of my new boots. Surely if Grandmother and Great-auntie could live with cramped feet I could manage a few blisters. A cold wind snarled and whined at my back. Soo Tie fastened his new hat firmly under his chin.

Near water, Second Brother swims beside me. Away from it I cannot keep him close. That day four men rode by on a wagon. One pretended to pull a pigtail from under his hat and tie it to the wagon's iron frame, while his friends pointed to us and laughed. Then he got out a bone-handled knife and pretended to slice off his imaginary man's leg. 'Yum, yum,' he said, holding the make-believe limb up to his mouth. His companions licked their lips. The youngest man had grey skin and a harsh expression. He pulled a smaller knife from his boot and gestured as though he was about to slice off my arm. Ida told me later that a newspaper article around that time printed an article about an Aboriginal tribe in Australia who tied three live Chinese men to a tree branch, eating them, one by one, over several

49

weeks. The same article said we tasted sweeter than Britons because of our rice-eating habits.

A red-faced man with untidy grey and white whiskers, travelling on the wagon, yelled, 'Scum of China!' and 'Thieving barbarian vagabonds!' as he passed. We were to hear such words often during our time in New Gold Hills.

'Why do they taunt us? Is it because we look different?'

'Even villagers from Pong Woo are wary of those from Naam Tseun,' said Soo Tie. But not rude in this way, I thought. 'I hope there is enough gold for everyone.'

'A patient man always finds what he wants,' he said, grinning. The scar on his cheek curved into the shape of a half moon. 'Where is your map?'

I took it from my jacket pocket, remembering how back in Dunedin the Chinese merchant's eyes had travelled down to my chest and back up to my face. In the same strong voice Second Brother used with BaBa after a beating, I had said, 'You do not know me,' which caused the merchant to drop his eyes and study the money in my palm. Inside I was shaking, but outwardly I appeared, if not confident, at least unconcerned.

We checked our whereabouts on the map and carried on to the Taieri River, which we crossed by ferry. Two men swam over in order to save the fare. 'They must have many relatives to feed back in China,' said Soo Tie.

Our route to the goldfields crossed mountainous land littered with surly men who displayed little tolerance or forbearance towards us. By the time we reached Lawrence, I knew that men similar to the Pong Woo river pirates lived in this country also. Some travelled by coach or wagon, others walked. Their cold eyes slid across our group, often resting on me longer than the others.

One evening, while I gathered brush for a fire, a miner with a shiny red face and a bald head sauntered menacingly towards me. My bones turned soft and my heart raced, as it had on the south path in Pong Woo. Once again I imagined Second Brother telling me to behave like a man. I spat on the ground. The miner swore and pushed me aside but did not stop.

That night, when we set up camp, I made sure I had a large rock behind me. I wrapped myself tightly in my blanket, sleeping like an animal, half listening to what the wind carried. The following day I paid particular attention to who was nearby, never relaxing, and being especially vigilant when we arrived in each new town.

At Alexandra a Chinese interpreter spoke in English to a wagoner who was waiting for his mate to come out of a hotel. He then switched to Chinese and said to us, 'An Irishman was recently robbed and beaten in the Tuapekas for a single nugget. So watch your backs.' Despite this worrying news, I was impressed by the way he had moved between the two languages. I vowed to achieve the same fluency.

We followed the Clutha River to where it joins the Karawau River at Cromwell, another gold town. The turquoise-blue Clutha danced its way down the valley, while the Karawau gouged a wilder path through the gorge, sending ripples of white foam into the air as it thundered over boulders the size of wagons.

The ground became drier and stonier the further inland we travelled. Clumps of golden grass lined the roadside, which made me feel hopeful, even though the hills were covered with inhospitable men and cumbersome wagons and a strong wind still blew.

Since my hair was in a queue, it could not dance in the breeze as it had when I'd run to the fields with Second Brother. His love still travelled with me. But on the day I arrived in the Arrow valley I felt lonely and apprehensive, even though a rainbow created a splendid archway for me to walk beneath, into my new life.

FOUR

Sojourn Begins in New Gold Hills

We arrived in Arrowtown early one Saturday morning. Two-hundred and eight people lived in the town, seventy of whom were Chinese. An assortment of drab wooden buildings lined Buckingham Street, the narrow main thoroughfare. I recall a general store, a bakery, a draper's establishment, a tea shop, two butchers and a post office, as well as a blacksmith. Municipal buildings, such as the Bank of New Zealand, did not look like those in Pong Woo. Nor could I see any ancestral halls or temples. I felt out of place, and full of longing for MaMa.

Merchants shouted across the street to boisterous miners spilling out of the various hotels. These scruffy specimens scratched their whiskers and belched loudly before sauntering over – pushing us aside as though we were insects – to inspect the merchants' goods. I did not understand all their words, only their actions. Bullying looks the same in any language.

Their women wore long skirts, jackets and bonnets. Wisps of colourful hair sat like small surprises on their pale foreheads. They had shopping baskets over their arms. Perhaps they'd been talking among themselves, like Pong Woo women on market days. But as we drew closer they fell silent, apart from one with green feathers in her felt hat. 'Not more John Chinamen!' she said, shaking her head from side to side, causing one feather to fly off and land on a small boy's ginger hair. He flicked it away and poked his tongue at us. I lowered my eyes and walked faster.

'Who is John Chinaman?' I asked as we headed down a steep track to the Chinese camp, located on the south bank of Bush Creek and upstream from where it meets the Arrow River. Twenty sod huts and one larger building stood on flat ground. Most had wooden planked doors and faced northwest. At the rear, fences, hawthorn hedges and stone walls bounded a garden. Young willows, plum trees and a stand of poplars softened the camp's austere appearance.

'I think "John" is you and me; maybe it's a bad name with no honour,' said Soo Tie.

We lived for months in caves above the camp. The best ones had overhangs, which we used as roofs. Some had solid banks that acted as back walls. If a miner found a cave with an overhang and a good bank he could build a shelter quickly, which was important, especially in winter.

To keep out evil spirits I hung an empty rice sack over the entrance to my cave. It did not stop rats visiting, though. They ate everything: my rice sack, dried vegetables, even the soles of my boots. I went to Su Sing's Long House to buy containers. Chests of tea were stacked against the walls. Jars of salted radishes, pickled lemons, garlic, shrimp sauce and preserved ginger lined wooden shelves. Brass and iron wok ladles and light-green glazed condiment bowls sat on the counter. I chose a pottery jar to store my food in and a tin box for my clothes. Su Sing told me about a tea to ward off chills, so I bought that as well, along with a bag of rice.

I placed a flat river stone on top of the jar and another on the lid of my box. My food and clothes were safe, but not me. Two nights later I woke to find a rat chewing my queue as though it was a strip of pork. I almost screamed in my girl voice but, thankfully, managed to swallow my disgust and chase the rodent from the cave.

The following winter was particularly harsh. Wind howled through the valley. Thunder cracked open the sky as though it was a ripe walnut. The rice bag hanging over my cave entrance froze, and my breath turned white as it flew into the air. Each morning my queue was stiff with frost: I feared it would snap like an icicle. And cold was not the only hardship.

Bad spirits rolled boulders over the bank above our camp. We ran from our caves thinking the sky had fallen. Rocks knocked us to the ground, denting our long-handled shovels and gold pans and spilling buckets of night soil. We screamed until the spirits ran away. Soo Tie rubbed a cut on his head. 'Maybe it's not evil spirits,' he said, 'but men who do not want us here.'

'There are devils in all towns,' said another miner, gathering up his tools.

'Good people, too,' I said hopefully.

Su Sing nodded respectfully. 'Yes, Mrs Ida cares for us. Last year, on her way home from Macetown she heard a man call for help. She went to look and found a Chinese miner with a broken leg. She talked quietly so as not to frighten him; gave him a drink from her water bottle. She tore her undergarment into strips and tied his bad leg to his good leg to act as a splint. When the miner was comfortable she left him her water and walked to the Long House. She arrived hot and puffing, and asked for two strong men to carry the injured man back to town.'

Su Sing accompanied Ida and the Chinese stretcher-bearers to the injured miner, and he told this story every time we were treated badly. 'To balance the scales,' he used to say.

I first saw Ida walking along the river with a boy close to Day-Day's age. To my surprise, she nodded and brought her hands together. The boy did the same. I gave them my best bow. After they had disappeared around a bend I gave thanks to Lo Shen, Goddess of Rivers, because my Chinese ways had been respected.

No Chinese women lived in Arrowtown other than me, and I did not count. This situation caused great loneliness among our men, although Soo Tie did not seem to mind. Sometimes he seemed more woman than me, for instance noticing that I'd lost weight after a bad chill.

'Soon you will fly away in a little wind.'

'Little Wind – that is what MaMa calls me.'

'Does she? I will call you Little Wind too, because you send puffs of sadness into the air.'

'It's important to work hard, not behave in foolish ways.'

'Even industrious workers need to laugh, especially skinny young ones.'

Had he noticed my girl shape?

Whenever the men in camp congregated at Su Sing's, I took the opportunity to wash myself. Not a quick wipe of face, arms, hands and feet, but a long, careful clean. My little buds stiffened like beaten egg-whites in the cool air. Soft hair, darker than ink, covered my private pocket. I washed carefully, taking in every change, for I did not know when I would next see myself. Once dry, I swung my hips like the village girls in Pong Woo and imagined the woman I might have become. But each morning, before leaving the cave, I climbed into Second Brother's skin which, although difficult at first, grew easier as time passed, until I almost believed that he did not swim like a fish, but lived inside me.

Bush Creek and the Arrow River also had secrets. The early miners had not found all the gold, only the easy colour. Patience was a virtue of sojourners. So was learning about water and its moods.

Winter was the best time to find gold. Then the rivers were low and heavy with sleep.

Throughout my first week in the goldfield I watched seasoned miners lower their pans into the river and scoop up alluvium, the clay, sand and gravel in which specks of gold can be found. They used a swirling movement to wash the alluvium with river water. I also listened to conversations in the camp and discussed the merits of each miner's technique with Soo Tie.

My first golden happiness came in late September, after I had raked and turned the rough sand and gravel for four weeks, swirling the water then swinging it back and forth in my pan to wash out the rubble. My back ached as I sifted the black sand. I had not expected to see colour, but three golden suns shone up at me. Soon I could repay Chang Huan for Second Brother's fare and the food I had taken.

Over the next few months, even though it was summer and the river was high, I found more small nuggets. Soo Tie, who panned a few yards down from me, found worthy amounts as well. We tallied up at the end of each week.

'How much did you find, Little Wind?' Soo Tie asked one Sunday as we walked back to camp.

'Two taels of silver for Chang Huan, five tins of salted fish, a fine cut of pork and one jar of shrimp sauce.'

'One fat duck, a large bag of rice and two jars of salted radishes for me,' he said, 'as well as a warm blanket; maybe wood for a cradle, too.'

Not a baby's cradle like the one Con-Lan made for Fang Yin, but a gold cradle, which is more efficient than a pan.

Sometimes I rocked the cradle while Soo Tie ladled water using a tin can tied to a wooden stick. Other times, I ladled and Soo Tie rocked. We worked the gravel and tailings the same way, shovelling as much as five cubic yards every ten hours. Yes, we learned the settlers' measurements so we would not be cheated. Our arms and backs ached but we smiled when we found colour.

At first I kept MaMa's gold in a pocket inside my jacket, which I had made from a piece of rice sack. After I moved to Swipers Gully with Soo Tie I buried my gold in a bag under a stone inside our hut. Soo Tie hid his in the hills. That way we could not be robbed at the same time, unlike two men working in a gully near Macetown; one had his leg broken in three places and his heart in ten. 'How will my family eat?' he cried as the thieves ran off with his and his partner's savings.

After that incident Soo Tie showed me where his gold was, in case something happened to him.

'It will be safe in there,' I said as he stacked stones back over the entrance to a desolate cave in the hills.

'Nowhere is safe, Little Wind. Always look behind you.'

His words reminded me of Second Brother's the day he warned me to stay away from the mountains and Tsung Fa. Soo Tie was also watchful, and he arranged his mind logically. Unlike me, he did not have to wait for his brain to remember where he had placed his shirt or shovel or sugar; everything had its place. Even so, unexpected events did not appear to unsettle him. Like the morning I woke early with pains in my back. Since I had shovelled wash dirt all week I thought the dull ache would pass. But over the next two days it travelled around to my stomach and down my thighs. Nothing helped. Not rest, or tea, or strong thoughts. Eventually I fetched a bucket of water, hoping to wash the pain away. Soo Tie remained at the creek. After taking off my trousers and placing a cool cloth on my stomach, which brought comfort, I noticed blood between my legs. I was bleeding like First Sister did before her stomach grew large with river babies. Despite my boy skin, I had turned into a woman.

I hastily made a pad from a piece of rice sack, filled it with soft grass and placed it between my legs. To hide my woman smell I rubbed the area with Soo Tie's Shao Hsing, a demon drink like Old Tom, which makes men laugh and cry and fight, and sometimes loosens their tongues until words slip and slide as though travelling across ice.

When Soo Tie came back to the hut he said, 'Why do you smell of Shao Hsing?'

I said, 'Better to smell of demon drink than other things.'

Soo Tie tugged at his queue, which helped him think. 'So each month I bring you a bottle.'

My face grew hot, but he smiled. 'Don't worry, Little Wind. Shao Hsing and I will look after you.'

'When did you realise?'

'On the *Jean Sands*. I saw a brave girl who needed help.'

Had anyone else noticed? Perhaps they had not bothered me because Soo Tie looked like a fighter. Also he did not smoke opium, and rarely drank alcohol, so he was always alert.

Around the time of my fourth bleed, Lok Yem, an ill-tempered man who mined alone in a gully near town, and who used his fists more freely than words, called me 'Soo Tie's Bad Smell' during a game of fantan. My protector answered, 'Better him who smells bad than a man who loses his money.' Luckily the coins fell my way and everyone laughed, but I wondered if this loner had noticed more than my smell.

If only I had looked after Second Brother as well as Soo Tie cared for me. Why had I not leapt from my hiding place on the junk and pushed the river men into the water? In my dreams I was a brave warrior. But when I woke, Second Brother had not been saved.

I wanted to write to MaMa, tell her I was safe in New Gold Hills and still her daughter, even though I wore men's clothes. But how could I tell her that I had not protected Second Brother? So instead I talked to MaMa in my mind, remembering how she hummed like a throat singer while brushing my hair. One night such reminiscing caused tears to fall into my cooking pot, where they sizzled along with pork and ginger, reminding me of my many failings.

'Our supper has plenty of salt tonight,' said Soo Tie, using chopsticks to lift a piece of pork from the pan to his bowl.

I filled my dish but only poked at the food.

'Come on, eat up,' said Soo Tie.

'Do you miss China?'

'I miss many things, Little Wind. China is one. Seeing you smile is another. Sometimes you look so sad. I want to see you always happy.'

Silently I counted my blessings. Friendship is a precious gift – one Ida would also ultimately give me. I turned towards Soo Tie and made a small bow. 'Thank you for getting me around a black corner.'

'We will work hard until the next flood. Then you can send lots of money back to your family.'

But it wasn't only money. Each day I sent love on the wind. I also gave and received love in Arrowtown. Not openly, though. I will tell that story later.

Soo Tie and I worked together for many moons. Over time, pieces of our lives fell into each other's hands: some too small to remember, although they return now that I am revisiting these times. If only I had Soo Tie's tidy brain. Mine still changes direction, tripping on wayward thoughts. I often forget what made it go down a particular path. All that remains is a feeling that something waits in the shadows.

We lived in caves in the Chinese camp through another harsh winter, when cold crawled into our bones. Nights were unbearably long. The creek and river froze so we could not work, and blankets of ice covered the ground. Our supplies dwindled. We had to give Su Sing IOUs, which we later exchanged for gold. Occasional or light opium-smokers went without the black beads after their evening meal. Heavy smokers, who usually spent between seven and fourteen shillings a week on a koon or small tin of opium, sucking in the thick smoke until feelings of elation, then comfort and drowsiness overcame their cold and misery, could not afford to satisfy their craving unless they denied themselves food. No one wanted such a man as a mining partner, since even in good weather he might spend several hours each day smoking. That's why heavy smokers worked alone. Soo Tie never bought Fook Yeun, or any other opium brand, not wanting to place himself in social or financial peril. Instead, he spent the winter playing fantan, pakapoo and mora.

Fantan, as you know, is played with copper coins. Pakapoo is different. You buy tickets, each of which has a certain number of characters. Each buyer punches out some of these characters. The person with the ticket that most resembles the one that was punched and sealed earlier wins the prize.

Mora is played on birthdays. The winner of this game makes the other person drink a cup of whisky. I did not play mora in case my tongue grew loose and my young woman's voice sang and laughed. I liked playing fantan and pakapoo, though. Some nights I won. When the prize was pork, I shared my good fortune with Soo Tie and our friends Ah Sip and Wong Yet Song. Ah Sip had the best garden in Arrowtown. He helped me and Soo Tie with ours after we moved further up the gorge, where the riverbed was rich with gold. At first we lived in a cave like the one I told you about earlier. Later we built a hut on a hill, facing the river, with good feng shui. We sealed the schist walls with mud-mortar. Our roof was made from sacking and thatch woven from tussock. Demons could not enter because we made sure there were no straight lines. Soo Tie broke an empty bottle and set it in the wall near his bunk. Outside, underneath the neck of this bottle, he placed a bucket. He could relieve himself at night without leaving the hut. This method did not work for me. Some men's ways are too hard for women. I used a bucket. Every morning I tipped the contents into a pit and later used the compost on our garden.

One Sunday afternoon Ah Sip brought us five cabbage plants and a story.

'For many nights bad spirits have been visiting me. They blocked my night bottle with mud so my bunk got wet. First I was mad, then I became frightened. Last night I decided to be brave and stay up late. I filled a spray pump from my night bucket. When the spirit came, I crept outside and aimed well. The spirit jumped and made an awful noise! I screamed and the spirit ran off. I could see small boy shoes. I don't think that spirit will be back!'

Soo Tie laughed and nudged Ah Sip. 'He was probably more upset than you!'

'And smellier,' I said, thinking this boy would stink worse than me at pad time.

'Boys are not always funny,' Ah Sip said. 'Remember the two who set fire to some sticks on an old man's back? He was badly burned.'

What would these boys do to me if my secret was revealed? I shivered, but not from cold.

Ah Sip put an arm around my shoulder and gave me a friendly squeeze. 'Time we put in some plants, Little Wind.'

I reached over and took the seedlings from the bucket where they had been soaking, confident that Ah Sip's varieties would do well in the Arrow climate. Soo Tie wanted a visiting photographer to take a picture of me holding a large pumpkin, but I worried that this stranger's magic box might capture my woman self. 'It only sees outside things, not inside,' Soo Tie said, but I was not convinced.

Vegetables from our garden, lightly fried with rice or added to soup and stew, filled our bellies. My favourite meal, though, was lean pork, a belly cut, chopped into pieces and stewed slowly in a cast-iron billy with turnips, carrots and greens. We could not afford meat often. During hard times we survived on a few shillings each a week.

One winter the river iced over completely. Icicles hung like swords from buildings. A hatter – a miner who works alone, often in isolated gullies – froze in his bed. No one could work. Soo Tie spent hours inside our hut building a table and two chairs from wooden boxes. I made cushions from rice sacking, which I dyed red with bottled berry juice and filled with snow tussock. Night after night we sat by the fire, talking about ordinary things, but one evening Soo Tie took a sheet of red paper from his swag and said, 'Little Wind, please show me how to make characters.' He told me later these words had hung upside down inside his head for months like bats in a cave until he'd found the courage to let them fly into the light.

The following evening Soo Tie proudly nailed his first sign to our front door; 'Five Blessings Come Here'.

'You have made fine characters,' I said, handing him a bowl of tea.

'I have a good teacher.'

'You are a fast learner.'

Spring came late that year. Gold was plentiful right through to November, enabling us to buy a pig to fatten for Chinese New Year in February. We started festivities by letting off firecrackers to scare demons away from our hut. Soo Tie made new inscriptions on high-quality red paper that I had bought him as a gift, shaking his head in amazement each time a new character appeared on the page. I made a shrine to Hung Shing, God of the South Seas, and burned sticks of incense to connect me with the past.

Sweat poured off Ah Sip as he turned the spit on which our pig was firmly secured. Ah Nuey, another friend, and Wong Yet Song, also came to celebrate this auspicious day with us. We ate pork with noodles and vegetables, and later enjoyed candied sweets with green tea, which our friends had bought from Su Sing's store. Everything tasted of China. We sat outside the hut with tears in our eyes. Later we consulted the lucky book to see when we should go back to work. Many times we told each other, 'We'll save one hundred pounds, then return home.'

I have stayed in Arrowtown longer than I intended. Now my ancestors call to me. But I cannot answer them yet. Hold my stories close. They are told with love, even those weighed down with sadness.

Sorrow nipped at Soo Tie's heels because he did not love the wife he had been given in a 'live fowl' marriage that took place without him in China. She came from the same village and was only nine years old when Soo Tie left for New Gold Hills. A live cock represented Soo Tie, the absent husband, at the ceremony.

Many wives wait in China for their husbands to return so they can have a son. In the meantime they live as widows. Someone wrote a song to describe their loneliness:

> *Do not marry your daughter to Gold Mountain man,*
> *He would not be home in one full year out of ten.*
> *Spider webs would cover half of her bed*
> *While dust covers full one side.*

Soo Tie's wife's family often had a school teacher write saying they needed money, which he always sent. But he did not want a young girl to wait for him. 'I must tell her I cannot be a good husband. Will you help me write to her, Little Wind?' In his letter Soo Tie asked for forgiveness, but his wife died of river fever before his words reached her. This tragedy re-awakened Soo Tie's memories of his parents dying from a similar fever, causing him to go for long walks and dream at night about washing bones. It is our tradition to bury a body twice: once in a shallow grave – exposure to the air hastens decay; and seven years later, after the bones have been carefully gathered and placed on a cloth to dry in the sun, then cleaned with a stiff wire brush. Finally we rub the bones dry and lay them in a box or urn to deposit in the family tomb, where they will remain undisturbed.

There was no river fever in Arrowtown, only gold fever. And, for me, love fever. Yes, I know my stories are not going in straight lines. But remember, I do not want demons to carry away my words.

Imagine a music box, not a fiddle which Con-Lan played, but a concertina that makes music when squeezed from both ends. I am like that box. Push on my life and I let out important memories. Some good, some bad, like the day Ah Nuey and Wong Yet Song returned from town with new shovels and a tale about a Chinese miner who had gone to Bannockburn to collect a small debt.

'When he returned, everything in his cave had been burnt or smashed,' said Wong Yet Song, wiping tears from his leathery cheeks.

'All he has left are the clothes he was wearing and a few shillings in his pocket. He has such worries,' Ah Nuey said, 'and he is so far from Tang Mountain.'

Ah Nuey and Wong Yet Song burned incense to appease the spirits before going back to work. Two weeks later a Chinese man who had lived for ten years in Queenstown arrived in Arrowtown with money in his pocket and a wish to set up a market garden. He asked three young lads who could sell him land. 'Sing song Chinaman,' they teased, pushing him from one to the other. After they wearied of that game they put him in a large barrel and rolled it around to the lane behind the New Orleans Hotel. Thankfully Ida's husband, Alfred, saw them and intervened. 'Me upset. Me cly,' the man told Alfred, who took him down to Su Sing's. His bad memories stayed with him. Mine have, too. Sometimes they grow so heavy I almost stop breathing.

FIVE

Secret Pocket Grows Heavy with Sadness

An old Chinese Proverb says: 'One who plants a garden, plants happiness.' A garden is also a teacher. Each season brings new learning. Seeds turn into vegetables, and blossom to fruit. In spring the sun melts snow that has sat like a flock of silent, lumpy birds on the tree branches. And mountains stretch their bones, sending icy torrents down vast gullies into rivers and creeks. The power of nature reveals the smallness of human life. Mine resembles a frail twig. I must travel to the next world to reach a higher stage of knowing.

Until then, I work in my garden, talk to Ida, and visit Fang Yin and Con-Lan's fung mu. A simple life is best. Wanting too much brings trouble. I will talk about that soon. First I have more to reveal about mining for gold.

As I said earlier, Soo Tie and I started with pans, later moving on to a cradle. Three years passed before we made a sluice. Not a sluice box — that needs wood, which is in short supply in this area — but a ground sluice. We dug a ditch, placed flat stones in the bottom and shovelled gold-bearing dirt into the stream that flowed through, hoping to trap colour under the stones. Every few hours we lifted them, then washed, broomed or shovelled the mix into our cradle for the final separation. I rocked while Soo Tie poured water over the wash-dirt into the top sieve, which had holes the size of a small fingertip. This action separated the gold and fine sand from the bigger stones, causing the sand to run out and the gold to catch in the sacking on the bottom. We always inspected the sacking nervously. Colour meant money for MaMa and food for us.

That is how we worked, day after day, month after month. In the evenings, before the light completely faded, I weeded the vegetable garden while Soo Tie mended tools or made rabbit traps. Sometimes we ate rabbit stew with steamed cabbage and a morsel of satisfaction. Left unchecked, these pests stripped our tender plants down to their roots.

In the early years we got supplies from Su Sing, as I did not like walking down Buckingham Street to Ye Goon's shop, even though it allowed me to see other women and take note of their fashions which, although exceedingly different to those worn by Chinese wives, reminded me of what lay concealed beneath my trousers and jacket. I was usually ignored, or stared at, as though I was an odd creature, not a person with hopes and dreams. So I was surprised when Ida greeted me a second time.

I asked Ah Sip what he knew about her.

'Mrs Ida is married to Mr Alfred. They have a big farm and a small boy called Jack whose mother died on a boat.'

'He is not their son?'

'No, but Mrs Ida, who was Miss Ida then, and Mr Alfred cared for him until they arrived in Dunedin, where they got married at the barracks. They put advertisements in British newspapers asking for the boy's relatives to contact them.'

'No one has?'

Ah Sip shook his head and worked his mouth into a frown. 'Which makes Mrs Ida and Mr Alfred happy for themselves but sad for Jack.'

'How do you know their business?'

'Mrs Ida talked to me while we were making a special broth to aid digestion. She is clever. Funny, too.'

Ida laughed when I later relayed Ah Sip's account of her life. 'There's a bit more to it,' she said, 'but he's covered the main points.'

If Su Sing did not have certain goods I had to go to Ye Goon's. Small boys waited outside with sticks to knock off our hats. 'Chink snake!' they yelled when my queue unwound and slid down my back.

A boy with dirty brown dots across his nose once poked a stick at Ah He, who chased him down the street. The boy's screams alerted his mother, who ran out of Pritchard's General Store with a sack of flour in her arms.

'Him devil,' said Ah He, pointing to the boy.

'You should be ashamed, running after a child and frightening him half to death. Spreading your germs too, I bet,' said the woman, making Ah He feel dirty, even though he washed every month.

A week later this boy died from sun sickness, after working all day in the hills alongside his father with no hat or water. Ah He was upset when he heard the news and placed a jar of green ginger on the doorstep of the boy's house.

'His mother and father will be very sad,' he said, drinking tea at Su Sing's. 'They loved their small devil.'

I loved my garden. Each evening I watered the plants from buckets I carried up from the river on my shoulder pole. This ritual helped me feel close to Second Brother and my old life in Pong Woo.

When the river rose and we could not make 'good tucker' – a term British miners use to describe a good find – we thinned turnips for local farmers, trudging up and down long rows, ten hours a day, with our backs bent, stopping only to eat salted radishes at midday. Some farmers – but not Ida's husband, Alfred – paid Chinese workers less than those from the 'home countries', meaning England, Ireland, Wales and Scotland. Wong Yet Song, whose chin stuck out – which, according to siang mien, the ancient art of face-reading, means he is stubborn – got mad with one farmer. 'You pay me five shilling, I weak; you pay eight, I strong.' The farmer laughed and said, 'For six, can you be a little bit strong?' Wong Yet Song sighed. 'Seven shillings and I will be best worker.'

In '73 our claim froze for weeks, forcing Soo Tie to work for the borough council. He helped build St John's Presbyterian Church, which now has Californian redwoods growing either side of its entrance. When the boss man, Peter Walker, was not looking, Soo Tie made a Chinese character in the mortar at the back of the building. 'To show I was here,' he said.

I, too, will leave reminders. Always my Fang Yin and Con-Lan's bones will rest in this earth, a thought that causes sadness to rise in my chest like waves until I cannot breathe. Even now, all these years later, I must untangle my breath, before I can take another crooked path.

Remember Su Sing, who gave us goods on tick when we had no gold to sell? Well, when Soo Tie played fantan with him at the Long House one Sunday, he mentioned to Su Sing that I was teaching him to make Chinese characters. The next time I went to the store Su Sing asked, 'Will you write letters for our people?'

Without the slightest hesitation I said, 'I would be most honoured.'

That was how my work at Su Sing's began. Two nights at week, while Soo Tie played card games in the store and opium smokers gathered in the back room, I sat at a table and, under lamplight, wrote letters for my countrymen. I also read out the letters their families sent back.

'You want tea?' Su Sing would ask.

'Thank you,' I would say as he poured me another bowl from his urn and placed it on the table beside me.

One evening a solemn miner brought in a letter that a missionary had given him upon his return from China. 'Will you read it to me, please? I fear it is bad news.'

'Only son has died,' I read, putting my hand on his arm to give comfort.

Seeing tears in the man's eyes, Su Sing took him through to the opium room and gave him a pipe, saying, 'Visit your son in dreams.'

Another night I read a letter to a young man whose family had fallen on hard times. Su Sing listened then, too:

It is five months since your father died. There is much hardship. We have no harvest. Your brothers and sisters cry at night with hunger. I am sad at heart. I pray that on receipt of this letter you send money.

When I finished, Su Sing said to the young man, 'Your mother does not know of your own hardship. Send some of your money, not all.' To me, he said, 'Write what a good son he is. Tell his mother to send love in her next letter.'

I worked at Su Sing's Long House for several years. During this time I wrote a letter to MaMa, having thought about my words for days and nights, as I had much sadness to send. My letter was started and abandoned seven times. After much effort, I wrote:

MaMa,

Don't fall down when you read my words. I am sending them to you from New Gold Hills. Second Brother has gone to the next world. I sent him off with food and money. Love, too. He was very brave,

71

MaMa. I burn incense for him and have built a shrine of stones close to where I live. Like the one he made near our hut in Pong Woo. I wear the shirt you made him like a second skin. I hope our family is well and that Day-Day is growing enough food for you all. The money in this letter is for you. Will you write to me? I call to you across the sea. I will send more money soon. I keep you in my heart.

Your Third Daughter, Ming Yuet

I gave this letter to a trusted missionary to take to Pong Woo.

One year later a letter from MaMa arrived at Su Sing's store. I placed it in my secret pocket, keeping it close to my heart until I was back at Swipers Gully. Soon I knew MaMa's words as well as my own face:

Ming Yuet,

How happy I am to know you are well. So many nights I called for you across the delta. When you did not answer, much sadness grew in my heart. Then your words came, and money too. Thank you. Many blessings go to you. May you be preserved in peace and comfort. You honour your family and ancestors with your goodness. Don't take bitter regret into your heart. Fu Ling is with Grandmother and Great-auntie in the next world. Day-Day takes good care of the fields. There is enough food to eat. You and Fu Ling taught him well. It is hard writing to you, Ming Yuet. This letter cannot give you all my words. I hold you close to my heart and wait for your return. I am your mother. You are my joy.

After receiving MaMa's letter I worked even harder. During the day I mined or thinned turnips, depending on the season. Each evening I wrote letters or helped Su Sing serve in the store. Slowly my secret pocket grew heavy with earnings. When the price was high I sold my gold for fifty pounds. Having such a large sum of money made me nervous, as robberies had increased in the goldfields, including Arrowtown. Also, the Arrow District Miners' Association was causing problems again. Their members thought we brought misery to local merchants by not spending our money in their shops. But their storekeepers did not always sell the food we wanted, and they often charged higher prices. We could not afford to buy from them, as well as pay the rice tax their government had introduced. So we bought from those who gave us the best goods for the lowest price, usually our own merchants.

Such unrest convinced me to send all my money back to MaMa. When a missionary arrived in town I went to see him. After we exchanged the normal pleasantries, I asked, 'Are you going back to China soon?'

'Yes, next month,' he replied. 'Do you want me to take a letter for you?'

I looked at his ears. Their placement indicated intelligence. 'Yes, to my mother in Pong Woo.'

'I'm taking letters for several others.'

Relieved to hear that he was trusted, I said, 'I will come by again tomorrow.'

'I'll be waiting,' said the missionary.

That night I told Soo Tie about my plan. He had been drinking Ng Ka Py, fermented sorghum, with Ah Sip at Su Sing's to celebrate his decision to go to Dunedin for Chinese New Year, so he was in a cheerful mood.

'Keep a little money for yourself. What would you like me to bring you back from Dunedin?'

'Only your safe return,' I said, carefully folding money inside my letter to MaMa.

Soo Tie watched me seal the envelope. 'You have made Fu Ling's promise come true. Happiness will visit you.'

'Thank you for your kind thoughts.'

'I learned them from you, Little Wind.'

My cheeks grew hot with foolish pride. 'How will you get to Dunedin?'

'I have bought a ticket for the Cobb and Co coach. I will stay there about three weeks. You be careful.'

'Yes, I will.'

Next morning I walked into town to give my letter to the man with well-placed ears. He put it in his bag, along with those I had written for five miners who had come to see me at Su Sing's store. One had said to me, 'Write that I am well and will return soon.' I did as instructed, although I knew he would not go home because he was coughing blood into his handkerchief. Another said, 'Tell my wife I am lonely for her skin.'

Skin remembers. I still feel Fang Yin's in my dreams: soft as peach down. Her father's skin was the colour of ripened wheat. He moved in me like wind through a cane field, sometimes gentle – a feather touch; other times twisting and turning until he exploded like a firecracker. I still hunger for him. At night, in my dreams, he bathes me. Other times I am a banquet and he eats me. Always his skin calls to mine.

Soo Tie returned from Dunedin with a red shawl wrapped in white tissue paper. 'If anyone asks, say I bought it for your MaMa.'

A lump formed in my throat. 'Thank you, Soo Tie.'

'It is to remind you of your woman's skin.'

Soo Tie came back with something else – happiness. 'I have met a man like me.'

I was not sure what he meant, so I said, 'Tell me about him.'

'First I will explain how I got this scar.' He touched his cheek. 'Chinese river men take boys as well as girls, Little Wind. One found me working alone in a field late one afternoon. He crept up behind me and put his hand over my mouth. At first I thought he was a friend playing a trick. Then a sharp blade travelled down my

74

face and a solid body pressed against mine. I panicked and, wanting to escape, sank my teeth into the man's hand. He yelled, and in the struggle that followed he gouged my cheek with his knife. We fought like angry pigs until I managed to flick dirt into his eyes. He cursed, but I fought with such strength that he had to release me. I ran as fast as a hare to my village. That night I told a friend what had happened. He said, "Show me." I put my arms around him. He did not struggle. We kissed.'

What he said raised more questions than answers. How could a man want another in this way? I did not understand. But because I respected Soo Tie, I trusted his story.

Also, whenever he talked about his new friend, Lai Jau, the son of a Dunedin merchant, his face danced with joy and his eyes glowed as bright as new lamp wicks. Although I was pleased to see him happy, it took months for me to accept that Soo Tie's love for his young man was a treasure and not a sign of madness.

Why do people want different things? How do desires begin? Why do some stay a lifetime and others disappear without a trace? What would Fang Yin's love have been? Music, which was her father's pleasure; or words, which are mine? Is it that simple? An either or? I no longer think so. Does Lai Jau still make Soo Tie happy in the same way Con-Lan made me? Or is it different? Perhaps I will never understand. Maybe I do not need to.

My friend and protector was in Dunedin visiting Lai Jau when Su Sing heard that the missionary I had entrusted with MaMa's letter and money was in Australia, not China. An Irishman who had worked at the Tipperary mine near Macetown saw him – without his white collar – enter a place in Melbourne where men pay women to lie with them. The Irish miner knew a Chinese man who had given this missionary a letter and money. Because the Irishman liked the Chinese miner and did not want to see him cheated, he waited for the thief to finish his business. One newspaper report said the impostor was still doing up the buttons on his trousers when the Irishman hit him.

'Have mercy on a poor man?' the thief pleaded as blood poured from his nose.

'Where's the Arrow miner's money?' yelled his attacker.

'I was robbed, honest to God. All letters and money were taken.'

The Irishman did not believe him because the man was dressed in fine clothes and looked well fed. He shouted, 'Shame on you!' and punched the villain until he stopped protesting. Bystanders called the constabulary and the miner was arrested. The incident was printed in newspapers in Australia and New Gold Hills, which is how Su Sing got to hear about it. He called us to the Long House and showed us the article.

Back in my hut, I cried tears of anger, rage and sadness. Why had I trusted that faan kwai, foreign devil? Because he had dressed and talked like a gentleman and his ears were well placed. Also, I had feared being robbed and having my woman's body revealed during a struggle, even though I still wore the dead man's red sash under my work-shirt to flatten my breasts, which had grown to the size of firm young pears.

This misfortune turned me gloomier than the hut windows young boys covered with black paint to make us think day was night. I had not saved Second Brother, and MaMa had not received my money. BaBa and First Brother's shadows visited me in my dreams. 'Ming Yuet,' First Brother said, 'go to Su Sing's store, fill a pipe and light a path through this darkness.' BaBa danced across the walls of the hut. His dreamy eyes rolled like conkers around their bony sockets. River men moved their arms and legs across First Sister's stone body.

Soo Tie did not know me when he arrived back from Dunedin. I was talking to the wall and punching at the air. He took my hands in his and said, 'Little Wind, tell me what you see.' But I could not find words. Only tears. Soo Tie said later that my sorrow echoed around the hills, frightening even the crows.

I don't remember much about that time, other than Soo Tie looking after me as if I was First Sister's river baby. He spooned rice gruel into me each morning, and soup or stew at night. Each evening he took me down to the river to wash. 'Turn,' he would say. 'Now bend.' I had lost my way, but Soo Tie led me back with tender care.

A letter came from MaMa during this hard time. Ah Sip brought it to me one Sunday when he came to visit:

Ming Yuet,

It is time to tell you why BaBa mistreated Fu Ling. Years ago when I was younger and still dreamed of a different life to the one I have in Pong Woo, a man came to our village. He was a poet and very handsome. His eyes shone with happiness. His voice sounded like music. Every morning the villagers gathered around him. Old people, small children and women who should have known better, such as me, sat at his feet and watched him draw characters in the dirt. Soon I learned to read and write. I wanted more than I had with BaBa in Pong Woo. So I neglected my work and found fault with your father. All I thought about was the poet and his magic characters.

One day I went to meet him at the marketplace. BaBa followed me. I had barely sat down at the feet of the poet when your father grabbed my arm and dragged me back to our hut, where he pushed me against the wall and said, 'This is your life. Live it.'

I never saw the poet again, although he visited our village many times. After Fu Ling was born with bright dancing eyes, BaBa thought I had dishonoured him. In a way I had, but only with thoughts. Some years later our village was attacked. Fu Ling hid you in the pines. Afterwards BaBa took to smoking opium. The more he had, the more he wanted. So he worked for the river men to get it. Then he sold Li Mei. I couldn't stop him. I tried to love your BaBa, but he had disappointed me too many times. Even so, I found ways to show him respect. I cared for his mother and aunt when he brought them to watch over me. I kept his house clean and fed everyone well. The only other bad thing I did was teach Fu Ling to make characters. Then Fu Ling taught you because he wanted to share this gift.

Do not fear love, Ming Yuet. Embrace that which comes to you. Better to feel heat once than live in the shadows forever. Forgive me. You are my daughter, BaBa is your father, and Fu Ling showed you the way to New Gold Hills. All are important.

Your MaMa

Soo Tie, who had listened intently as I read it out, said, 'Your mother has written a fine letter.'

I imagined MaMa hiding from BaBa in the fields until her best words came. Had her worry-vane pointed skywards? I hugged my red cushion and wept for my family, and for myself, so far from China.

Sadness rearranged my mind. I grew quieter and even more watchful. A hard shell formed over my heart. More of my young girl self disappeared. I lost hope of ever wearing pretty clothes, brushing my hair in front of a mirror and letting it hang free, or laughing and talking in a soft voice.

Soo Tie tried to cheer me up with stories about his trips to Dunedin. One night, while we mended the sieve on our cradle, which we still used occasionally, he talked about the first time he had loved Lai Jau. 'I had the strength of a buffalo. Our bed collapsed. A wire went ping, ping, ping and flew across the room. Later I picked it up and tied it to a piece of string. See?' It hung around his neck like a good luck charm. He shook the spring at me in a teasing way. 'Little Wind, your time will come.' Then with a serious face he said, 'I will never get enough of Lai Jau.'

It was a long time before I knew what he meant.

SIX

Man Who Makes Music in Mountains

I heard Con-Lan before I saw him. He came to me on the wind, playing joyful music that swept away my darkness. I stopped rocking the cradle. Soo Tie ceased ladling. Even the birds went quiet. A great calmness entered the gully, as though the earth, water and sky worked in harmony. I remembered MaMa's words – 'a gift to share' – and thought, yes, music, like words, brings joy.

At dusk I climbed back to the hut with Soo Tie. My arms ached and my hands were crinkled like chicken skin because I had shovelled four cubic yards of wash-dirt into the cradle. As we passed the place where the music-maker had stood with his fiddle a small ribbon of hope curled around me. I decided to save money again for MaMa.

But the easy gold was gone, and much had changed. Chinese miners who had saved one hundred pounds returned home. Others, like Wong Yet Song, who now called himself Sandy McPherson to stop him being teased about his Chinese name, found work on farms. Kong Kai stayed on as interpreter at the Warden's Court. Another friend applied for a position on a farm as a cook, also using an English name. The station master looked surprised when the applicant jumped down from the dray, saying, 'Yes, I Chinese but good cook all the same.' I had eaten his delicious turnip cake and jellied bean curd, so knew his employer would not be disappointed.

Soo Tie's trips to Dunedin increased. He sometimes travelled part way with Kong Kai, who set his homing pigeons free in Alexandra. Each pigeon was named after a mine. The best homers were Tipperary, Homeward Bound and Defiance. Ah Sip waited at Kong Kai's hut for their return. Betting on pigeons gave him almost as much pleasure as gardening.

Lai Jau was Soo Tie's delight.

Con-Lan's music was mine.

He matched his tunes to the weather: loud and powerful when it rained and blew, soft and gentle on warm, still days. My nerves frayed like the sacking on the bottom of a gold cradle and I became forgetful and clumsy if his music did not surround me.

One morning, after I had emptied wash-dirt in the wrong place, Soo Tie said, 'If I bang stones together to make music will you work better?'

How embarrassing. I hoped I had not gone red. 'My thoughts are flying in all directions, Soo Tie. From now on I will think only about gold.'

Soo Tie shook his ladle in a joking manner. 'Music is good, but gold is better.' I laughed and clapped my hands to my ears. 'Call me Foolish Wind.'

'At last – a happy face! It's been too long since you smiled.'

I was still angry at myself for trusting the man who spent MaMa's money instead of taking it to China. My foolish ways had caused family hardship and lengthened my stay in New Gold Hills. I also worried that the music that was helping to heal me might be a fleeting gift, one I could not keep. So I replayed the music-maker's notes in my mind, holding them close, along with the feel of MaMa's hand on my cheek and the smell of peach blossom. I made up words to go with one tune and sent them into the air:

Wind blows sweet and grass grows soft
Music flies across mountains on golden wings
To hold up the stars and light the moon

'You sang a good song in your sleep last night,' said Soo Tie as we walked to our sluice.

I had said the words out loud! 'It was the spirit of three lights.'

'Ah, sun, moon and stars. I think your heart is singing, too.'

A red heat spread across my face. 'I was making up a returning song.'

'I will not return to China, Little Wind.'

'Why not, Soo Tie? It is your first country.'

'I am not the same man who left China. Lai Jau has settled in New Gold Hills. I wish to stay too. Yes, love will keep me here.'

'I will not find love, only gold.'

'And music.' Soo Tie danced around me, clapping his hands.

'You can love music as well as people.'

'Wait until you love a man, Little Wind. Then you will sing more sweetly than a bellbird.'

At that moment vigorous fiddle music filled the space between sky and earth. I glanced up. Con-Lan stood like a beacon on the hilltop, as though he and Soo Tie had somehow conspired. I lifted my hand to shield my eyes from the sun. Con-Lan may have thought I waved because he stopped playing and pointed his bow in my direction. Ah Sip waved back but I picked up the shovel and set to work, wishing my hands would stop shaking.

That night I dreamt Con-Lan played while I flew like a bird. The more sweetly he played, the higher I soared. Red and gold threads – maybe like the ones Second Sister Nuo makes at the silk factory – streamed behind me. Fire shot from my wings as I spun through the air.

Next morning Soo Tie watched as I poured tea into a bucket and put my boots on the wrong feet. He did not comment until I said, 'I'm tired, that's all.'

'Me too; I chased Lai Jau in my dreams.'

My fire dream returned many times. It is still in my night thoughts. So are stones.

Each time Con-Lan played I added a single stone to a shrine I was building for Second Brother Fu Ling, a stone that felt warm in my hand and had a pleasing shape.

Years later, when I showed this shrine to Ida, she said, 'Jewish people place stones on the graves of their dead to let them know they called. Con-Lan's people also mark death with a cairn.'

So, I was not the only stone-gatherer in the world.

Nor, like other miners, was I guaranteed a long life. Death followed us like a looming shadow. We never knew when it might descend.

Plenty of miners died in Macetown, a small village a day's walk in good weather from Buckingham Street, and half a day from Swipers. To travel there in winter, packhorses wore shoes sharpened to a point and held on with frost nails. Saddle horses had lost their footing on the ice and fallen with their riders into the gorge. John McCrae, and later his sister Mrs Hood and her grand-daughter ended their lives this way. No Chinese, though, because we did not ride horses, and we wore rough sack slippers over our boots for better grip. Our music maker travelled on foot too.

Gin, Woon, Sue Dok and Ah Wak mined in Macetown, building a stone wall in the middle of the river before diverting the water from one side to the other. This method allowed them to work the dry side and bring good fortune upon themselves. Ah Wak, who still does not speak good English, worked in a store after the gold was gone. One afternoon two little girls teased him unkindly. As punishment he locked them in the stable at the back and stood outside calling, 'I kiss, kiss, kiss!' The little girls knew Ah Wak was joking, so were not frightened, but they screamed anyway.

Ah Wak laughed every time he told this story, unfortunately not everyone thought it was funny. A miner from Skippers heard it one evening in the Royal Oak. He shoved Ah Wak against a wall and yelled, 'Mongolian filth – stay away from our children!'

This reaction was typical among members of the Arrow District Miners' Association. They even issued a poster to promote their petition: 'We are free men – they are slaves; we are Christians – they are heathens; we are Britons – they are Mongolians.' In a letter to the newspaper the association's president, James Miller, wrote:

Did we come here to explore and prospect a country for these Mongolian hordes from Asiatic shores to fatten on the fruits of our industry? No it shall not be! Rouse, miners of Otago, rouse! Shake off this lethargy, and if union is strength, let us combine as one man, and from Associations such as the Arrow has done; let us not relax our efforts till they extend from shore to shore, and then power and influence be felt throughout the length and breadth of the land.

Miller thought we lowered the standard of morality in the province by not bringing out our families. Those who agreed asked the government to make a choice between us and the Britons, and threatened bloodshed and anarchy if we did not leave.

At the time I wondered if the fiddle player shared these views, but told myself that surely he would not play for us if he did.

When the petitioners asked Ida's husband, Alfred, to buy a subscription to their association he wrote to the newspaper defending the Chinese miners' right to live in the district without being harassed. After describing us as quiet and inoffensive, patient and frugal, and successful contributors to revenue derived from the country's gold export, Alfred asked the settlers to tear down the posters saying 'John goes home to China with his pile', and urged them to ask themselves if they had ever thought about returning home. His final statement – 'Regardless of whether we are settlers or sojourners, we share the same stars' – reminded me of the night

Second Brother Fu Ling and I sat under the moon in Pong Woo. Maybe that's why I liked Alfred straight away.

For a while we sojourners imagined demons on every street corner, until Su Sing reminded us that plenty of good people, like Alfred and Ida, also lived in Arrowtown. 'Name another,' he said during a cheerless card evening. When Ah Nuey said, 'That fiddler from Kent Street seems friendly,' my foolish heart sang.

Two weeks after Alfred's article appeared, a rock was thrown through his and Ida's kitchen window while they were eating supper. 'I jumped three feet,' Ida told me after we became friends. The following night a fire destroyed their stable, where Jack kept his horse, Sunny Boy. Con-Lan, who was dining at the farm, helped Alfred carry water from a barrel at their back door but the intense heat drove them back. Jack's horse did not die quietly: he neighed and cried like a human. Jack was distraught and blamed us, even though the magistrate said there was no proof of 'celestial involvement'. Sunny Boy's pain entered Jack, along with the beliefs of the Arrow District Miners' Association.

Su Sing called another meeting. I stood with Soo Tie by the door and listened to the talk go around in circles. 'Miller and his men need locking up.' 'We are in danger.' 'Fight back; don't let them drive us out.' The loner, Lok Yem, who rarely came into town, knocked against my shoulder as he hurried to buy Shao Hsing from Su Sing.

After all our angry, hurt and sad feelings had been expressed, Su Sing made a suggestion. 'Hate often comes from ignorance. Why not invite the settlers to our camp? Treat them honourably.' A long silence followed but we eventually decided, with Ah Nuey's guidance, to prepare a feast for the following Saturday. 'Each man will contribute gold for supplies and share in the work. We will feed our detractors well. Little Wind and Soo Tie can write notices to paste on buildings.' Soo Tie grinned at Ah Nuey's acknowledgement of his new writing skills. I wondered if a particular musician would come to our feast, and if he did, whether he'd bring his fiddle.

We swept and cleaned and polished until the Long House gleamed. On Saturday morning we mixed goodwill into black bean sauce and spring rolls. Ah Sip picked carrots, beans and corn from the expansive camp garden, while I sweetened my dumplings with musical memories.

Twenty-eight guests attended, including Ida and Alfred, the Butel brothers, the chemist and blacksmith and their wives and children, along with three farming families.

'No fiddler?' said Ah Sip to Alfred.

'No, he's is Macetown; otherwise he'd have joined us.'

'What a pity,' said Soo Tie, avoiding my glare.

We sat our guests on chairs under the lip of the hill, where the sun would not burn their fair skin. I passed sïumáai, an open-topped steamed pork dumpling, to Ida, who said, 'Thank you for inviting us to spend an afternoon in your camp. This is delicious.'

'Small boy not come?'

'Jack prefers the company of lads his own age these days.'

'Please take some food home to him.'

'You are very kind.'

'Do have a second dumpling.'

'Thank you, they are extremely tasty.'

'You have fine dress. Did you make it?' Instantly I regretted my foolish comment. A man would never ask such a question. Ida looked puzzled and bent over to inspect the dumplings.

'Yes,' she said kindly, without looking up, 'but I can't cook fine food like you.'

Ida's kindness also benefited the hospital, which opened in 1880 on the edge of town. 'I went to the opening,' she told me on a walk, years later, 'with no intention of saying that Miss Nightingale thought flowers and newspapers cheered the sick. It doesn't pay to tell doctors what to do; best to seek their opinions. I simply asked

Dr Dickinson if he'd like me to bring anything for the patients. He looked at me thoughtfully, as though measuring a bandage for a wound, finally saying, "Perhaps you should talk to Matron." He took me to meet a stout woman in a grey dress and navy cape standing by the hospital door. Her steely-blue eyes and hooked nose suggested that she could easily control the wardsman, several patients and a doctor.

"Matron, I don't think you've met Mrs Chynoweth," said Dr Dickinson.

"No, how do you do?"

"I'm in fine health, thank you."

"Mrs Chynoweth is impressed with the hospital," said Dr Dickinson.

"Yes, it will serve the community well," said Matron.

"Are you wanting flowers and reading material for the wards?" I asked, testing her knowledge of modern nursing practices.

She looked surprised but quickly recovered and gave me a thorough inspection from head to toe. Thankfully I'd worn a tasteful blue dress rather than my red party one, which I'd been tempted to put on since it puts Alfred in an amorous state. She was not to know that I was wearing the scarlet stays he'd given me for my birthday!

"As you please," she said. "No insects or dust, mind."

"I'll make sure everything's clean, Matron, thank you." I said.'

Each year Ah Sip bought a ticket to the hospital ball, mostly because he supported British medicine and doctors, but partly because the local newspaper published stories about the people who attended, and Ah Sip liked seeing his name in print. He also loved telling stories about these balls.

'The billiard room in the New Orleans was lit with candles. The dancing got rowdy. The noise of boots and shoes on the wooden floor drowned the music of the single fiddler. I stamped my feet like the settlers too!' Ah Sip told me and Soo Tie with a laugh. He demonstrated by flattening the grass around our hut.

'Tell us more,' I said, eager to know who the fiddler was.

'Mr O'Rourke got very drunk and fell to the ground with Mrs O'Rourke still in his arms! Everyone laughed except his wife on the floor. Mrs Stafford got angry when Mr Stafford helped Mrs O'Rourke up and gave her a big kiss on the cheek. Mr Stafford watched his wife's face turn sour as old cream. She threw a candle, which hit him on the chest and set his beard on fire! Mr O'Rourke tipped champagne on the flames and the fire went out. But Mrs Stafford said her husband deserved to burn. She was so cross I was glad I was not Mr Stafford!'

Ah Sip's admiration for British doctors developed after he was injured in a mining accident shortly after arriving in the district. A young doctor from Edinburgh walked three hours in the midday sun to treat him. Ah Sip never forgot this good deed and faithfully supported anything medical. He said doctors had only once made a mistake. One gave him a tonic to stop wind, but it made more wind, not less. He didn't take it again.

Unlike Ah Sip, Soo Tie and I avoided anything to do with the hospital. We treated our cuts and scratches with what we found in the countryside or could buy from our own merchants. When Ah Nuey got an abscess he made a poultice from grass, moss, fern and herbs. Lok Yem smoked opium to relieve his back pain. At one time Chinese miners with serious ailments saw Dr Leung in Queenstown because of his 'no cure, no pay' policy. British miners liked him for the same reason. One sufferer, whose toes turned black during a bleak winter, went to see Dr Leung, who amputated three toes on the spot. Afterwards the miner asked, 'No toes, no pay?'

'Chop, chop, chop,' said the doctor. 'Three toes, three shillings.'

The miner paid up, but insisted on taking his toes away so the doctor would not have anything to show for his time and trouble. 'He's not keeping toes if I have to pay to lose them,' the indignant miner told Su Sing, who had accompanied him. I laughed at this story, although I did not usually enjoy hearing about medical misfortune, fearing that my second skin would be discovered if I was taken to hospital.

'Do not send for a doctor if I become ill, Soo Tie.'

'Well then, you must promise not to get sick,' he replied.

I kept the hut and myself very clean after Ah Sip said Ida thought cleanliness helped to prevent the spread of germs. Ah Sip believed everything she told him, and was quick to praise her. 'If she hears that a woman is low, she takes a basket with baking and funny newspaper stories. Sometime she brings ladies to stay with her and Alfred. They go to concerts at the Athenaeum Hall to hear songs like "Razors in the Air" and "Can You Lend My Mother a Saucepan?" She tells ladies who can read and have money to take out a library subscription at ten shillings a year. Mrs Ida thinks an active mind cures misery. Mr Alfred is always laughing. He is a lucky husband.'

Talking about husbands makes me wonder what BaBa was like before MaMa learned to read and write and made him feel inferior. Did his eyes dance when he saw her? Or did BaBa die inside, along with First Brother, on the Day of Fire and Knives?

I have a memory of MaMa from that time: her hair tangled and her eyes red, coming to the pines to take Second Brother and me home. 'Be kind to everyone,' she said, 'especially First Brother. He is badly hurt.' I don't think she said anything about First or Second Sister but my memory is unreliable.

First Brother thrashed about on the bed, screaming like a pig whose throat had not been cut properly. Ehhhhhh! Ehhhhhhh! Ehhhhhhhhh! BaBa knelt beside him, pressing a stained cloth, red like delta earth, below his stomach. The village doctor, a small misshapen man with oversized hands, said, 'Your son will live.'

'But he is no longer a man,' BaBa said.

'It takes more than one muscle to make a man,' said the doctor.

90

Second Brother put his hands over my ears but I saw with my eyes. Now I remember through them. Second Sister Nuo was sprawled in a corner beside First Sister Mi Lei. Their clothes were torn. Second Sister lay still as a statue. First Sister rocked. A few minutes later, without warning, she banged her head against the wall of the hut, making a din like a lid being slammed on a pot. I jumped. Second Brother shivered. Blood ran down First Sister's face. Second Brother took his hands away from my ears, placed them on my shoulders, and turned me away.

'See to your daughters,' the doctor told MaMa. 'Yes, it is hard, but you are not alone. Other families face this shame.'

Nine months later many babies were born in our village but there were no celebrations, not even for boys. MaMa's baby was born dead. First Sister, who was thirteen, maybe fourteen years old, had a baby who lived only two days. BaBa found him outside with his head smashed. These babies were not placed with our ancestors. MaMa took them to the pines, where BaBa dug a small hole. Second Sister did not get a baby because she was too young, only ten or eleven.

Laughter did not visit our family for a long time. Any happiness had been buried, along with the dead babies. Crops were planted and fish were caught in silence. But late the following year Second Brother Fu Ling drew a funny story in the dirt about a greedy chicken, and MaMa smiled again. BaBa was not amused. 'Your foolish words don't put food in our mouths.' He kicked the characters until they could no longer be read. Maybe BaBa was upset because it was his son, not him, who had made MaMa happy again.

MaMa was often in my thoughts as I worked the ground sluice and waited for my heart to lift when music rolled down the mountains into my lap. I studied each note as though it was a fleck of gold. That was my life until a great calamity came upon me.

PART TWO

Conran

SEVEN

A Great Flood Brings a Muckle Surprise

We had an awful winter in '78. Right blashy weather, familiar to an Orkneyman. Everything froze, even the river. Sheep died under rookles of snow. Farmers worked day and night. Some went gyte from lack of sleep, their hearts freezing, along with the carcasses buried beneath the blinding whiteness that covered the valley. One man set fire to his home after internal voices told him to restore the fields to their rightful lushness or his children would be taken as human sacrifices. According to his wife, who was mortified by his actions and sought refuge at Ida and Alfred Chynoweth's, he hoped the flames would melt the snow and, at the same time, cleanse his sins, which included regular visits to a 'daughter of seduction'.

Less dramatic events, but still distressing to the sufferers and those who cared for them, also took place that winter. Bairns came down with fevers. Their young brows burned hot as the coals in a smiddie's furnace. Fathers struggled through deep snow to the chemist or sought advice from Ida, who was respected in the district for her nursing skills and healing potions but scorned in some quarters for her forward-thinking ways. When a mother of five died from the pleurisy Ida despaired, complaining that the committee for the proposed hospital was slower at raising money than a team of three-legged horses climbing the Remarkables. 'If women were on the committee it would have been built by now,' she told me and Alfred. 'I'll pen another letter to the newspaper.' Once Ida took up a cause she roared like a furnace. Impatient as she was bonny.

Miners suffered too. Hunger scratched at their bellies. Those who could still get supplies on tick ventured into town wrapped in sacks, icicles hanging from their beards, giving them an ancient Icelandic appearance. Even the merchants looked sickly, although some greedy blighters made money during the freeze. The price of butcher meat jumped fifty per cent.

Afore coming to Arrowtown I was a crofter in Stromness, a village in Orkney. Me family owned a flock of sheep, a milking cow and a fishing yawl, but our gloondie landlord ate the best food, leaving us to survive on a plate of gruel in the morning, herrings for dinner and neeps at night. If a lamb died or an icy wind pulled seedlings from our kail-yard, or the sea thrummed and groaned and kept the fishermen indoors, we lay hungry in our neuk beds, which Mother piled high with bracken, having first stuffed the mattresses with seaweed to keep down the fleas. Our house had a sloping floor so the animals' piss flowed away from the fire, where smoldering peat gave off a bitter reek. Aye, it was darker than a murderer's soul, the only light coming from the lum hole.

I built me Arrowtown house with schist, which learned men say is a metamorphic rock. A grand living can be made if a man can pick first-rate stuff from a stack of rubbish.

Mother and me sister-in-law, Annie, still live in Stromness. I write to them twice a year, enclosing money to see them through. Annie writes back with the claik, despite still grieving for a husband and two sons, lost years ago during a flyan storm, when three generations went under the water between two tidal islands known as the Holms, leaving it up to me to keep the women in food, even though I wasna ready for the responsibility. But nor could I watch them grow thin. I came to New Zealand, hoping to make a fortune. Turns out it was stone, not gold, that put food on their table.

During winter months hoar frosts can split rock easier than a drunkard's fist opens a lip. That's how it was in '78: snow, ice and frosts, along with odd hues in the sky and faint tremors underground. A newspaper reporter reckoned a sudden thaw would bring severe floods, since snow was eighty feet deep in a ravine in the Carricks. Gad! Orkney gets snow, but not that much. Nor does it stay long.

It was all we talked about in the Royal Oak.

'Is that anither tremor?' said William, me assistant stonemason. William also hails from Orkney – Kirkness, mind, a fair distance from Stromness, but still on the Mainland.

'Could be the six whiskies you've just tossed back,' laughed Alfred Chynoweth.

Our blacksmiddie, Elias de la Perelle, a melancholic man, put down his glass and walked to the door. 'A big one hit the Maniototo yesterday. Maybe the tail's heading for Buckingham Street.'

'You're thinking of a twister – they have tails,' said the hotelier. Afraid of losing his customers, he added, 'Come back in and I'll pour you a free one.'

'Not much to knock down in the Maniototo,' said Anderson, the baker, rolling his wrists across the bar as though kneading dough instead of reaching for ale. 'But our mountains could do with being hammered flat,' he added, pointing towards Mt Soho.

I liked the grand peaks, despite being raised on undulating land, more akin in appearance to a mass of whales slumbering in soft green blankets.

Anderson liked to hand-wrestle. As I was younger, free drinks often came me way, but I couldna beat the smiddie. Elias had the strongest arms in town. Picked up an anvil like it was a feather. He could make metal sing sweeter than a choir of angels. Good with animals, too. We listened when he said they were edgy, thinking worse weather might be on the way.

A few evenings later I was back at the hotel chin-wagging about grain prices with Alfred and William when Butel, the miller, came in, saying, 'That odd sky's back again.' Sure enough, a distinct emerald-green glow hovered over the town. James Healey, the town clerk, who'd cut all his yackles, as we say in Stromness, which means he wasna born yesterday, reckoned we were in for a downpour. Even so, we didna expect the amount that fell the following day, Tuesday, 24 September. Warm at first due to a nor'wester.

Within thirty-six hours the district was awash. Tons of icy water poured down braes into gullies and creeks. The Shotover, Arrow and Kawarau Rivers tossed boulders and mining equipment around as though they were a bairn's playthings. Bridges disappeared from their foundations quicker than a half-crown can vanish off a card table.

The mayor called a special meeting. Businesses like Lock's Bakery at the back of town and close to the river were considered unsafe and abandoned. A dozen families who'd built on low ground were forced to leave their homes. All over the district, people saved what they could and helped others to do the same.

William moved his belongings from his hut near the river to mine on the rise. While he unpacked, me unruly mind wandered off to the gully where two Chinamen mined below a brae similar to Brinkie's in Stromness, the rise on which I first scraped bow over strings. Grandfather made that fiddle. Knowing me tendency to daydream and misplace all manner of things, he carved an elaborate decoration on the back, so there was no mistaking it. Within six months I could do shakes and trebles and shivers. Stromness music lovers reckoned me notes soared sweeter than a guillemot on the wind, which was a right compliment since these seabirds are graceful creatures. Music has always been me joy. After discovering that the sound changed depending on where I played, I roamed the moors, neglecting chores at the croft in search of sites that produced dulcet notes.

The brae above the Chinamen's claim sweetened even the sourest of notes, and both miners seemed to enjoy me impromptu concerts, bowing after each tune. The smaller one was light on his feet, like Annie afore her loved ones drowned. She'd be working in the kail-yard, her skirt swaying in the wind, then she'd run inside waving leaves in the air, sometimes tickling me or encouraging me to dance a few steps, causing a mix of embarrassment and confusion, for I was gleckit lad.

I learned to dance properly in Arrowtown with twenty-five other men. We wanted to attend a ball organised to raise funds for the hospital, but not feel foolish if we had to accompany various dignitaries' wives in a Gay Gordon. Also, an Irish fiddler from Alexandra was coming to play and I wanted to hear him. Couples, like Ida and Alfred, who could already dance, came along to the town hall, where we took lessons from our teacher, who was French. 'Dancing eez natural, like breathing,' he said. But I didna feel right holding on to another man. So I laughed and jostled and played the fool until Pierre stamped his foot and told me to leave if I couldna follow his instructions. Ida took pity and partnered me in a waltz, her golden-brown curls bouncing up and down as we made our way around the room. Alfred and William also tested Pierre's patience by dancing with more exuberance than the tunes warranted until Ida rectified that situation, too, by having a word in Alfred's ear.

The majority of men in town thought Ida had Alfred in the palm of her hand and feared their own wives might get similar ideas if they mixed with her too often. 'Women are designed to be pudding, not the main course,' Billy Anderson told Alfred after Ida pasted notices to various buildings urging women to put forward their views on the proposed water supply since it would affect their lives as well. 'Some men like pudding better than meat and vegetables,' laughed Alfred.

During Arrowtown's early gold years women were in short supply. A coach arriving with a dozen new dancing girls was a major event. Miners abandoned their sluices, scrubbed themselves clean – which took a strong bush, a bar of soap and several buckets of water – and dressed in their Sunday best. Each man hoped to pick the ripest for himself, as though she was a plum on a tree. One hotel proprietor got so tired of lassies never starting work that he asked for the ugliest one in the country to be sent. Even she was married within a fortnight.

Ida lent her wedding ring to couples who couldna afford to buy their own. When she got it back, Alfred insisted on marrying her all over again. 'You're the most desired woman in town,' he'd say, kissing her full, laughing lips. I played at their re-marriages, and William sang between drinks. Aye, we had some grand times; it wasna all work and floods.

But we didna laugh when the rain continued. Realising the two Chinese miners in Swipers Gully might go hungry, I bought supplies from the general store and meat from the butcher, although it aggrieved me to pay his high prices, and headed up the gorge, intending to leave a food parcel on their doorstep. I was motivated by childhood memories of belly pains when fishing boats couldna go out due to fierce storms.

I reached the brae overlooking the gully by mid-afternoon. The younger Chinaman was shifting his cradle to higher ground. No sign of the older man. Afore I'd reached their hut, a roar, like that of a Viking from Scandinavia marauding westwards, filled the gorge, forcing me to scramble down tussock, shouting, 'Git oot! Git oot!'

A huge force of water from a flooded tributary of the Arrow River spilled into the gully, knocking the Chinaman off his feet. I slipped and slid down the brae, fearful and keyed up at the same time. His oriental features froze as a piece of mining equipment rode in on a surge and tossed him into a roil of debris, snagging his pigtail on a loose piece of timber. I threw me swag and jacket on the ground and leapt into the water. Its coldness wrapped around me like a shroud. I flapped awkwardly over to where the Chinaman had gone under, memories of Nuckelavee, the Orkney sea monster, rising along with panic. Had Father and the others thought of him as they slipped under the Pentland Firth?

I grabbed a pole from a pile of wreckage and poked beneath the churning water. Surely I could rescue the peedie miner since I could only save me kin in dreams. A length of timber jammed hard against the pole. Something like plaited rope brushed me palm, then a mouth latched on as though I was a hunk of fish bait. I shoved a knee hard into the Chinaman's back and tugged at his pigtail. He came out with a pling, like a plug from a sink. Our bones rattled like two pails of cattie-buckies being bounced up and down by a bairn as rubble crashed around us and water surged through in waves. I tightened me grip on the struggling miner. Swallowing terror, along with mouthfuls of water, I struck out for a cluster of rocks that jutted out from the left bank like a stack of rusty wagon wheels.

The Chinaman couldna get onto the ledge unaided, so I pushed and shoved until he was safe, then clambered on meself. His face hung limp as a dead fish over the edge. I pressed on his chest, as me sister-in-law Annie had done when a bairn fell into a chilly-bin I'd made from flagstone, sunk into the earth and filled with water to keep her whelks and limpets alive. Murky water spurted from the Chinaman's mouth.

'Aye, that's right, spit it oot,' I said, turning him on his side and banging on his back, which caused him to cough and groan a heap of times. 'Are you all right?'

He blinked his eye-plinkers as though he couldna believe the bedraggled sight in front of him. Alarm set on his face like a plaster mask. His eyes widened in terror. I stepped back, thinking he'd settle once he recognised me.

Mother has a saying – 'Daft actions lead tae trouble' – which I hadna heeded on the croft. But resting on the ledge, thinking of a fire back at me schist cottage, a mug of sweet tea on the hob, her words came back to me. How quickly could I get the Chinaman to his hut and be off home?

'Can you stand?' His face creased with pain as he tried to lift his head and shoulders. 'Best keep still if you're injured,' I said, placing a hand on his back to prevent him falling back into the water. 'Rest a minute. We'll try later.'

'Thank you.'

'You speak English?'

'Little. Not good.'

'Where's your mate? Ah'll take you tae him.'

'Soo Tie in Dunedin. I walk to hut.'

He tried to stand but collapsed against the bank, clutching his chest.

'Does it hurt?'

He nodded. 'Leg too.'

Ragged purple flesh protruded from a large rip in his breeks. My mind flashed back to Alfred's slaughter shed where, last week, Ida had stood, knife in hand, waiting to dissect a sheep's liver. 'I take any opportunity to learn,' she'd said in response to me quizzical expression. I'd have welcomed her company now.

'Ah'll help you tae your hut.'

'Leave, please.'

'You canna stay with the river risin'. Mark me words. Ah'll take you home.'

Afore he could argue I eased him onto me back, folding his arms around me neck as though they were the front legs of a sheep. His sodden clothes squelched against mine, a cold, clammy combination. We'd not last long in the open.

The ground was slippery as lard, requiring crab-like movements to avoid ending up back in the water. Sharp-pointed speargrass plants we call Spaniards slid through my hands. Nothing felt solid. The sodden brae evoked watery images: Father's restless bones moving like bleached sea creatures across the ocean floor; me brother, a mirror image following in his wake; Annie's husband stretching sinewy arms towards their boys, whose long blond hair spins in the current.

Me jacket and swag waited on the ridge like two faithful dogs. Both would be sorely needed.

Somewhere between the gully and his hut the miner squawked like a diver, a rain-goose seen in Orkney skies, and went hirple. In the fading light his youthful face set me thinking about Annie's dead sons again. I tugged on the Chinaman's necktie but failed to rouse him. Maybe he wouldna survive either. Even so, I couldna leave him. The Orkney deaths still haunted me. I skittered on, aware that any chance of getting back to town afore nightfall had gone.

The door to his hut flapped in the wind; its eerie clatter echoed around the brae. Me puggled feet crunched along a stone path.

Strong odours of seaweed and sugar emanated from the hut. I laid the Chinaman on one of two bunks. He didna move or open his eyes. I wasna sure what to do next, being a man who generally minds his own business, whereas Ida goes out of her way to involve herself in the troubles of others. Our friendship surprises people, given me reticent temperament and her fiery ways. Perhaps her exuberance reminds me of me younger, livelier self. I hankered after that carefree lad in much the same way a well-fed dog longs for the stringy contents of a rabbit burrow.

I found matches on a stone shelf above the fireplace. A flame revealed a tidy dwelling. I lit an oil lamp that sat on a small table. Wind rattled the flattened kerosene tins. The miner's raspy breaths sounded like they came from a badly strung instrument. Was his chest injury serious? Or did Chinamen breathe differently? What a crazy thought. I'd been at Ida's when her friend Ah Sip visited. His breathing was as regular as mine.

After taking off me jacket and shirt I took a closer look at the hut. A well-stacked river-stone fireplace bonded with mortar and straw. Speargrass and matagouri stacked close by. Pots and pans hung from metal hooks. A tin box, as well as a fancy green ceramic jar, with large stones on their lids, sat on the packed-dirt and partially stoned floor. The jar's foreignness stood out like a boil on a backside. What had I got myself caught up in? Easy enough to leave a food parcel on the Chinaman's doorstep, but to cross over the threshold and enter his world was an entirely different matter. Sooner I was off the better.

After I lit the fire, I put me wet jacket back on so he'd not be scared out of his wits if he woke and found a half-naked settler in his home.

Shadows flickered across the rough stone walls. One shape resembled a moorhen, another darrow, which we used as fish-bait on Orkney.

Holding the lamp aloft, I inspected the miner's leg. Bloody pulp oozed from the wound. I cleared my throat. He flinched and edged closer to the wall.

'I am good,' he grunted. 'You leave please, thank you.'

'Ah'll see tae your leg first.'

'You not take off clothes,' he said, clutching his jacket. 'You go away.'

'Sorry, but ah need tae make you comfortable.'

'Not need help.'

'Oh yes you do, young man. Noo bees still.'

I removed his square-toed leather work boots. They were similar to mine with their U-shaped steel heel-plates, but several sizes smaller and with common crescent toe-plates, whereas mine had the fancier V's. No socks.

Using a bone-handled knife I'd found on a shelf among some cooking utensils I cut away more of his breeks.

'I tell you not take off clothes. Not want you stay.'

'Stop mitherin', man. Lay still or it might be your throat that gets cut.'

That shut him up.

The wound went from just below the knee to mid-thigh. A drop of Old Tom wouldna have gone amiss – for him and me – but none was in sight, just a small brown bottle containing a fishy substance. Grim as a reaper I picked up a pot and placed it outside to collect rainwater, watching it fill to the brim in less time than William can empty a whisky bottle. As water ramped in the pot over the fire, I studied the Chinaman's face, for he'd fallen asleep again, perhaps from shock – I shouldna have been so harsh. High cheekbones, a well-shaped nose and a generous mouth; his body, although slight, was well proportioned, reinforcing the notion that brawn wasna necessarily required for mining. His pigtail, which dripped onto his chest, felt slippery as a dancing girl's taffeta petticoat when I moved it to the side. No wonder laddies screamed each time they knocked a hat off and a reptilian creature unfurled as though from an ancient slumber.

I ripped me shirt into pieces and dipped them in boiling water like Annie did afore cleaning a cut.

He woke as soon as the hot cloth touched his leg.

'Feels most bad.'

'Aye, sorry.'

'Bad you stay. Go now. Thank you.'

'Your wound needs cleanin'.'

He shook his head forcefully but I paid no attention, dropping a blood-stained shirt scrap onto the hearth and fetching another from the pot. 'You're too hurt for me tae leave.'

He bit his buddom lip as a fresh strip went on.

'Not good you stay.'

'Ah'll not harm you.'

His chin trembled, so I quoted Bunyan: 'He that is down need fear no fall/ He that is low, no pride/ He that is humble ever shall/

Have God to be his guide.' A foolish choice, maybe, since few Chinese are Christians. Still, he sighed and closed his eyes. Perhaps fine words, said or sung, also comfort non-believers.

Likely his wound would turn bad afore I'd had a chance to stitch it. Shock and infection claimed lives faster than the Ballarat went through dancing girls.

'Pays to keep them clean, warm and well fed,' Ida once said, referring to her patients during a Sunday supper at the farm.

'Surely the same principles apply to dancing girls,' said Alfred.

Ida threw a tea-towel at him but laughed all the same.

Feeling like a thief, I searched through the lad's belongings for a clean shirt.

'Take your blashie one off,' I said, tapping his shoulder, 'and put this dry one on.' I held up a thick flannel work-shirt.

His eyes flew open. 'Go. I yell.'

'Don't skrek,' I said, backing away with both hands in the air as folk do when caught in a holdup. 'You'll get a chill.' I hung the shirt over the back of a chair but he made no attempt to reach for it. 'Hold still while ah bind what's left o mine aroond your leg.' He didna even murmur when I knotted the ends and pulled tighter than intended. Me desire to do good deeds had faded along with daylight. Bugger caring for an ungrateful lad. I was tired and irritable. Hungry, too.

'Whit aboot a bite o supper?'

No response. I cut the pork into small pieces and put them in a pot anyway. An hour later I sliced vegetables and dropped them in as well. While the concoction shimmered and the miner rested, I composed fiddle music in me head, believing a man with a diversion is less likely to bring calamities upon himself or those around him.

Once supper was ready – smelling better than it looked – I fetched two bowls, drained the vegetables and divided up the meat. When I couldna find any spoons, I gave the lad a nudge and pretended to shovel food into me mouth.

He pointed to a shelf. 'See, chopsticks.'

Ah well, if he was prepared to eat me stew, I could use his odd-looking sticks.

Although he was still in his wet clothes, I decided not to make a fuss until after we'd eaten, but I did pick up a cushion and place it behind his back, which produced another rant.

'Bad, most bad. Go away. I beg leave.'

'Stop frettin'. Ah want to help. Noo eat ap.'

His chopsticks darted back and forth but they didna work too well for me. It took a few blinkies to nab a piece of carrot. Then, afore I got it near me mouth, it fell to the floor.

'Like this,' he said, demonstrating in a slow, measured manner.

So there I was, wet, cold and tired, in a hut high on a brae in the middle of a storm, taking instructions from an injured Chinaman.

'Use hands,' he said after another chunk of carrot proved evasive. 'Bad luck if chopsticks fall.'

As if to ward off the possibility, he put his own chopsticks aside and ate with his fingers, which suggested he wasna entirely indifferent to me predicament. I thought again of Annie's lads and how they'd helped me make the chilly-bins. After we'd finished, I grabbed the peddie one by an arm and leg and twirled him around until he squealed like a piglet. I also helped Jack, Ida and Alfred's lad, to make a similar bin for his tadpoles. 'Is this right, Conran?' he'd said, positioning a stone slab, and later, 'Am I a good helper?' 'Aye, you're doin' a grand job, Jack.' No exaggeration. He was a goodly laddie – always following, though, rather than leading.

'More stew?' I said to the Chinaman, pointing to the pot. He shook his head. 'Right, off with your wet jacket.'

'No,' he said, crossing his arms defiantly.

'Ah canna leave you drookled.' I tugged at his sleeve, hoping to slide an arm out. He screamed. I jumped back and hit me head on the wall. A string of curses flew about the room. A twitchy young fellow can set a man's teeth on edge. Ask Alfred about Jack's hooligan ways. I rubbed the injured spot and said grumpily, 'You'll do as ah say.'

A drock of sweat, possibly the start of a fever, had broken out on his forehead. I pulled his jacket off, despite his protests. His narrow shoulders and compact chest reminded me of Annie's eldest boy, the year the sea took him. I thought of Annie never seeing her sons again and wondered if somewhere in China a mother waited for this lad.

EIGHT

Ah Visited Orkney in Me Dreams

Rain was falling on the tin roof when I woke. The fire had gone out so the hut was bitter cold. The Chinaman lay still as a corpse. Even the air felt dense. Was the end of the world nigh, as Elias had predicted? That man's tendency to read any unusual occurrence such as queer skies as a sign that God was about to shut up shop had cast a gloomy shadow over the land.

A tickle in me throat led to a splutter, which awakened the Chinaman. He looked around the room, but avoided looking directly at me.

'Ah need tae tend your woond,' I said, pointing to his leg. 'Or will your friend be back soon?'

A web of pain flickered across his young face. 'Yes, Soo Tie velly back soon.'

I nodded but didna get off the second bunk, sensing it might alarm him. 'You need help until he does. Whit can ah use tae stitch your woond?' I sewed the air with me hand. In and out, like a fisherman mending a net.

'Ah,' he said, and pointed to a cotton bag.

Inside was a purm of blue thread and a bone needle, along with an assortment of pins and buttons, fancier than miners usually keep. Thinking China cotton might be different quality, I unwound a strand. It was no stronger than ours. 'Ah need somethin' firmer. Do you have anythin'?'

He put a hand to his mouth as though shocked and looked around the room, eventually gesturing towards a cushion, which I took over to the doorway to inspect in better light. Mist hung like a bride's veil over the brae, hiding all matter of things, including the gorge where the flooded Arrow no doubt lurched and swayed and raged in the manner of a Saturday night drunk.

The red cushion cover was neatly stitched with horsehair. 'This'll do grand,' I said, pulling the hair out in two long threads. If only it would fly through the air and form rows of soldiers standing to attention along the lad's leg. I dreaded piercing his skin, being of queasy disposition. Such things are best left to medical men and women such as Ida and Annie. But I didna have a choice. So I prepared me rudimentary tools, re-lit the fire and put the pot outside again to collect rainwater, talking constantly, more to settle me own nerves than the miner's.

'Ah'll make us a hot drink first, all right?'

'Thank you. See.'

I found tea-leaves in a ceramic jar but I couldna find a teapot so I dropped a handful in the buddom of two bowls. What would Ida do next? Probably say, 'Cleanliness is the key,' since she believed unsanitary conditions spread disease.

After the '76 typhoid scare, Ida trebled her order of Prize Pale Soap from the Dunedin firm Bardsley & Sons. She urged us men to petition the government for a public privy to be erected in Arrowtown. We didna heed her pleas, being content to use an alleyway or a convenient bush. Ida fumed. 'If men had to wear split-crotch pantaloons and urinate in secluded alleys or behind a bush while attempting to hide the process under a long skirt, petitions would be travelling north each week on Cobbs' coach!

We weren't so cocky when a Dunedin friend sent her an article from the *Otago Witness*. 'See,' she said, ' "germ theory" – the latest medical discovery. I'll paste the story to the council chamber door so those in charge can read it. Come on, Jack, you can help.'

'Can't I go riding with my friends?'

But she wouldna hear of it. Promoting healthy medical practices took precedence over all.

I poured the Chinaman's tea and put the needle in the pot to give it a peddie clean. Would I sew his wound well enough? What if things took a turn for the worse?

'Maybe ah should fetch the doctor.'

'No! You fix, please.'

Coming into the hills had brought nothing but trouble. I should have known better. But since the drownings, and after meeting Ida, I'd developed a need to help others, which was fine until I was actually in the midst of folks' problems then I wanted to be a million miles away. Good intentions are not always matched by praiseworthy actions. As Ida says, 'Consult the lips for opinions, the conduct for convictions.'

'Do you have anythin' for pain?'

He pointed to a globular-shaped bottle. 'Soo Tie say Ng Ka Py do good job when he upset.'

I didna ask about the cause of his friend's heartache, fearing another problem. One thing at a time – that's me. A quick sniff confirmed the liquid's high alcohol content. Gad! What a pong! 'Aye, that should do. Have you had it afore?'

'No, might have big end.'

Assuming he meant 'effect', I said, 'Maybe ah should have a sibble too,' but I quickly lowered the bottle when his eyes widened in alarm. He had every right to be fearful, being in pain and alone on a brae with a man who knew how to work with stone, not flesh. Hopefully I wouldna need to sit on him, as was the habit of one medical man when his patients protested. 'Noo drink ap while ah clean this horsehair.' He took a sibble and grimaced like a bairn being forced to eat a plate of greens. 'That's right. Keep it ap.'

I wiped the hair with a piece of ramped shirt and laid it on the table. 'Time tae thread the needle noo.' Me hands shook like a skirlo on a blustery day, making the task impossible until I licked two fingers and ran them down the hair, like Mother did with her thread. If men paid closer attention to women's work we'd be a sight more useful at times like these.

'Has Ng Ka Py done its job?'

His mouth slipped into a blootered curve.

Small yaps of pain escaped through his clenched teeth as I struck up a certain rhythm: pierce, sew, knot, cut; pierce, sew, knot, cut. Thinking about things in musical terms was a knack of mine. Didna help his pain, though. During one nasty section he inhaled deeply and held his breath as though in a trance. His pupils rolled like small black stones around a saucer of milk. 'Do you need a rest?' I said, noting his wet brow. He shook his head but I stopped briefly to wipe it with a cloth.

When I started sewing again I accidentally pulled an area of skin too tight and it split, then I overcompensated by leaving the next bit exceedingly loose, causing flesh to erupt in unsightly ways, and requiring me to poke and push it back into place. During this messy painful business he floated away, maybe to that place we're said to enter afore dying, although his hands continued to flutter like nervous doves on his chest. I prayed for guidance, hoping there was still enough good in me to attract a willing listener.

'Hang on, laddo. We're almost done.'

I tied and cut the last knot, then stood back to observe me crooked row of horsehair soldiers. His brow was drenched again, even though the fire had burned down.

'You can rest noo.'

'How many stitch?'

'Twenty-two.'

'Same as my age. How many you?'

'Ah turned twenty-eight last March.'

'Good you not sew them.'

'No enough Ng Ka Py in the bottle.'

'You do most hon-o-lable job, thank you.'

I'd be a heartless man to ignore such praise, even if he can't pronoun his 'r's.

'You're welcome. Ah've nivver mended anyone braver.'

That got a peddie smile.

By the time I'd washed the needle and placed it back on the shelf he was asleep, with his pigtail tucked neatly under his chin and both hands folded across his chest. A great weariness came over me as well, so I stretched out on the other bunk and dreamed about a treeless land with lush green fields that slid like dinosaur tails into an ancient sea.

Orkney has over sixty islands, made in the main from sedimentary rock, which, like Arrow schist, splits sweetly into slabs. Stromness is on the largest island, now called the Mainland, although in ancient times it was known as Hamnavoe, which means 'haven inside the bay'. As a laddie, just afore lessom, once all the chores had been completed, I watched ships sail between the Holms into a vast cobalt sea, heading for foreign lands such as Canada, America and New Zealand.

Stromness harbour is tucked into the southwest corner of the Mainland. A bonnie town, even when the kippering house blows its goo across the barley stacks. Vennels wind themselves between slate and stone houses all the way down to the nousts, which are scooped-out hollows on the beach where yawls are left over winter. Beyond Brinkie's Brae lies a croft on a wind-scoured moor. A flicker of memory and I'm back.

Peat burns in the hearth. Fish oil feeds a cruisie lamp, while a supper of clapshot, mashed tatties and neeps spoils. Mother and Annie watch the sea. Huge whitecaps twist and turn, resembling mythical creatures riding the waves with nothing but mayhem on their minds. We're all on edge. No one expected this storm. Father, me younger brother Peter, and John, Annie's husband, and their sons, James and George, are well overdue. This time of year they neeraboot always bring home a good catch of kippers for Mother and Annie to salt. Their absence is heightened by the sound of Mother and Annie keening across the moor.

I woke in the Chinamen's hut with the same feeling, made worse by a skreever rattling the door. A gale in the mountains sounds worse than one on the flat.

The lad whimpered in his sleep. Knorros of sweat covered his forehead. The flesh above his knee was red as a plum; puffy, too. Exactly what I didna want to see. What would Ida or Annie do? In the winter of '61 Annie healed four bairns from the Stromness parish of whooping cough when others from nearby crofts were reduced to a ruckle of bones in the kirkyard. Annie fed the lucky weans water of boiled elecampane roots sweetened with sugar. Like Ida, she has fine nursing skills.

Two almond-shaped eyes slid briefly across mine.

'You'll be all right, wait and see.'

'No fetch medical man – plomise?'

Why did he fear them? Perhaps he'd had a bad experience. 'You have me word. Noo, what would break your fivver?'

'Chinese medicine.'

'Do you have any?'

'No. Need Don Quoi from Su Sing to cool blood, and poultice to put on leg. Take money, see mat. Lift stone.' Each word was pushed out as though from an egg-bound hen. 'Do say not who you buy medicine to give.'

He surely could jumble words. Anyways, how could I've blabbed? I didna even know his name. 'Ah'll not say. Noo, let's cool you doon.'

I placed a fresh strip of shirt on his forehead and used another to wash his hands. Despite a string of callouses on his palms, I felt as though I was doing holy work. Saving him might help compensate for the Orkney deaths.

As soon as the Chinaman's breathing settled and his big moon eyes closed, I harked in his ear. 'Ah'll go tae Su Sing's store noo.'

'Get money,' he sighed.

A rice sack flakkie covered a section of floor between the bunks. Underneath a large stone a peedie drawstring bag full of notes and coins sat like a skylark on a nest. I counted out ten shillings and put the rest back. He obviously didna trust a bank. I piled matagouri into the fireplace, said a prayer and set off at some lick, hoping to be back afore he woke.

The braes were treacherous; whole sides were on the move. Navigating the bridle path required the stamina and surefootedness of a mountain goat. So did scrambling down willsome braes towards the gorge, where uprooted trees and timber from mining plants careered along the river like gyte trows.

During one crossing, while I was precariously balanced on rocks as whirls of white water churned and spun around me, a boulder the size of a hennie-hoose shot by. A man can have too many close calls.

Stones littered both sides of the river in no apparent pattern, unlike the cairn erected close to the lad's hut. Maybe I'd ask him about it later. Stacks of rubble impeded me progress until I reached the flat, where mud and slush had turned the land into a drab brown carpet square instead of the usual September green and gold tapestry.

Su Sing's Long House in the distance brought a pinch of relief, along with a belly of nerves. Despite working with Chinamen on the

Presbyterian church, and finding them industrious and courteous, less likely to fight than us, I felt uneasy. If the lad hadna reminded me of Annie's boys I might have scarped. Instead, I took a deep breath, cleaned me hands on a bundle of brush stacked high on the bank, and ploughed through sways of mud to what local church leaders call the 'Den of Sin'.

Su Sing, whom I'd seen around town, wore a knee-length smock over loose long pants. A green cap with a tassel fitted snugly over his crown and a shiny black pigtail hung down his back. Two men in work-shirts and rolled-up trousers stacked goods on higher shelves. Was more rain expected?

Despite me bedraggled appearance, Su Sing acted as though nothing was amiss.

'How can I help?'

'Ah need a poultice and Don Quoi, please, for a miner with a bad cut.'

'Has a doctor treated him?'

'Na, he lives tae far oot o toon.'

'Any fever?'

'Aye, so he needs your best,' I said, placing ten shillings on the counter.

'I will make him good poultice for five shillings and sell Don Quoi for three.'

Su Sing placed ingredients from vials on a dish set on a highly polished brass scale and weighed them. When each portion met with his approval, he tipped it into a jar. Once the final substance had been added, he placed a stopper in the neck and passed it over, saying, 'Mix with small amount of warm water and smear on wound three times a day until finished. Understand?'

'Aye, ah do,' I said, bowing and joining my hands together.

Respect – or was it amusement? – flickered in his coal-black eyes as he did likewise.

'Now for Don Quoi,' he said, handing over a vial while speaking

116

in Chinese to the shelf stackers, who answered in a joking manner. Their banter unsettled me. Was I being cheated? No doubt they mistrusted our merchants. Perhaps the lad at Swipers would teach me a few useful Chinese words in exchange for learning more English. Me accent might prove difficult, though.

'Tell the miner Su Sing sends him good health and prosperity.'

'Thank you, ah will.'

'Remember to take your change.'

I tucked the jar and bottle into different pockets, joined both hands together and bowed all the way out of the store. The shelf stackers, who'd watched the entire transaction, cheetered again, but maybe their laughter wasna directed at me. Too much can be read into unfamiliar situations.

The track up to town was littered with jars, kerosene tins, a baby's cot and piles of brush – all deposited by the flood. Buckingham Street was also in a right state. Rain had gouged a deep furrow down the centre, making it look as though it'd been ploughed by hooligans. I vowed to take the young fellow his medicine, make him comfortable, then return to town to help with the clean-up.

Edsall Gruber was sweeping rubbish away from his store door. I wondered if it might be worth taking back something from him as well.

'Good afternoon, Conran. Are you run off your feet repairing buildings?'

'Aye, it's a busy time, Edsall. Do you have anythin' tae clean a woond?'

'For you, is it?'

'Na, a miner ap the gorge has a cut.'

'Well then, you'll need one dram of carbolic acid in eight ounces of water, then five parts glycerine and four parts of the yolk of an egg. Mix well. Wash the wound with this mixture twice a day. You want it to form a varnish.'

'Whit if it has already turned bad?'

'Ah, then you'll need my special elixir and a prayer.'

Edsall leaned his broom against the storefront and went inside, returning moments later with a light blue glass bottle. 'Fix me up later, Conran.'

'Aye, ah will, thanks.'

'Mind how you go, and remember to pray,' he said, reaching for his broom.

I was pondering whether the lad at Swipers was still in this world or already on the other side when I collided with Jack outside the general store.

'Steady on, buddo. How are you? Where's that bonny Ida?'

'She's inside doing a shop. Can we go to the races this Saturday, Conran?'

'Not the weather for it, Jack. Maybe anither time.'

Ida explained years ago over a mug of tea how Jack came to live with them, while Alfred fed the hens and Jack played marbles on the veranda.

'His mother, Mary Sinclair, was a single woman who managed to conceal her condition until midway through our voyage. Not a long or difficult birth but shortly afterwards she became hot and feverish. Then her pulse turned rapid and thready. Two girls went for the doctor but as usual he was full of whisky. 'Call me when it's over, for over it shall be,' he told them. Unfortunately he was right. She died from puerperal sepsis three days later.'

'Whit happened then?'

'I don't recall who reported her death, but two crewmen came aft to steerage quarters, where we single girls were housed, and bundled Mary up in a blanket. The older one climbed the ladder with her slung over his back in an undignified fashion, while the younger man held the lantern aloft, inspecting us as though we were sides of beef. He said Mary would go over the side at first light and that she'd not be missed.'

'Whit a thoughtless blighter! Did you give him a piece o your mind?'

'I wasn't about to give him the satisfaction. Besides I had a baby to mind.'

'Weren't there any married women available?'

'Yes, a good number were housed in mid-section, but none wanted Mary's infant. Not even those with babies themselves.'

'Whit a klatter. You were naught but a lass yirsel'.'

'I just did what needed doing.'

That's Ida through and through.

'My, you look weary, Conran,' Ida said, coming out of the store with a shopping basket on her arm. 'Jack, stop tormenting that collar. Come here. Let me tidy you up.'

She couldn't let the boy alone. Perhaps it stemmed from not having had a child herself. Not for want of trying, according to Alfred.

'Are you busy, Conran?'

'Well, with the floods and all ... Whit about you, Ida?'

'We're waiting for the lower paddocks to dry before replanting the crops. Could be a while, though – further rain's forecast. A fever's doing the rounds as well, and Ah Sip's poorly. I took him a pot of chicken broth yesterday.'

'You shouldn't give soup to a Chink. They eat different food,' said Jack.

'Don't say Chink. Ah Sip's Chinese and he likes my soup,' said Ida.

'I don't.'

'Jack! Mind your manners. I'm sorry, Conran.'

The lad needed a clip. Ida kept him tied to her apron strings but no one could deny that she had his best interests at heart.

'The lad's growin' ap, Ida. Disagreein's a sign.'

Ida doesna always see the obvious where Jack involved, although she can defuse other tricky situations. Last full moon a flamboyant

Welshman ran naked down Buckingham Street. The magistrate thought he'd have to lock him up until Ida whispered to the galoot that the size of his manhood was putting the fear of God into church-going women. Apparently the imbecile agreed to keep on his breeks as long as he could take off his shirt. When Ida said, 'Well, your chest is also a magnificent specimen,' the fool said, 'yours is too. Want to join me next time?'

'Ah hope Ah Sip feels better soon,' I said. Along with the lad at Swipers, I thought.

Jack scowled and kicked a lump of mud. Pieces splattered me already filthy wet breeks.

'Jack!'

'Whit's a bit more mud when the whole toon's swimmin' in it?' I said. 'Ida, how would you treat a wound that's turned bad?'

'Has someone been injured, Conran? Can I help?'

Her question required an evasive answer if I was to keep me word to the Chinaman.

'An old drunk fell over a kerosene tin. Nothin' much, only a scratch, but he needs a dollop of something. Said I'd drop it in. No doubt he'll call by the farm if he needs further attention.'

She nodded thoughtfully. 'Well, have him clean the wound, then sprinkle it with boracic powder.'

'Will that do the trick?'

'It might, if he's lucky.'

'Does Edsall sell it?'

'Come back to the farm. I've a bottle in my nursing bag.'

On the way Ida told me about a bairn she'd delivered the previous night.

'Small enough to fit into a sock drawer but a good crier, so he might survive.'

Talk of bairns got me thinking about two English lasses who'd had children with Chinamen near Bannockburn. Several church-going Arrowites, keen on colouring the lives of others to feel better about their own, referred to them as harlots. Blabbing's a queer pastime. Give me a piece of schist and a plumb-line any day.

At the bottom of Suffolk Street I had an idea. 'Ah'll just nip up tae the cottage tae change. Can ah follow shortly?'

'Of course, come by when you're ready. Jack'll help me measure out the powder. He's got steady hands. You should see the new schist edging he's made around my herb garden. You taught him well.'

'He's a fast learner.'

Jack kicked a stone into the road. 'I'd sooner go fishing with my friends. You never let me go anywhere or have any fun.'

'I want you with me, Jack. There'll be time for fishing when you're older.'

Surely she could let him go down to the river with his mates.

After a quick wash and change of clothes, I wrote a note for William: *I'm off to a job up the gorge. See to those in town who've suffered flood damage. Stay in me cottage if you want until yours dries out.* Then I wrapped me fiddle in a woollen scarf, put it in the swag and set off to Ida's.

She was sitting at the kitchen table holding a glass jar.

'Sprinkle the contents on the wound. Make sure you give it a good dusting.'

I hoped it would help, along with the other medicines. 'Thanks, Ida. If you have a wall that needs fixin' . . .'

'Just let me know if it works. If not, I could ask Ah Sip for a Chinese mixture.'

Not wanting to pursue this line, I just gave a brief nod. Things were complicated enough. The last thing I needed was more questions. Maybe she'd insist on fetching the doctor or coming back with me. I mightna be able to save the Chinaman's life but at least I could keep me promise.

On the way through town I stopped at the butcher and bought a pound of chicken bones and another cut of pork. Thankfully no one in the shop asked why I'd deviated from me regular sausage and mutton order. Everyone had worries of their own, which included fretting over the amount of rain still predicted.

I entered the river, trying not to think of the cold or the crossings that lay ahead. A grey bleakness covered the land. Even the schist on either side of the gorge appeared dull. A bitter wind doubled me misery. But I thought of Annie's boys and pressed on, feeling increasingly apprehensive as the miles fell away.

In the distance, the lad's hut, high on the brae, resembled an ancient Pict lookout. Not a wisp of smoke came from the lum hole. Was he still alive? What would I do if he wasna? I felt a might uneasy as I opened the door.

NINE

Love Comes with Light and Dark

He was hot, despite dead embers in the fireplace and the hut being cold as an Orkney chilly bin. But he'd put on the flannel shirt I'd left over the chair. I raked the ash and built a mound of speargrass and matagouri over a scrap of paper. Even the bleakest of times can be cheered by a flame. The cloth I'd left on his brow had slipped onto his right shoulder so I rinsed it in fresh water and put it back. He stirred but didna speak. Good intentions mightna save him. Things could turn pie-eyed. I should have brought a bottle of brandy to settle me nerves.

I tossed chicken bones, vegetables and a pinch of salt into a pot, hoping the smell would bring him around. But though soup would warm his belly, it wouldna do much for his leg. I lined the medicines along the table as though drinks on a bar. Which would I try first: powder, poultice or elixir? Without medical knowledge I might as well be tossing a coin. Edsall's elixir might be as good as any.

I gave the lad a peddie shake. 'Best see tae you noo.'

His hand rose like an oystercatcher's beak coming out of a mudflat.

'What you do?'

'Ah plan tae fix you.'

'Fix?'

'Make better. Soon you'll be right as rain.'

'Please, not put outside.'

Mercy, what a pickle! As if I'd toss him out of his own hut into the storm. 'Not that kind o rain. Ah've good medicine. Make you stronger.' I thought of flexing a few muscles to convey the notion of strength but decided a fighter's stance might scare him. Instead I propped him up like a good wee wifey and tipped the elixir into his mouth.

'Not Chinese.'

'Na, but it'll make you better. Take anither sibble.'

Talk about a sour face. You'd think he had the back-door trots. I suppressed a laugh and pulled me scarf from the swag.

'No hang, please. I be good now not bad.'

Seeing his terror was real – he'd pulled the blanket up to cover his throat – I said, 'It's tae bind your chest, you fuilie thing.' He raised two fists. I was in no mood to toady to a girnie lad. Jack's nonsense earlier had been quite enough. The Chinaman would do as he was told. 'It'll hold your ribs in place until they mend,' I said, sliding the scarf between him and the cushion at his back. He groaned like a grullyan but I kept winding, recalling Ida's bandage slogan: firm, fulsome and fresh. Her hospital versions, made from old linen sheets ripped into strips and looped between two wooden rollers, were a far cry from a plaid scarf with frayed ends. 'There, your ribs are stiff as a board.' Not the wisest thing to say, seeing all of him could be rigid by morning. The wee blighter turned his head to the wall and placed both arms firmly over his chest.

'You'll thank me if it works.'

'I say thank you many time. You not listen.'

I sighed, which caused him to say 'thank you' again, loudly, as though deafness was another of me defects. 'All right, – ah've got the gist. Noo we'll try Su Sing's Don Quoi.' But what if it worked against the elixir? Ida knew about medical disasters. She'd told me about a young nursemaid who used a soda foment to relieve a child's abdominal distention when it should have been turpentine based. Hopefully she wouldna need to tell disastrous stories about me.

'Has the elixir helped?'

'Not make brave like Ng Ka Py.'

'Didna make you blootered, ither.' I put on a silly face and wobbled around the room as though drunk. 'Noo, take a drop o Don Quoi.' I supported his head while he drank a mug of water. 'Rest ap while ah mix Su Sing's poultice mixture with hot water. It's sure tae do the trick.'

'Why you want tlick me?'

'Ah'm not planning tae trick you, it's a sayin'. It means it'll do the job.' No wonder wars are fought between men who speak in different tongues.

'Not good. Go now. Please.'

'You're in na state tae leave. Ah need tae fix you ap.'

A groan with the weight of the world at its centre spilled into the room. He pulled the blanket up further until it covered all but his eyes and forehead.

'Whit would help you forget the pain?'

'MaMa told stolies to make pain go away.'

'What were her stories aboot?'

'Wise men who slept on golden pillows and roamed the night sky.'

'Ah know nothin' o them. Would a story aboot fairy folk do?'

'Yes, thank you,' he said, grinning shyly.

Although not certain that he'd fully understand I launched into a story. 'Orkney fairies are sometimes called trows, and are nasty creatures who take great pleasure in apsettin' folk. They're short and ugly with wizen faces and pale skin. They have red eyes and green teeth and wear charcoal grey tunics and brown mittens. Folk say they occasionally put on armour but ah nivver saw any dressed like that mesel'. Ah had trouble with them a while ago. They attack cattle, you see. Sometimes stealin' a healthy beast and replacin' it with a sick one. Ah lost a cow tae trow-shot but nivver found the weapon. Unlike Peter Tankerness, who locked his fairy arrow in a chest and wouldna allow anyone tae luk at it for fear the fairies would return tae steal him awa. Me own cow became thin and ill aroond the same time, so ah summoned a wise woman who, durin' the examination, foond lumps beneath its skin. Tae be sure, she pierced the cow in several places with a large needle. It didna bleed on the outside, which meant it was bleedin' inside from the fairy's blow. The cow died, even though the wise woman ripped a page from Mother's Bible, rolled it intae a pellet and stuffed it in the woond. Ah heard later that four Shetland cows survived this treatment but nivver an Orkney one. Noo whit do you think o that?'

All I got was a quizzical expression. Unsure whether it was due to pain or confusion, I said, 'Ah'll na put paper in your leg. You were not hurt by a fairy.' Still no response, not even a grin, so I said with a pouting face, 'Am ah a good storyteller like your mother?'

At last – a smile. 'Make happy. Thank I you?'

There's that funny order of words again but the meaning's clear. Being a right bletherskate, I added, 'Ah play well, too,' and pretended to draw a bow jauntily across strings. That made him smile.

'Yes, I like listen to music.'

While chicken bones and vegetables simmered, I gave a spirited rendition of 'Grant's Rant', rolling me eyes and grinning like a ninnie.

After supper he got in a right pizzo, wriggling and wincing, unable to lie still. It wasna till me own bladder was close to bursting that I realised why.

'Do you need a bucket?' I said, making piss piss sounds.

He nodded and gestured towards the back of the hut. I found a night bucket which I placed beside his bunk. Then I stood back, not sure how he'd manage without help, which I wasn't keen to give, mind. It's one thing to carry an injured lad to his hut and stitch him up, but it's an entirely different matter to help him go about his private business. He must have thought along the same lines for he waved me out the door with a flurry. Any faster and he might have taken to the air with speed of a razorbill.

The night was black as printer's ink. Rain pelted down, creating pools in the uneven ground. I added to the torrent, then wandered around like a knotless thread, wondering if William was working or drinking. Whisky flowed down that man's throat as often as salt went on his neeps.

Afore long, thunderspots had soaked me through to the bone, setting off shivers that grated on me already strung-out nerves. Every bit as bad as Jack's school chalk screeching across his slate. I hurried back to the hut, not caring whether the Chinaman had finished or not.

He lay on his bunk, pale as a ganfer. Plenty was in the bucket, though. He'd rest easy for a while. Despite the foul weather, I put everything back in its rightful place, since tidiness is a habit of mine: a good one for a stonemason. I never rest until a stone sits well.

I gave the lad extra drops of Don Quoi and smeared more of Su Sing's mixture on his leg. The poultice may have stung, as he bit his buddom lip, drawing blood. It was time for another story, one about selkies.

'One day long ago some angels fell from heaven. Them who fell on land were known as fairies – you already know aboot them – while them who fell intae the sea were called selkies. Selkies are gentle bein's who, in human form, dance on the seashore in the moonlight or bask on far-off rocks or skerries. Folk call them shape-shifters because they can change from seals intae beautiful nimble humans. Sometimes they come ashore for special raisons. Me grandmother knew a mortal woman who had a husband who couldna satisfy her, so she cried seven tears intae the sea at high tide. A selkie-man crept ashore, shed his skin, and pleased her night after night.'

'How man please?'

This could take some explaining. Best give a simple answer. 'He loved her with all his heart.' I pointed to my own and attempted to look soppy.

'Did woman love man?'

'Aye, they say she came tae feel that way.'

What would a young lad know about love? I knew nothing meself. Oh, I'd paid tent women ten shillings and hoped to last long enough to feel I'd got me money's worth, but that doesna count.

'Try tae sleep, lad. Let the medicine do its wirk.'

I piled matagouri on the fire and crawled under a blanket on the other bunk. Thoughts of Annie and John, and Ida and Alfred, and the love that passed between each couple, kept me awake. Would I ever care for a lass in the same way?

Next morning the Chinaman seemed a shadie better. I heated the previous night's soup and ladled some into a bowl. 'Here . . . whit's your name?'

'Soo Tie call Little Wind.'

'And back in China?'

'MaMa say same. What you call?'

'Conran.'

'Con-Lan?'

'Close enough.'

'What land you come flom?'

'Orkney, near Scotland.'

'Man with yellow head come Scot-Lan. Ok-nee long way?'

I assumed he meant hair rather than head, although William's skin can take on a yellow tinge after a heavy night's drinking. 'Aye, Orkney's a very long way.'

128

'You miss, be sad?'

'Aye, ah miss me soft green land. Do you miss China?'

His chin trembled and tears pooled in his chocolate brown eyes, reminding me of deep and mysterious lochs with histories longer than memory.

'We're both a long way from home,' I said quietly. 'Ah saw a cairn ootside. Did you build it?'

'What you mean? I not savee.'

'The pile o stones tae the right o your hut.' I pretended to build it in the air.

'Ah, yes. I make for MaMa's Second Son Fu Ling. He want come to New Gold Hills but he die.'

'Ah'm sorry,' I said, patting his arm. Then, to me surprise, I told him about those who'd drowned. Orkney sayings swam like herrings out me mouth but he seemed to catch enough, for tears soon ran down his cheeks. Mine, too; we were a right pair of sooks.

By the time I'd wiped away me blubberings, the water to clean his wound had finally boiled, and his cheeks were also dry.

'Noo it's time for a friend's powder.'

'Su Sing's all gone?' he said, frowning.

'No, but ah want tae give this a try. Ida's a grand healer.'

'Is she same lady who came to camp party?'

'Yes, she and Alfred talked about it for weeks.'

He cocked his head, maybe to check if I was telling fibbers, and although he didna look me directly in the eye, I got goose-bumps. Feeling meself turn red, I stroked me unruly beard while the lad rubbed his own smooth chin. Thinking he'd softened, I said, 'Ah'll take a luk at your leg then decide.'

'Chinese is best.'

'We'll see.'

Using a clean piece of shirt, I washed off a patch of Su Sing's mixture. The area near the knee was still red and swollen, but I grinned and said, 'Not bad, but ah'd like tae use Ida's boracic powder.' I showed him the bottle. 'What do you think?'

Once again he folded his arms and turned his head towards the wall. Sensing a fight was looming, I had a brain rush. 'Ida took a pot o chicken broth tae her friend Ah Sip a couple o days ago seein' he was poorly with a chill. It helped. He asked for more.'

'Ah Sip not gleedy.'

'You're right,' I said, cursing the exaggeration. 'He was grateful for the one pot.' Trying to make up lost ground, I added, 'Ah Sip also liked the vapour treatment Ida used tae clear his head.' I put a blanket over me own and pretended to lean over the steam rising from the pot.

'Ah Sip like funny things.'

'Then, please, be like Ah Sip. Try Ida's powder.'

His arms remained crossed but I could see he was thinking. I raced on. 'Whit aboot Chinese for you and Ida's for me? We'll see whit wirks best.'

A smile hovered at the edges of his oystershell-pink lips.

'We make bet?'

'Aye. One shilling?'

He propped himself up. 'Five?'

Pain and something else shot across his face – a memory, perhaps – not an expression I'd seen afore. Tenderness, tinged with sadness. A moment later it was gone.

I washed away more of Su Sing's ointment, then dusted Ida's powder above and around his knee until it covered the wound like a sprinkling of fresh snow, an image which called to mind a bad winter on Orkney when Annie's boys came down with fevers. She'd wrapped them in sweating blankets and used a month's supply of peat on the fire, hoping to burn out their illness. Several days later they woke, pale and weak, but with no fever. We celebrated with music and ale. I hoped this lad would recover too.

He didna protest when I trussed his leg up in the blanket that had covered me the night afore, thinking a good sweat might also work for him. Nor did he say a word when I fed the fire until it belched and roared. Fearing he'd close his eyes and slip away if I didna keep him occupied, I said, 'Do you know any tongue-twisters?'

'What town do twist tongue live?'

'They're not people. Just words that soond like each ither. You have tae say them fast.'

'Show, please.'

> *Whither wid yi rither?*
> *Ur rither wid yi whither?*
> *Hiv a stewed soo's snoot?*
> *Ur a soo's snout stewed?*

He looked puzzled, so I said it again, this time slower and in best English.

> *What would you rather?*
> *Or rather would you what?*
> *Have a stewed sow's snout?*
> *Or a sow's snout stewed?*

He studied me thoughtfully. Like a puzzle he needed to put together. Finally, he pointed to his nose and said, 'Not eat mine?'

I rubbed me belly, which might have caused a commotion if I hadna accompanied this action with comforting words. 'Easy buddo, while it's a fine-lukkin' specimen, ah'll bees cookin' pork for supper.'

'Ah, pork, you want cook me. Be kind and good, thank you.'

No point untangling his sentence. He'd got the gist and I his. Still, that lick of praise unsettled me. I didna deserve it. Not after deserting Mother and Annie. Money didna make up for me absence. Chinese sojourners also left their families for economic reasons but usually returned. I'd not see me relatives or Orkney again. A lump rose in the back of me throat.

Needing to lift me mood, I told a joke. 'Did you hear the story

131

aboot the two miners who had a fight and were brought ap afore the magistrate?'

He shrugged and scowled.

'Well, ah've na idea why it started – over gold, maybe. Anyways, they'd been brawlin' ootside the hotel for ten minutes when things turned nasty. One man bit the other's ear right off.' I tapped me own so he'd not miss the significance. 'The magistrate charged him with assault and boond him ower tae keep the peace. 'Keep the piece,' the ear-biter yelled. 'I can't do that. I swallowed it!' I waited for the lad to laugh but he just blinked his plinkers.

Finally, he said, 'Not undee-stand.'

I should have kept me gabby mouth shut.

'No speak well English. You teach, please?'

What could a man with a few years' schooling teach him? Then I remembered a story I'd heard from Edsall after he'd been to Cromwell for a celebration dinner to mark the end of New Zealand's provincial councils. Maybe it would show the lad that he could learn English more easily than a daft Orcadian could pick up Chinese.

'Ah'll tell you anither story.'

'Thank you.' An expectant look spread over his face.

'There was this celebration.'

'Chinese?'

'Na, it was English. It took place in Cromwell. Many important people such as mayors were present. An American was seated next tae a Chinaman. Dinner started with soup.'

'What kind?'

'Ah don't know.' His face fell, so I added, 'Maybe chicken.'

'Ah, is good soup. Please, go on.'

'Efter they finished their soup course, the American leaned ower and said tae the Chinaman, "You likee soup?" The Chinaman nodded and smiled. After they had eaten all courses ...'

'How many?'

'Four,' I said, making it up to keep him happy.

'Big meal.' He pushed out his stomach, which made us both laugh until the effort caused him to clutch his ribs, which turned us serious again.

'Efter the meal wis finished,' I continued, 'the guest o honour wis asked tae speak. The Chinaman sittin' beside the American wis an Oxford-educated philosopher . . .'

'What mean?'

'That he wis a clever man who went tae a very good school where he thought aboot important things.'

'Like Ah Lum?'

'Who's Ah Lum?'

'Illus-tee-ous Chinese who speak most good English.'

'Yes, same as Ah Lum. Anyways, Dr Wellington Koo stood ap and walked tae the front o the room, where he made a grand speech in flawless English.'

'Fwoo-lis?'

'Dr Koo didna make any mistakes.'

'He talked good?'

'Yes, he had excellent English. Much better than the man who sat next tae him.'

'Ah, so big shame.'

'You understand well.'

He beamed like a well-maintained cruisie lamp. A fine-looking lad when his face wasna screwed up with pain.

'When Dr Koo returned tae sit beside the American he leaned ower and, in a very serious voice, said, "You likee speech?"'

The young miner laughed so much he nearly fell out of his bunk. His chest must have hurt because he asked for Ng Ka Py. After taking several sibbles he passed it to me.

'Likee Ng Ka Py?'

'Likee soup?'

We carried on in this manner, laughing and drinking, until our stomachs rumbled. 'Drinkee now?'

'Wantee tea?'

Later we played 'I Spy' in Orkney and Chinese. I learned dōu, knife; wún, bowl; yuhk, meat; and dang, chair. He did better because he already knew many English words. But he liked to win honestly. When I played dumb a couple of times, like I used to with Annie's lads, he said, 'You not think well.' So off I went again spluttering out nouns, which seemed to amuse him.

His eyes shone like wet flagstones and his voice softened as his tongue curled around his own language. And he clapped each time he won. I got caught up in his happiness. We played well into the night.

I brought him the bucket afore we settled to sleep and went out for a walk while he tended tae his business. Me head whirled with strange thoughts. Why had his voice changed during the evening? At times he'd almost sounded like an excited lassie. And something about his chest was odd. Aye, he'd hurt it, which might have caused the swelling. But why did two mounds sit like gimmer shells? Not big and squashy like tent women's. Nor were they like mine. The longer I thought about them, the more I wanted to race back into the hut, open his shirt and take one in me mouth. Then I remembered something else. His necktie, which I'd tugged in an attempt to rouse him after the flood, hadna concealed a well-developed Adam's apple.

On the way back to the hut I heard him greet, gentle and low like Mother and Annie. Gad! Why hadna I realised? What nyaff doesna recognise a lassie's ways? I shoogled from side to side. Me mind birled like a wobbly wheel. Instinctively I knew she'd send me away if she thought I'd discovered her secret. That's if she didna take to me with a meat cleaver first. A surge of longing came over me. I wanted to hold her. Take those small hands in mine and kiss each inch of callused flesh.

But I walked in as though nothing had changed, picked up her bucket and went outside to empty it. Afterwards I sat on a schist outcrop, trying to make sense of the situation. Had she always dressed and worked as a man? Did anyone in Arrowtown know her real identity? Why pretend to be someone you weren't? Safety reasons perhaps, since the goldfields could be dangerous for unattached women. An image of a meadow thick with grass-o-parnassus, an Orkney flower with honey in its white caps, arrived out of nowhere, a bit like this mining lass. My pilly thought so too, rising like one of God's serpents. I couldna go back inside for fear it would burst from me breeks. So I took it out and gave it a right good working, and, queer as you might think, sent seed down the brae to mix with her piss.

After wiping me hand on tussock and dunking that fuile head of mine in a puddle of cold water, I sat back on the rock ledge. Seems love can arrive without warning. Mine had snuck up quiet as a mouse, though I'd always felt content playing on the brae above where while she and Soo Tie mined. Had some part of me known even back then? Annie used to say when she and John were courting that she wouldna want tae live without him. I imagined never seeing or talking again to the lass inside the hut. Annie was right. Life wouldna be worth living.

Me heart raced ten times its normal speed. Gyte, I know, for if I declared meself a suitor, she'd be unlikely to accept. And, even if she did, Arrowites wouldna fancy a Chinawoman winning the heart of a single man with a stone cottage and money in the bank. Not a month went by without merchants with daughters of marriageable age inviting me to supper.

Back inside the hut I joked about the weather. 'We might grow old afore the rain stops,' a thought that now pleased me.

'Stitches come out. Then you go please, thank you.'

Despair surged and swirled like the wild and dangerous waters of Pentland Firth. I poked the fire with a matagouri branch, which burst into flames. I held on to it as if to prove that nothing could deter me. 'When will your minin' partner return from Dunedin?'

I also wanted to ask if he meant anything to her but suppressed that urge.

'Octobee, then go back for Chinese celeblations. Please, put down stick.'

Sparks flew in all direction as the flaming object landed in the hearth. Something similar happened inside me. 'Will he stay for your New Year? A special time, isn't it?'

'Yes. We settle debts, clean hut and take bath. Light tom-thumb bang-bangs – make new messages. You likee?'

I laughed, and so did she.

'What you do at New Year, Con-Lan?'

'We sing and dance and drink ale. And we visit folk. Years ago, wanderin' bands of young men went from house to house. The one known as the "Kyerrin Horse" carried a straw basket for householders tae put gifts in.'

By the time I'd finished telling her what Orkney folk got up to she was asleep. I lay on the other bunk, hoping to nap, despite not having a blanket. Mine was still around her leg. Mostly I wondered what might be coming me way.

TEN

Skin Gives More Pleasure than Stone

The blanket was back on me when I woke next morning. Little Wind was on her bunk, still as a tattie-bogle in a field on a windless day. The idea of her getting up in the night to cover me was right pleasing. Then I thought of the hurt it would've caused.

'Yaase min,' I said, in a dipped-in-the-honeypot voice.

'Jóusáhng.'

Over the next six days, rain, torrential at first, then a thick drizzle, drenched the countryside. We passed greetings back and forth, tangling ourselves up in each other's words, sliding them along our tongues like sweeties. Little Wind learned how to shape Orkney vowels by watching the position of me mouth. At one stage I considered shaving with the sharp bone-handled knife to give her a better view, but decided against revealing me ghostly white chin.

In between language lessons we shared meals and told stories about our lives afore coming to Arrowtown. I recalled those that shone a low but steady light on me better aspects, hoping to impress her but not come over as a braggart. She described China in such detail that I could almost see the paths and fields and people in Pong Woo. Each time she told me about a family member, she rearranged her features until they resembled that person's. Her contortions for Grandmother and Great-auntie were amusing but it wasna funny when she got to Fu Ling. Her beautiful almond eyes filled with tears and washed away her previous joy. All I could do to ease her sorrow was make tea.

I was jumpy when it was time to check her wound. Whatever the condition, a change was coming.

We briefly caught each other's eye as I rinsed away Su Sing's poultice and Ida's powder. The angry redness had almost gone. Just a peddie patch remained around her knee. The rest looked fine. She put out her hand for the money. I shook me head. 'Still a ways tae go. Money doesna leave an Orkneyman's hand that easy.' She clicked her tongue as though she was angry. I clicked mine back. Next thing we were laughing fit to spret.

'We both win,' I said.

She looked up at me and smiled. 'Most good.'

Like us, I thought, but didna say. 'Let's sprinkle more o Ida's powder around that knee.'

I removed her stitches three days later; cutting knots, then pulling the hair out with me teeth, briefly resting both lips on her skin, which was smooth. The last tent woman I'd lain with had had rough skin. She'd wrapped her hairy legs around me as though she was a grizzly bear and I was a morsel of meat she planned to devour. Even afore I'd truly got going, she'd drawn blood with her razor-sharp toenails. Little Wind's nails were neatly trimmed and her small toes perfectly formed. I longed to stroke them.

That night torrential rain made a right dunder on the tin roof. I sat in the lamplight while me thoughts raced faster than a white-tailed moppie crosses a hill. Little Wind seemed content to rest, only speaking when I put the last of Ida's powder on her leg.

'Ah Sip says Ida make good medicine.'

'She does. She has a way with plants and a desire tae help. Just like me sister-in-law Annie. Do you miss not havin' a family tae yap with?'

'What is this yap?'

I placed a hand aside me mouth and pressed fingers and thumb together which made her chuckle.

'I miss. But please not make laugh. Pain is bad in chest.'

'Ah'll be serious then.'

'You must go back to town.'

'It's too late tonight. And you need the bucket.'

A new set of worries took hold while I waited outside. What if her chest got worse or her leg festered and she died after I left? Perhaps I should confide in Ida. But what if she notified the doctor? Little Wind trusted me. I didna want to disappoint her. Me heart was closing to breaking and I hadna even kissed her on the lips.

I went back in with a fuilie smile. She lay on her side, facing the wall. I wanted to run a hand down her spine until the bones parted and let me in.

'Are you comfortable in that position?' I said, picking up the bucket.

She didna answer.

The ground steamed as I tipped out her piss, the only sign of warmth. A slice of moon slid behind expansive black cloud. Could an Orkneyman living in New Zealand span yet another world? China sounded so unfamiliar, despite Little Wind's stories.

'Ah'll play an Orkney ballad,' I said, coming through the door. 'This one's called "The Great Selkie o' Sule Skerry".'

She tucked the blanket around her chin as though ready to sleep.

I played that sorrowful tune with great feeling, sometimes lowering the fiddle to sing a verse. *I heard a mother lull her bairn, and aye she rocked, and aye she sang. She took so hard upon the verse that the heart within her body rang.* As Little Wind's eyes closed, I returned to a land where the sea rippled beneath a hammer-beaten sky and a beam from a distant lighthouse carved a path between two rock stacks. *I am a man upon the land; I am a selkie on the sea, and when I'm far frae ev'ry strand, my dwelling is in Sule Skerry.*

We didna speak afterwards, although I sensed she was still awake. The embers in the grate died down as the flames inside me gathered strength. By the time I got into the other bunk, I was as fearful of leaving as I was of staying.

Everything was different next morning. She seemed uneasy, and I was all fingers and thumbs, spilling tea, knocking over a chair. I didna know how to be with her any more. Even the rain had taken on a sombre tone. I fixed the fire, asking in a voice that bent like a sapling, 'Are you feelin' better today, then?'

'Yes, you now go,' she said firmly.

'I'll get matagouri for your fire first.'

I tramped the braes in a mood, pulling on brush and snapping matagouri like they were kail stalks. Me head spun faster than a thresher. What should I do? Leave as she wanted? Or find an excuse to stay? I considered falling off a ledge high enough to cause a reasonable injury, but not so serious that I'd break me neck and not be able to crawl back to the hut.

While I was clambering about looking for a possibility, two Chinamen came into view. One had a pole over his shoulder with two bags hanging from it. Possibly Ah Sip. I was too far away to be certain. The other man may have worked with me on the church, betting on everything, even which tree branch a bird might land on. Gambling was another thing the settlers disliked about the Chinese sojourners, while conveniently overlooking their own vices. I crouched down afore the two men saw me, crawling on hands and knees until out of sight. Me stomach lurched as though it held a day's catch of cod, haddock and skate, each fish swimming in a different direction. Our strange but wonderful time was coming to an end.

I burst through the hut door. 'Visitors are comin'.'

'Go, please.' She flapped her hands anxiously.

I stuffed me fiddle into me swag. 'Will you luk oot for me tomorrow night?'

She shook her head.

'Ah'll play on the brae. Open the door if you bees alone. Otherwise ah'll head back tae toon.'

'Leave now, thank you.'

I took her hand as though it was a delicate flower. 'Ah go with a heavy heart.'

For a brief moment her face softened, giving me reason to brim with hope.

By the time her friends had started their climb out of the gully, I was over the rise and back on the bridle path heading for town, already planning me next trip, desperate to kiss her sweet toes and work me way up to her pale pink lips, taking several detours along the way.

I arrived back in town exhausted. Freshly deposited rubbish was banked up against the storefronts. Merchants shovelled muck into barrows. I shot down the back lane, not wanting to account for me absence. But late that night on his way home from the New Orleans William saw the chimney reek and bashed on the door. He found a distracted man who couldna settle.

'Sit a-paece beuy, sit still, gilly. Whit's goin' on?' he asked.

I couldna tell him so paced some more.

He pulled a bottle of whisky from his jacket pocket and filled two mugs.

'Where have you been, Conran? Ah wis aboot tae form a search party.'

'Ah wis lost in the hills.'

'Well, you're home noo. Settle doon and ah'll tell you the claik. You won't have heard aboot the latest trouble in Alexandra?'

An icy chill rippled through me like sea foam. 'Na, whit happened?'

'An old Chinaman had his hut burned tae the groond. Came intae toon tae report it and was set upon by three larrikins. Rolled hissel' intae a ball so lived tae tell the tale, mind.'

I slumped into the fireside chair. 'Surely lads have better things tae do than play ball with an elderly man?'

'Celestials ask for trouble, livin' they way they do. They should mix.'

'Ah work with you. Drink with you.'

'Mark me words. Fresh trouble's comin'.'

When William's full to the gunnels it's best not to argue. But I didna want to collude with his prediction either. I slumped further into the chair and pretended the whisky had taken its toll.

Next morning I checked William's repair work, thinking the drink might have distorted his eye, but he'd laid stone like there was magic in him. Something fairy-like was in me too, although it had nothing to do with masonry.

Afore the smuttereens of day, that faint light in the sky at twilight, I was back playing on the brae. Three nights went by afore a cruisie lamp flickered in the doorway. I raced towards it, love increasing with each step.

She stood by the fire stirring a pot with a long-handled ladle. I waited on the doorstep, grinning like a nout. 'I cook you,' she said, nodding towards the table. 'Sit please, Con-Lan.'

I grinned and handed her a bag of toffees I'd bought earlier. 'Thank you. Ah'd be honoured.'

She moved gracefully, like a swan gliding across a loch. Her loose blue shirt concealing what I wanted to lick and suck and kiss.

'Fish soup,' she said, carrying over two steaming bowls.

A ton of words formed inside me tappie head, each phrase more foolish than the previous. Since it proved impossible to find the right sentiments I swallowed me kringlie-headed thoughts, along with her sweet-tasting soup, feeling sixteen, not twenty-eight, and a blithering nyaff to boot.

'Ah Sip give fish. And spice to warm blood.'

How long had Ah Sip and his friend stayed? I pushed these jealous thoughts aside and said, 'You have good friends.'

'You man good, too.'

Her words melted over me like butter on hot toast, leaving luxurious trails of golden warmth. I grinned, then realising she might think I was gyte, bowed and said, 'Alwis your friend, ah hope?'

I held out me hand, hoping she'd take it so I could feel her skin again. A moment's hesitation, then, with the lightness of a feather, her fingers rested against mine. A lump formed at the base of me throat, another nearer the heart. One lodged further down, which I hoped she didna notice. When our hands finally parted I felt happier than a fisherman with a yawl weighed down by a good catch.

'You know, don't you?' she said, turning away.

'Aye, but ah'll not tell. It's your affair.'

'Af-faa?'

'Your business, for you tae keep private.'

'Yes, must stay quiet, Con-Lan. When MaMa's Second Son Fu Ling die I put on his skin.'

Relieved that she'd not ordered me out of the hut, I said, 'And ever since you've dressed as a man?'

'Yes, to keep safe.'

Images of Little Wind fending off burly miners flashed through me mind. 'So you sailed all the way from China like that?'

'Must stay man. Find gold. Repay Chang Huan forty taels.'

'Is he a relation?'

'What mean lay-shon?'

'That he belongs tae the same family.'

'Ah, like clan.' She shook her head. 'No. He lend money.'

She opened her arms to show the size of the debt. I fought off a desire to walk right into them.

'Do you send money back tae your family too?'

She made a peddie circle with her hands.

143

'Small amounts?'

'Yes, but two autumns ago I find much gold. Give to faan kwai.'

'Who's he?'

'He devil man. I think he take to MaMa. But he not go to Pong Woo. He sail Aus-ta-lia. Spend money on women sleep with men not husband. Now I must find new gold.'

What would she say if she knew I'd lain with similar women? Best keep those stories tae meself. 'You canna trust many in the goldfields. Does anyone else know your secret?'

'Soo Tie, but he not tell. Ah Sip, I think he suspect. Maybe Su Sing, too. Please, you not say. Not even to fliends.'

Ida would love to hear the ins and outs but she might spread the news like treacle across the borough. Not meaning any harm, like; just needing to be at the centre since she views everything as an extension of herself. 'Ah promise, Little Wind.'

We spent considerable time together during the winter of '79 while Soo Tie was in Dunedin. Snow flurries were no obstacle. I lived for our evenings by the fire, drinking tea, eating sugar candy, discussing topical events, learning new words.

When Soo Tie returned in late August I was reduced to playing me fiddle on the brae near their hut, never sure when I'd next step inside, wretched at being close but unable to touch her. Then towards the end of October, Soo Tie arrived in Arrowtown with his travel bag. We nodded to each other as he boarded the coach. I rushed home, packed a few supplies and was on the bridle track afore he'd have reached the Arrow Junction.

We talked for hours – I can't remember what about, but I do recall feeling content in her company. We accidentally touched as she handed me a bowl of tea. She jerked away and, thinking she'd been scalded, I reached for her hand.

She pushed it aside and walked to the door. In a firm voice she said, 'You must go.'

'Ah'd rather stay.'

'Not good me and you. Please leave, Con-Lan.'

I walked over heavy with despair to where she stood watching the stars. In a moment of recklessness I rested her head on me shoulder. We stayed like that until the moon slid behind milky-grey cloud. Later we lay together on her bunk in our clothes. Not a word passed between us. The only sounds were the beating of our hearts and the occasional crackle from the fire. I moved a hand across her face like an archeologist uncovering lost treasure, peeling back layers of her life until, in a strange and beautiful way, I found her centre. Time slowed as we hovered on the cusp of longing.

I woke with her still in me arms. She stirred as I said, 'Ah'll nivver hurt you and ah'll nivver tell.' Two fingers ran across me eyelids until they closed. Then she shifted slightly. Next thing her lips rested on mine. Gad, what a feeling. Me insides turned to fish oil.

Two days and another night passed afore I kissed her toes. Skin, I learned, gives more pleasure than stone.

In between loving, we ate black beans and salted duck eggs, which Ah Sip had also brought. I teased her with the beans, making her come close afore popping them into her mouth. Afterwards we licked each other's lips. Then she placed an egg between her breasts and put me head under her shirt to nibble at it. An explosion – bigger than forty sticks of dynamite – blew me clean through her skin and into her bones. I couldna get enough. To me joy, she felt the same way.

Later we heated pots of water over the fire, tipping them one by one into her wash bucket. Although she wouldna remove her shirt, saying, 'Show too much skin feel ashamed,' I treated every part of her body like a holy place. Some say love's blind. But I kept me eyes wide open so I wouldna miss a thing. She trembled as I ran a finger around her mouth. Moments later she poured water over me and bent to catch the droplets that ran down me beard into her mouth. 'I sip from bushy pool, Con-Lan.'

There are still others to taste, darling lass, I thought, but didna say.

Another day passed afore she unwound her queue, which is the proper name for a pigtail. I soaped her slate-black hair until she resembled a frothy sea creature. Rinsed clean, the jet-black strands flowed down her back in luminous ribbons of grace.

She was perched on one elbow looking at me when I woke next morning.

'Lass, whit are you starin' at me for?'

'I put in mind.'

Why? Was she sending me away? The earlier warmth contracted. 'There's na need for that,' I said, with more confidence than I felt.

'Soo Tie back soon. You must go. Best he not know we lie like this.'

Leaving her, even for a day, was unimaginable. 'How long will he stay?'

'Maybe up to twelve weeks.'

'Will he return tae Dunedin then?'

'Yes, he say is best place to enjoy Chinese celeblations.'

'And he'll stay awa?'

She nodded. 'Soo Tie has found big love in lucky city.'

This revelation made me reckless again. 'Love is important, Little Wind.'

She brushed a lock of hair from me forehead. 'Yes, Ok-nee man.'

I rested me head against a wall. As the fire burned low, and a pot of broth simmered, we loved each other with our eyes wide open.

When I walked into the cottage two days later William was cleaning his boots, which meant he was getting ready to go down to the hotel for a drink and a dancing girl, in that order.

'Come with me,' he said, spitting and polishing.

'Na, thanks. Ah've some catchin' ap tae do.'

'A man canna disappear for days withoot his chores mountin' ap.'

146

'You're right aboot that.'

I went outside to the water barrel. Me hand shook as I dipped in the ladle. I was turning into a right gushel.

Over the next few weeks I repaired barns and built walls but me mind wasna on the job. Little Wind was all I could think about.

Early one November morning I couldna stand it any longer. I left a job unfinished, having told the store-owner, who was paying to have his premises extended, that I'd be back once a certain cornerstone had been found. 'It could take some doin'. Ah might bees gone all day.' Then I skittered home for me swag and fiddle.

Me bow had hardly touched the strings when she looked up from the sluice. You canna imagine the willpower it took not to run down the brae and swing her off her feet. Because the day was warm and light I played 'Come under me Plaidie', a happy tune. Soo Tie took off his hat and clapped in time to the music. Something light and graceful as a kestrel landed on me right shoulder.

At dusk Little Wind walked back to the hut as though in a trance. I waited on the brae, thinking she might come to the door after she and Soo Tie had eaten supper, but me only visitor was a shooting star.

I kept the number of trips the same as afore. William was right. Folk had their hackles up. The previous Sunday, after church service, a stable-hand, standing close to me, had said to a saddler, 'The time's come to put those Chinks in their place. If I'd known they'd find gold on my claim, I never would have abandoned it.' His wife fanned the flames. 'Have you noticed how dreamy and odd they look after smoking that foul opium? Their disgusting diseases could travel into town on that smoke.' I kept quiet, not wanting to attract attention. But that night I couldna sleep. I went off me food as well, a development that didna escape Ida when she called by ten days later with a message from Alfred asking if I wanted to go to the races.

'But first tell me why your trousers are falling off? Are you working too hard?'

'Aye,' I said, thinking love was the hardest work I'd ever done. 'Tell Alfred ah've got too much on. But thank him for askin'.'

'Come by for supper tomorrow. Bring William. I'll give you another dancing lesson. You both need to improve if you want a wife like me.'

She waited for me to laugh but I didna oblige. Part of me wanted to tell her about Little Wind. But another larger bit worried. Ida's a fine woman and a good friend, almost like a sister, but she's also gloonie in the head. She wants to know everything and she loves telling stories. What if she told someone? 'That would be grand, Ida.'

'I'll make you a tonic.'

She left, shaking her head as though she'd come across an illness she couldna identify. I sat on a box at the back door and watched the sky turn bleak and broody, wondering if the men who studied the heavens knew what it was like to love a lass so much that you didna feel whole without her in your arms.

That night I dreamed I was walking down Buckingham Street with Little Wind on me arm. As we passed the general store three women spat at us. Opposite the New Orleans, a crowd of men, many of whom I would have called friends, yelled 'John Lover!' and 'Mongolian Filth!', words that then turned into rocks. Although I tried to protect Little Wind by gathering her into me arms, something or someone stronger pulled her away. Next thing she was flying through the air, her queue on fire. I ran for miles, arms outstretched, only to see her disappear into the clouds on the wings of a giant harrier hawk.

I woke in a sweat, wanting to rush up the gorge to see if she was safe. Madness, I know. Soo Tie had looked after her for years. It would be better if I carried on as normal.

The following evening I went to the New Orleans with William. Anderson, the baker, was telling an old tale about an Irishman who was arrested for drunken and disorderly behaviour. 'The constable of the time chained him to a log, seeing it was afore the gaol was built,' he said. 'Anyways, like William here, the Irishman wasna happy away from the drink, so he picked up the log – said tae weigh as much as six men – and carried it with him to the nearest bar. When the constable called by later, his eyes nearly popped out when he spied the Irishman stretched out on the log snoring loudly.'

'Whose plannin' tae appear in next month's court notices?' said William.

'Me if I turn a Celestial into sausages,' said the butcher. 'But the magistrate will probably let me off. One less would be no loss!'

The barman wiped a glass until it gleamed. 'Their money's as good as yours.'

'They should stay in their own country, not come and ruin ours,' said a wagon driver whose wife had recently died and who wasna above using this loss to his advantage. 'Now, whose turn is it to buy me a round?'

I wanted to ask where he and the butcher had been born, knowing full well they'd probably come from a London slum, but kept quiet, fearing that if I opened me mouth I wouldna be able to stop defending Little Wind and her countrymen.

'Listen tae those gisless buggers,' I muttered a few minutes later to William.

The vein on a farmer's meaty neck pulsed faster than the tailor's eye twitch. I ducked his first punch. William, who rarely shies away from a brawl, retaliated with one in the imbecile's guts and another on the chin. Both noses were soon bloodied and William lost a tooth. I helped him outside while Alfred held on to the wagon driver, who was threatening to scythe William into two-inch squares. During the skirmish the butcher polished off everyone's ale.

William wasna fit for work next morning, so I set off alone, doing repairs for the borough council, only stopping at midday for bread and cheese. Resting against the cemetery wall, looking down the gorge, I wondered if Little Wind knew about this latest bout of unrest.

I'd just finished eating when two Chinamen passed by with firewood tied in bundles on their backs. They gave a friendly nod but didna stop, just walked towards the track that leads to their camp. People from the same country tend to stay together. I'd done much the same. What's best? Staying with your own or mixing with other folk?

Such thoughts occupied me for days. One minute I decided it was better to stay with your own. The next, I wanted to learn more about Little Wind and her Chinese ways.

'Whit's ap, Conran?' said William a fortnight later, after I split a slab of rock into three instead of two pieces. 'You're like a hennie withoot a head.'

That night I was back playing on the brae, hoping to see lamplight, all the while telling meself that even if Soo Tie was in town, I'd not stay long if she invited me in. I'd just make sure she was all right.

ELEVEN

A New Life Begins in the Mountains

All November I played for her. She never looked up straight away, although Soo Tie sometimes put down his shovel or stopped rocking the cradle and danced his version of a jig. I wanted to thank him for caring for her, so noted which tunes made him happy and played them on each visit. The rest were for Little Wind. Music was all I could give her while Soo Tie was near.

Back in town I laid stone, drank with William and Alfred, and took extra dancing lessons. 'You're getting the knack, Conran,' Ida said, after I managed a waltz without standing on her feet. 'But look at those two.'

William had a firm hold of Elsie, a pretty new dancing girl. Every time another man tried to cut in, William tightened his grip and whisked her off in a flurry of fancy steps.

'Looks like he's smitten,' said Ida.

'Ah reckon.'

'Did you hear Mr McDonnell gave the committee back their

money after they purchased his land for the hospital?' Ida said, as we finished dancing. 'He'll be remembered for his generosity.'

What would they say about me? 'You'll be pleased tae see it finally built.'

'We've waited a long time, Conran. Ever since Dr Douglas treated early miners with pleurisy, fractures and gunshot wounds under canvas on the riverbank.'

'A miracle any survived,' I said, edging out of William and Elsie's way.

'Having our own hospital will help keep women and babes out of the graveyard.'

'It'll benefit those still minin', too.'

Last year a Shetland lad got trapped under a rockslide. Unable to stand the pain, he begged his mate to cut off his leg with an axe. Poor bugger died of shock hours later. His mate went mental and hanged himself.

'Did you see the poster about the ball?' Ida said.

'Aye, it was a grand idea tae offer free medical care tae ticket-buyers.'

'The draper sold out of dress material within hours of the poster going up. And William arrived at the farm with a bolt of red velvet under his arm asking me to sew a gown for Elsie!'

'William bought velvet? 'He must be in love.'

'What about you, Conran? Anyone caught your eye?'

I was saved from answering by Alfred, who came to fetch his wife for a dance.

They'd stand out at the ball: Alfred in his best jacket and trousers; Ida wearing a grand new gown, dancing around the billiard room in the candlelight. Maybe I should look for a wife like her. Courting would be less complicated.

That daft idea didna last. I was back on the brae early next evening, playing to Little Wind with more love than a bairn can fit turnip pieces into his pen-gun. As her hut door opened, lamplight shimmered across the tussock, making it glow like polished brass. I was torn between cleaning me boots on the grass and patting that wild hair of mine into place or racing to her in me dishevelled state. A second later I'd licked a palm, pressed me hair down, and was running like a right klumbung.

She greeted me with a bow. Her hair, although still plaited, gleamed. A bright red sash, which I longed to untie, encircled her waist.

'Come. Supper I cook you.'

'It smells grand.' I looked around, half expecting to see her mining partner sitting at the table.

'Soo Tie away go poison. Need money to take lucky city.'

After the easy gold was gone, miners went rabbiting to supplement their income. Small groups walked abreast, each man holding a box of contaminated grain, which they scattered over the ground with a spoon or occasionally by hand. It usually contained strychnine, although sometimes phosphorus and arsenic. They worked from spring onwards, often staying away for weeks. The larger groups went out just afore winter, when the rabbits had been without green feed and were more likely to eat the poisoned grain.

'Ah'm pleased Soo Tie has foond wirk.'

A smile fluttered like a butterfly onto her lips. 'You happy now can hold me.'

I laughed and took her in me arms.

Later we ate braised pork clay-pot, which Little Wind had made with ginger, pork, onion, spices and a peddie drop of Chinese wine. She served it with rice and pickled cabbage. I savoured each mouthful and praised her abundantly.

'I make to thank you,' she said.

After supper she told me about the river men around Pong Woo. I described the clearances in Orkney. We talked through the night. She made me feel better, and I was able to comfort her, too. Only after the sun came up did we love each other with our bodies.

Afterwards she ran a finger around me face.

'Eyes blue like sea.'

'Hair shiny as wet slate,' I said, joining in the game.

'Face as hot as sun.'

'Skin shines like gold.'

'Please do not sell me.'

'Nivver. Why do you think ah would?' I took her in me arms and smothered her with kisses but couldna bring back her earlier joy. 'Whit's troublin' you, lass? You can tell me.'

'If I stayed in Pong Woo, BaBa would sell me.'

I didna want to criticise a man I hadna met, or a practice that might have been common in China, so I said, 'Ah'm sorry for your sadness, Little Wind. It must be hard tae carry such a burden. Do you want tae tell me more o these goin's on?' She shook her head. 'Na, then perhaps you'd like tae talk aboot Second Brother Fu Ling's cairn. Which are your favourite stones?'

'Each is special. When place new stone say two things. One: I visit you. Two: I keep plomise to MaMa. Be much sad when devil steal money.'

'Ah'm sure she'd understand.'

'But plomise now take long time to keep. Make me feel bad.'

'You're too bonnie tae be sad.'

'I act much foolish.' She climbed out of the bunk and into her clothes.

I offered to help her fetch water for us to wash in but she refused, saying, 'Not be good if someone see you.'

She made her way down to the creek with two buckets balanced on her shoulder pole. I was amazed at her physical strength and also her courage. She'd taken on her brother's identity, along with her family's expectations, and come to this distant land, and now she'd given her heart to a feckless Orcadian.

The sun dried our hair as we sat in the doorway, nestled against each other like young starlings, while I described me dancing lessons. 'Me feet aren't made for such shenanigans.'

'I not undee-stand she-nan-gin?'

'It means acting foolishly.' I got up and took a few cuffy steps. To make sure she didna think I was a complete gappus, I danced a few fancy ones too.

'Man who make beautiful music dance most well.'

Her words stuck to me insides like honey. 'Does anyone in your family play?' I said, blowing into an imaginary instrument.

'Long time ago MaMa's Second Son Fu Ling make Day-Day a flute.'

She leaned against me bare chest. I nuzzled the soft velvet skin at the back of her neck.

'He show how to blow. But Day-Day goes squeak, squeak, squeak. He mouse boy, not music boy.'

'Ah'd help your peedie brother play his flute.'

'I not see Day-Day long time. Must save hundred pounds to take back to China.'

Surely she wouldna return now. Couldna she just send money back, like me? Wasna it enough to remember where she'd come from and whom she'd left behind?

Maybe that was Jack's problem. Not knowing where he belonged. That, and Ida keeping him tied to her apron strings. Alfred had done his best to track down the lad's relatives. Letters with British postmarks or unfamiliar handwriting caused Ida to collapse in a dramatic fashion. A Chinaman working on the farm painted funny faces on two eggs he found under a hedge and gave them to her, saying, 'Missus look glum. Eat happy eggs. Feel much good.'

Ida soon practised what she preached with regard to busy hands and applied for the matron's position at the new hospital. Jack stormed off, saying he always knew she'd abandon him, leaving Ida completely baffled. 'One minute I'm writing my letter and the next I'm searching for Jack so I can tell him it was a foolish idea.'

When Jack came home with bloodshot eyes, looking as if he'd been gnawed by a goat, Ida threw her application in the fire. Around the same time the Chynoweths' barn burned down, trapping Jack's

155

horse inside. Jack was inconsolable. Ida turned herself inside out trying to make up for his loss.

'She stifles the lad,' William said.

I remembered how I'd felt when Mother had clung to me after Father and the others drowned. 'He'll find a way to escape.'

Jack was soon keeping company with a wild bunch from Skippers. Now that's a bleak, harsh place. I once built a stone dwelling for a merchant whose teeth froze during a cold snap while he slept under canvas. 'Blighters took over an hour and three mugs of whisky to thaw. No Chinks came by with tea. Stick to themselves, they do, the yellow little blighters.'

Sitting on the doorstep with Little Wind's head resting against me chest, not a breath of wind rustling up the gorge, or any sound from the crickets, I prayed for harmony between our two races, since we'd moved further down the path of love during the night. I encircled Little Wind's waist with both hands, imagining them to be a wedding band.

Shadows criss-crossed the land as the day wore on. Mountain goats formed a guard of honour along a ridge, their dusky-cream horns catching the last of the sun.

I kissed Little Wind's shoulders, neck, ears and lips. 'You're sweeter than music.'

'You play me same as fiddle, Con-Lan.'

We scorched the air with such intensity that afterwards we lay exhausted in a pool of love.

We parted just after dusk, since livings had to be made and appearances kept up. A secret love has limitations. I wanted to introduce Little Wind to Ida and Alfred and William, which seemed possible when we were together, but doubts and fears crept in the closer I got to town.

At Bush Creek, three miners stopped to gab. They were on their way to a party in Macetown, their packhorses laden down with whisky and ale.

'The whole town's invited,' said the tallest, after establishing I was the stonemason who'd built a cottage at Twelve Mile Creek.

'No Chinks, though,' said another.

'Yellow bellies very smellie,' said the youngest with a laugh.

Their lunatic antics set me thinking about the ill-feeling William had mentioned. It might pay to listen to the claik.

A few evenings later, while having supper with Ida and Alfred and Jack, I said, 'Why do you think this "them" and "us" nonsense is rearin' its ugly head agin?'

'Men are without work,' said Alfred. 'They're looking for someone to blame.'

'It's the same everywhere. That Kearneyism labour movement's gained strength,' Ida added. 'Some newspaper reports . . .'

'Ah canna imagine anyone believin' those gyte stories,' I interrupted. 'Chinamen are na that different tae us.'

'People believe what they read and hear,' said Alfred.

'Newspapers are full of wild stories from the Queensland goldfields,' said Ida. 'Remember the Aboriginal tribe near Cooktown? Papers reporting that incident sold out.'

'Chinamen taste sweeter than us because they eat rice, not mutton,' said Jack, pushing aside his plate of stew.

'That's not amusing,' said Ida. 'After reading that story a Cromwell miner tipped a bucket of urine over a Chinese storekeeper.'

Jack pulled his eyes into slits with his fingers. 'Catchee catchee Chinaman. Cover him with pee. Catchee catchee Chinaman. Eat him for your tea.'

Ida picked up a heavy serving spoon and banged it on the table. Peas, carrots and barley flew off Jack's plate onto his lap. 'That's hot,' he screamed, jumping up. 'I wish you'd thrown me into the sea with my real mother!'

Ida gasped and gripped the chair arm.

Alfred placed his hand on hers. 'Take a walk, Jack. Cool down, then come back and apologise.'

157

Jack slammed the front door. Crockery skittered across the table. I steadied the salt cellar.

'Why is he so difficult?' Ida said, wringing the tablecloth as though it was wash day.

'He's confused, love. But time's a good leveller,' said Alfred, looking to me for support.

'Aye, he'll come tae his senses, Ida. Remember that pup he nursed back tae health after its hind leg got caught in a trap? The lad has a good heart. He's just misplaced it.'

'He used to help me find medicinal plants,' said Ida, dabbing her eyes with the edge of the tablecloth. 'Now he's off with those larrikins at the slightest provocation. Goodness knows what they get up to.'

Ida eventually served burnt apple pie camouflaged with custard. What was Little Wind's favourite pudding? There was still much to learn – her real name, for a start.

She didna want to tell me. It took weeks of soft talking. 'Ah'll hold it in me heart,' I pleaded. 'Only use it in your company.' But she wouldna say. So I played me trump card. 'Ah need tae know what name your MaMa gave you since she'd have chosen it with love and ah want tae say it with love.'

'What sound love make?'

'Close your eyes and imagine water lappin' on stone.'

'Love not quiet, it loud,' she said, flicking her queue playfully.

'And it comes in different colours,' I said.

'What one we have?'

'Ah need a name afore ah can give it a colour.'

She looked at me and sighed in an exaggerated manner. 'My name is Ming Yuet.'

I said it over and over. 'Ming Yuet, Ming Yuet, Ming Yuet,' then alongside mine, 'Conran and Ming Yuet, Ming Yuet and Conran.' The rhythm sounded grand. I wanted to pen a ballad but settled for wetting a finger and writing our names on the stone fireplace, where the letters sat like musical notes until the heat dried them. Later we recorded each other's names in the air.

Afore leaving, I sneaked a present, which I'd bought earlier through a catalogue, under her pillow. On the way back to town I imagined her opening the parcel and finding a pair of red satin slippers with yellow buttercups embroidered on the front.

Soo Tie returned to Swipers in mid-December. Christmas came and went without me seeing Ming Yuet. Instead of moping around the cottage, I helped Alfred and Ida on the farm, as Jack was spending most of his time with his mates. As we pitched hay into stacks, Ida told me about Jack's latest foray.

'You know those larrikins who stomped around the Chinese camp garden, ruining everything, not a single cabbage or bean left? Well, Jack was involved.'

'Are you sure, Ida?'

'He came home with mud and foliage on his boots. When I asked where he'd been, he called me a nosey parker. Do you think I am?'

'All lads get ap tae mischief, it's their nature.' I wiped me brow with a handkerchief, for the sun was fierce that summer.

'We took vegetables from our garden as compensation and Alfred promised two pigs and timber for a pen. How can I help Matron when I can't even manage Jack?'

'You canna prevent Jack from mixin' with scoundrels unless you tie him tae a tree. He'll stop in his own time. Now tell me aboot the preparations for the New Year ball.'

'I'm in charge of the decorations. They'll be the best ever: bright red, orange and yellow. Save me a dance, Conran. I want to see if those lessons paid off.'

'Ah'll be first efter Alfred tae mark your card.'

Hopefully the fiddler from Alexandra would play me favourites – 'The New Brig o' Dee' and 'Ben Doran', as well as faster reels, many of which would leave the dancers gasping. Even so, I was in two minds about attending, despite taking those dancing lessons and paying for a ball ticket, since I'd seen Soo Tie board the morning coach to Dunedin. He might be away for weeks, perhaps until after Chinese New Year. I didna like to think of Ming Yuet alone at Swipers. But I also knew I'd be missed if I didna go to the ball. Awkward questions would follow, especially from Ida.

After much to-ing and fro-ing I decided to attend, dance once or twice with Ida and Elsie, then slip off. That way I could join in later with the gab about the fiddler and the decorations and the dancing, but still be with Ming Yuet. I bought bread, tomatoes and cheese from Pritchard's and salted fish from Su Sing, hoping to persuade Ming Yuet to have supper with me among the tussock grass, figuring we'd be safe with everyone at the ball.

Folk arrived at the New Orleans well afore time. The women looked grand dressed in their finery. Several admired the new tailored jacket I'd bought to impress Ming Yuet. I stayed for three dances: two with Ida magnificently decked out in bright green silk; the other with Elsie, in sways of red velvet. She quizzed me about who I'd dance with next. 'All the single girls are waiting, Conran. A few married ones as well.'

'Oh, ah'm more interested in fiddlin' than dancin'.'

I also drank ale with Alfred and William, who asked what I thought of the fiddler.

'He's very pleasin' tae the ear with his simple bowin' style and little slurrin', hardly any vibrato ither.'

Once the dancing turned exuberant and conversation became impossible I slipped outside and raced like the wind into the hills. To the best of me knowledge no one noticed me leave.

Ming Yuet laughed when I swung her high in the air and caught her like she was a star and I was the mountain she twinkled above. 'Thank you, most beautiful shoes,' she said, stroking me cheek. Her touch sent shivers down me spine. 'I have you, too, a gift.' She reached under her bunk and pulled out a parcel. 'Blue same as eyes.'

I held the beautifully stitched shirt close to me heart, letting each thread weave its way in. 'It's grand, dear lass. The best present ever.'

It was well past eleven o'clock but still light when we reached a perfect picnic spot. The wheat-coloured tussock made a grand backdrop as we wound our arms around each other and loved with such warmth that the land took on a burnished glow.

Later I spotted a clump of red poppies close to where we'd lain. 'Luk, Ming Yuet, a miner from California's been here. Maybe he left them especially for us.'

She looked from me to the poppies and back again. Her eyes reflected the sorrows and joys from Pong Woo, along with her hopes as a sojourner in this land, and something else, too – maybe a dream connected to mine.

We placed our food near the poppies and ate and drank and talked until the light faded. Then I asked her to stand. While other Arrowites lived it up in the New Orleans, I danced Ming Yuet across the mountaintop.

It was a night full of love and laughter. She even unwound her queue while I sang 'Auld Lang Syne', spreading her hair over her breasts until she was covered by a soft black tent. We loved again and again. I swear we could have reached up and touched the sky; that's how close we got to paradise. And although we didna know it then, three of us came down the mountain early next morning.

TWELVE

Blowin' Kisses intae the Hills

If I wasna with Ming Yuet, I was thinking about her. Her hair, her smell, her smile, the way she arranged words. Me heart became stretchy as droo, a type of Orkney seaweed. There wasna a bit of her I didna love. When I cut stone, I thought of her curves. If I wiped me brow, I recalled the tingle of her skin as it touched mine. When I cooked supper, I remembered a meal we'd shared. I smiled at everyone, especially Chinamen. And, twice in one day, I blew kisses into the air. How gyte's that? Afterwards I chided meself, but minutes later I was doing it again. Aye, she was always on me mind.

I couldna visit her once Soo Tie returned, so I paced around the cottage in a twitchy manner, ending up with more nicks from careless wood-chopping than Ida had pleats in her parlour curtains.

One morning, after I'd laid stone in a cuffy way, William said, 'Whitever it is, Conran, you have it bad. Luk at that wall!'

'Could be heatstroke,' I said, taking a drink from the water bottle.

'Funny it's only affectin' you,' said William, giving me a friendly shove.

Although embarrassed about the state of the wall, I couldna say what had turned me into a gappus. William might've got blootered and blabbed all around town – not meaning any harm, like.

'Maybe you need tae lay doon?' William said with a wink. 'A dancin' girl could fix that heatstroke.'

He threw a handful of schist chips at me, which I fended off with a mock growl.

'Ah'm a bit off colour, that's all.'

'Feeble-minded, more like.'

We joked some more afore sitting on a knoll to eat bread, cheese and pickles.

'Is somethin' botherin' you, Conran?'

'Na, just tired, that's all.'

Me love for Ming Yuet was getting harder to conceal. Some nights I got into a terrible state, ramming me pilly into the mattress until it almost went through the flock and got tangled in the wire bedstead. Just as well William was back in his own hut. Otherwise he might have thought an earthquake had hit the valley.

It wasna just an unruly pilly that longed to be with her. Don't get that idea. I wanted to look into her eyes and wrap me arms around her as we talked. I would have given anything just to hear her breathe. Love's about more than putting your pilly in and going for it. It means caring for your lass as much as yourself.

Ordinary things took on new meaning. Colours appeared brighter. Cats fighting at night sounded joyful, whereas previously their screeching had affronted all me musical sensibilities. Aye, love had me by the throat. I wanted to marry her, but I worried what the settlers would say if she accepted, and whether the sojourners could forgive her masquerade.

Dreaming about being with her was a poor substitute. Time dragged. Me only pleasure was thinking up ways to please her. I bought silk thread from the draper, hoping it might have been made by her middle sister. Another time I got a cake of sweet-smelling soap from the chemist.

'Not your normal kind, Conran,' said Edsall with a grin.

'Ah might send it home tae Orkney.'

'Don't they have soap there?'

'Not this kind,' I said, backing out the door.

I also collected interesting stones, hoping Ming Yuet might fancy them enough to put on Fu Ling's cairn. The notion of making memorials appealed to me. I hoped Mother and Annie had built something similar for our dead.

Mother and Annie wouldna be at our wedding. No male relatives either, only the distant roll of wild seas. Loving Ming Yuet had helped me appreciate the chasm that must have opened in Annie and Mother. Strange to think that one storm took their men away while another brought love to me.

Soo Tie remained at Swipers for weeks. Between visits to the brae to play, I shadow-boxed, hoping to improve me physique for when Ming Yuet and I next loved.

'Chin-aps and press-aps, laddo,' said William when I asked how he kept his own body in shape. 'That, and runnin' ap and doon Tobin's Track.'

William was what Orcadians call a whiddie fellow. One minute he'd be drinking himself legless, the next, training to be a world-champion weight-lifter.

'Imagine it's a dancin' girl, not a rock,' he said, one afternoon, lifting a slab of schist the size of a sea stack over his head. 'Noo put her doon in whitever position you fancy.'

'Ah like safter women,' I said, thinking of Ming Yuet's sweet bosom.

'If a dancin' girl isna in your arms soon you'll have forgotten whit it's all aboot.'

'You got the best in town, you cheeky beggar.'

'Keep your eyes off Elsie. Find your ain lass.'

We laughed and joked for the rest of the day. William was nivver in poor cut, even when drinking. The wagoners whose barrels he holed with a gimlet while they were inside hotels collecting money for their deliveries always had a good word to say about him.

Few would have guessed, though, that I'd stand on a brae and play to a lass who dressed and worked as a man, or that I'd buy a snuid. That ribbon almost gave the game away. I was walking along Buckingham Street when Ida spotted me.

'That's a dainty parcel, Conran.'

I pretended to re-tie a bootlace while thinking of something to say other than a fibber. That's when I noticed a piece of the snuid sticking out of me paper bag. 'Aye, it's small enough,' I said, shoving it back in. 'So I have a spare hand tae carry your shopping, Ida.' Not that Ida put much store in domestic undertakings. She'd sooner bandage a leg than bake a loaf.

'Thank you, Conran. I've a heavy bag of flour.'

'Do you have a special occasion comin' ap?'

On Jack's thirteenth birthday, Alfred organised horse rides for all the children in the district, hoping the lad would take to one of Scoles' mares, which he'd hired for the day. I composed a new tune that I played while Jack blew out candles on a lopsided chocolate cake that Ida had baked. But we didna get a smile out of him all day.

'I'm giving an afternoon tea for women who raised funds for the hospital. Did you hear it's opening on New Year's Day?'

'Will there be a celebration?'

'The committee's still thinking about drains and tenders, but, yes, a small gathering's planned. Mrs Gruber said Kempthorne Prosser and Company has sent up medical supplies from Dunedin – liquid strychnia, paraldehyde and chlorodyne. And surgical equipment has arrived from Edinburgh.'

'Did she say whit?'

'She mentioned clamps, bone-lifters and a butcher's saw with two spare blades.'

The saw would be for amputations. I thought again of the Shetland lad buried in the kirkyard, far from home, no mother to care for his grave. 'Maybe you'll get tae wirk at the hospital after all.'

'I'd like to meet the doctor before I say yes to matron. We might have different views.'

Ida had had a run-in a while back with a medical man from Queenstown who was bent on saving a bairn during childbirth at the mother's expense.

'So you'll give him a thorough goin' ower?'

'It pays to be vigilant. Edinburgh-trained doctors have been known to take up mining and quacks scalpels. Imagine the likes treating a child.'

Ida always championed for the unfortunate, which partly explains why Jack was her joy and her sorrow. She'd be full of fun one minute, but unravel like a reel of cotton if the lad as much as poked a face at her.

'Why do you think Jack's so querulous, Conran? Did Alfred tell you his mates from Skippers think Chinamen lit our barn fire, deliberately burning Sunny Boy?'

'You're not the only family with a cantankerous lad. Whit about those who borrowed five buggies last Saturday night and mixed them up well and truly afore returnin' them. The owners spent half o Sunday sortin' out their mischief. As for your barn fire, the culprit's more likely a careless pipe smoker.' I shifted Ida's basket to the other arm. 'No doubt Jack will develop his own views. He's a good lad at heart.'

'Maybe I'll help deliver your baby one day.'

I bent over and retied me bootlaces, muttering, 'Aye, could do, Ida.' I should have told her about Ming Yuet then. Why didna I? It could have been to do with me need to examine things from every angle afore talking about them. Ida's loose lips might have been another reason. 'Do you know o any on the way?'

'Three for sure, and there's bound to be a surprise or two.'

'That there could be, Ida.'

She gave a peddie smile and took her basket back. 'Where are you off to with that parcel?'

I waved to two acquaintances outside the smiddie's and hurried over, leaving Ida to ponder over the shortcomings of men.

'I can't feed my family on the wages farmers are paying,' said Bill Harris, an odd-job-man, as I joined him.

'There are too many Celestials working on farms now. They're driving down everyone's wages,' said Fred Harper, the night-man. Clumps of white hair sprouted from his misshapen ears, giving him the appearance of a gone-to-seed boxer.

'This new petition is badly needed,' said Bill.

Ice-cold rage snapped and crackled deep within me. The last thing Little Wind and I needed was another petition. A funny thing happened, though, with the '71 version. Penned to prevent further sojourners coming to Arrowtown, it lost steam when several Chinamen signed, saying, in their opinion, enough of them already worked in the district. Ha! Clever tactic.

But what might a new one mean for Ming Yuet and me?

Back at the cottage, over a mug of tea and mutton sausages with mash, I ran through me options. After deliberating until sunrise, I decided it wasna the right time to make a public declaration. Best wait and hope the current bad feeling faded along with summer. To ward off dismal thoughts I went for a walk and came across Soo Tie and another Chinaman waiting for a coach. Several pigeons cooed in a wicker cage at their owner's feet. 'Good homers?'

'Fly back all way from Dunedin,' said Soo Tie, flapping his arms as though they were wings. His friend laughed. I did too.

'Is that where you're goin' noo?'

Soo Tie nodded.

Me heart leapt. I almost jumped in the air to catch it. 'Have a safe journey.'

'And you play happy music,' said Soo Tie.

I bowed and walked away in what I hoped was a dignified manner.

At dusk I set off to Ming Yuet's, taking a different route since the Miners' Association members might be on the lookout. But the only person I saw on the outskirts of town was Lok Yem, who drinks more than William. He was too busy gathering firewood to notice me.

The night was still; barely a cloud smudged the dusky sky. A large moon, whiter than a sun-bleached mast on a yole, illuminated Big Hill. I stopped briefly to study it. Like me, it had a public and private face. Mother and Annie would marvel at how time and love had altered their callow lad. Love might strike Jack one day; could be the making of him as well.

Ming Yuet ran towards me with outstretched arms. We kissed until our lips stung, while all around the air buzzed with a hypnotic current.

'Where o where is Soo Tie?' I crooned.

She laughed and sang back, 'With his love, same as me.'

I studied her face; noted softer eyes and a radiant skin. 'Ah love you, darlin' lass. Alwis will.'

'I love too you.'

We grinned like daft creatures. Then, realising we were out in the open, hurried down to the hut, slid the plank across the door and loved each other again and again and again.

Afterwards she lit the lamp and sat on the side of the bunk. 'No blood two times.'

I looked at her blankly.

'You think big?'

She placed me hands on her bosom, which had filled out some. A queer feeling came over me. I felt nine feet tall and strong as an ox, and a minute later full of panic. 'Is it a bairn?' When she blinked anxiously I added, 'You can tell me.'

'Must stay man, not woman; much bad.'

With no mother or sister or woman friend to help, and still in disguise, she had every right to be concerned. 'It'll be all right, lass. We'll git married.'

'I most upset.'

'We'll go further intae the mountains. Stay there until the bairn comes. In Orkney we say, "There's a time for the hearth and a time for the wind in the hills." Maybe this is our mountain time.'

'Too big snow will come.'

'Don't worry. Ah'll think of something. In the meantime ah'll go back tae toon for supplies, tell William ah've business far awa, and come back tae stay with you.'

She shook her head vehemently. 'Not safe. Only visit same as now.'

Her body trembled as though balanced precariously on the edge of a crumbling cliff. I steadied her with both arms. 'It will be all right, lass.' I turned the conversation to practical matters. 'Tell me whit supplies you need. A bairn brings the hunger. Annie ate bread and kippers day and night.'

'Belly will get fat. You not like.'

'Ah'll love you even when you're a gruelly-belkie.'

'What mean that?'

I drew a mound in the air.

'I wear Soo Tie's big clothes. You not see.'

'Ah'll find a way.'

I put a hand under her shirt but she pushed it aside and started to greet. I felt quite emotional meself. We'd created a tricky situation. I didna know what to suggest. 'Whit if Ah Sip notices?' I said, after a while.

'I say sick belly make me fat.'

'Me ain hungry worm wants tae get inside you right noo.' I raised me eyebrows, which usually made her laugh. She gave a wee smile when I pulled her towards me but we didna love, only talked until the sparrows stirred. Such a mix of emotions rushed through me: love for her and the peedie bairn, but fear too.

170

Another two nights went by afore she said, 'Please, Con-Lan. Too long gone be notice.' I kissed her with great fervour, partly to reassure meself that love would sustain us through these worrying times, but also to take her taste into the night. Her eyelashes walked like timid crickets across me cheek. The thought of leaving her and the bairn with no one to care for them brought back painful Orkney memories. I had to do better this time. 'Ah'll bring supplies each week and play on the brae so anyone watchin' will think ah'm still the same mad fiddler.'

We lived like that for months. At night, back in me cottage, I turned a gin case – bought for three pounds – into a bairn's cradle, hiding it under a sack when anyone knocked on the front door. Ida caught me sanding the rockers one Saturday morning when she dropped by with a pot of jam. She didna ask any awkward questions, which I was grateful for at the time, although I nearly told her the whole story as we said goodbye on the doorstep. What held me back? Saying it out loud would have meant facing up to the consequences and I wasna ready. So I listened to Ida's claik as though as I didna have a care of me own.

I visited Ming Yuet over the early part of winter, despite heavier-than-usual snowfalls and bitter hoar frosts, which made travelling perilous. Ice hardened like armour on me wet clothes. On the way home from a trip around mid-July I became breathless. Within days I'd developed knife-like pains in the chest, which worsened with each breath. Ida found me propped up in a chair a few mornings later barely able to speak. Next thing I was in the hospital with a cheery fire in the ward but a dull ache in me heart. How would Ming Yuet manage without me visits and food parcels? Worry consumed me. I couldn't tell anyone our news while I was unable to protect her. Treatments were administered and broth supplied, which helped the pleurisy but not me concern for Ming Yuet. A full night's sleep was impossible. I spent the wee hours composing lullabies. Blowing the words into the air, hoping they'd somehow float up the gorge on the wind.

I was discharged early August on the condition that Ida called twice a day and the doctor every second evening. Cook offered advice as well. 'You're as weak as a kitten, Conran. Liver's what you need. That'll put iron in your blood.' What I needed was Ming Yuet in me arms. But a trip to Swipers was out of the question with Ida and the doctor's regular visits and me legs feeble as a newborn colt's.

We had mighty snowstorms right through August. By the first week in September I was desperate for signs of a melt. Then three o'clock one Thursday morning the air softened. I chose the time and route carefully. Staying upright proved difficult even on the flat because the ground resembled a curling rink. The thick white crust would take weeks to disappear. I cut steps on the steepest sections of the track with me axe. Even so, the journey was hazardous. The land groaned and cracked like a North Sea ice shelf. I half expected it to send chunks bigger than icebergs down into the gorge, taking an Orkneyman in its wake. I prayed for the good Lord to watch over me. Ten steps up, four down, followed by several yards on me backside, landed me spread-eagled with considerable force against a rock and cursing like an ill-nettered lout.

Her door was shut but a wisp of smoke rose from the lum hole. I called softly, not wanting to scare her, and was relieved to hear stirrings inside the hut. Next minute she was in me arms, her cheek pressed hard against mine. She looked a shaddie tired around the eyes. Her puggie was no longer small. I lifted her shirt and bent to kiss her stomach. A wave of skin skittered afore me. 'Our bairn?'

She nodded. 'Be-nui, baby daughtee, says hello.'

I removed both mittens and placed me hands on Ming Yuet's rounded belly, softly tapping out three kisses to our wean, who moved as though to face me. What joy! I canna put it into words. Some things are beyond the arrangements of letters. I shook like a lassie-boy.

'You cold,' Ming Yuet said, hugging me. 'Sit by flames.'

'You luk bonny. Ah've missed you somethin' terrible.'

'I miss too you. Such deep snow. Come, I unlace boots.'

While she rubbed me frozen toes back to life, I told her about being in hospital.

'I sad not know, Con-Lan. Most bad you do big walk today.'

'Ah'm sorry not tae have been here for you, dear lass. Did you have enough food?'

'Baby and me fine now.'

'Orkney folk think rainbows are a bridge for a boy child.'

'What Ok-nee say if not boy?'

I didna know, so said, 'We have lots o feasts, regardless of whether it's a girl or boy.'

'What feasts?'

'First there's Blide-Meat. That's when the family and neighbours come tae view the bairn and congratulate the parents, who give oot scones and ale. Then there's Fittin' Feast. That's when the mother starts doin' her household chores agin. Cirsenin' Feast happens efter the bairn's baptised. The father shares a bottle o whisky with ither men tae bring the bairn good luck.'

She patted her stomach. 'What come to this baby? I think not good.'

I worried that she might be right but held her like I was a man who knew what to do.

After sharing a bowl of thin turnip soup, I reached into me pocket. 'Ah've a gift.'

She ran the ribbon through her fingers. 'It is most beautiful. Thank you.'

I told her about the Swee-een o the Snuid ceremony, saying, 'We'll burn it efter we marry.'

'Tie in queue now, please.'

I kissed the back of her neck as I worked the ribbon through her hair. 'Ah've made a cradle for our bairn, Ming Yuet.' I rocked back and forth until she understood. Her eyes filled with tears. Mine got watery too. We hugged each other like two crabs in a shell.

'Will you come tae the cottage one evening?' I said, after we'd lain for a while on her bunk. 'Tae see the cradle.' I also wanted to love her in me own bed so her smell would linger until she came to stay forever. 'We'll have neeps and tatties for supper. Should we ask Ida aboot arrangin' a weddin'? When she didna answer, I said, 'It's not impossible, Ming Yuet. A couple o European women live with Chinamen in Bannockburn.'

'Many say first step to spoil.'

Realising she'd meant to say 'ruin', a saying I'd also heard, I said, 'We'd be happy. I know we would.'

She raised a finger. 'Shhhhh.'

I closed both eyes while she traced the length and breadth of me face. Her touch caused me to shiver as though a bawkie had walked over me grave.

Two days later I returned to town afore dawn, half filled with hope, half pumped up with fear. Twice a twig snapped behind me. As I neared Bush Creek, even the familiar sight of Lock's bakery took on an alarming shape. Then close to the cemetery I jumped at what was me own shadow sliding past a barn.

THIRTEEN

Me Happiness wis Whuppid Awa

William told me about the murder of Mrs Young over at the Kyeburn diggings while we built a stone farmhouse out near the Junction.

'Poor soul wis bashed on her heid with a fifty-poond rock.'

'Fifty?'

'Aye, it wis on the floor aside her, covered with blood and bits o brain.

'Who foond her?'

'A neighbour, Lee Guy, noticed her door wis smashed off its hinges so he took a luk. The poor widow, still in her goonie, wis sprawled oot cold on a mattress. Seems there'd been a muckle struggle, for the place wis in a klatter. The Chinaman ran oot screamin' like the devil wis aboot tae fry him.'

A chill, solid as a hangman's noose, hovered in the air. 'Then whit?'

'Someone fetched the doctor but he couldna help. Her heid wis mushy as feeskid cheese. She died later the same day.'

'Whit do you think it wis aboot? Wis anythin' taken?'

'A thousand poonds in money and securities, along with a promissory note she'd planned tae take back tae Scotland.'

'Why wis she leavin'?'

'They say she wis fearful o livin' alone efter her husband died.'

'Perhaps she had good reason?'

'That's the gab in every hotel this side o the Clutha.'

Evil doings set tongues wagging faster than a dog's tail. 'Any suspects?'

'Aye, the constabulary arrested Lee Guy and anither Chinaman called Lee Tow.'

I continued tapping stone into place, not wanting William to detect any undue concern. 'On whit groonds?'

'They foond a pair o bloodied trousers and a stone in Lee Tow's hut.'

'Wouldna he destroy the evidence if he wis guilty?'

'Maybe. But mixin' apples with pears makes you think, doesna it?'

His comment unsettled me – for more than one reason. Did he know about me night-time walks? He'd made another odd remark a few weeks ago when I'd called by after he'd failed to turn up for work. The state of him! His mother would've walked by. He looked as though he'd been stung by a swarm of bees. Even the whites of his eyes were honey-coloured. I'd fetched a mug of water and sat it quietly aside him. His tongue, which resembled a blackened tree stump, curled out, as though waking from a long hibernation. I swear it sizzled as it hit the water. 'Would you consider easin' back on the drink, William?'

He raised an eyebrow and even that small movement seemed to pain him.

'"Let be for let be agin," as the Harray man said tae the crab. I'll not interfere with you if you don't interfere with me.'

I shrugged as though his words made no sense and picked up the mug to refill it. Was he referring to me visits to a certain brae and a particular Chinaman? Gad, surely he didna think I was a back-door operator! How many others thought the same?

A while back a young rabbiter came out of the hills in a right fluster, having stumbled upon two men behaving unnaturally. A councillor, who yearned for more drama than planning the pipes for the town's water scheme formed a posse to flush out the sinful pair, but they came back empty-handed.

Sometimes there's a bright side to unusual goin's on. Soo Tie's attachment to his young man meant I could spend time with Ming Yuet: that alone was reason not to judge him. Another being that I was far from perfect meself. I'd be first to agree that life's full of complications but fancying a man wasna one of mine. And I didna want William thinking it was. So, despite two Chinamen being implicated in the Kyeburn murder and knowing what might eventuate, I decided it was time to declare me love for Ming Yuet.

After buying pork at the butcher's, I purchased pickled lemons, salted fish, rice and eggs from Su Sing, and calming Chinese tea from another store. I said, 'Néih hóu' going into both shops and 'Joigin' as I left. Maybe that was foolish, for although Su Sing was friendly, the tea merchant seemed edgy. When I placed two shillings on the counter, saying, 'Each earned honestly,' he said, 'Honour not in words but actions.' Lok Yem, who was also present, sniggered, making me feel uneasy.

Other things worried me, too. Would Ming Yuet's milk come in? Or had binding her breasts for years made her dry? Should I buy a cow? How would I get it up the bridle path and down into the gully? Maybe a goat would be easier. But what if our bairn didna take to goat's milk? Should I write to Annie? Her youngest had trailed after her with a stool until he was five years old. Whenever she stopped to wash potatoes in a bucket or churn butter or shape wax into candles, he'd climb up and burrow like a mouse into her bodice. A glimpse of that nut-brown nipple had set me own mouth twitching. A curious laddie can be a shameful beastie.

Notice how the mind turns in on itself like the tide? How does an image or a smell or a single word dredge up memories buried deeper than seams of gold? A similar occurrence took me back to Stromness, during the months that Ming Yuet's belly swelled, to evenings by the fire and Annie's husky voice reciting nursery rhymes to her boys.

> *Kirstie kirstie kringlick*
> *Gae me nave a tinglick*
> *Whit shall ye for sapper hae*
> *Deer, sheer, bret an smeer*
> *Minchmeat sma or nane ava*
> *Kirstie kringlick run awa!*

Each time I imagined telling this rhyme to me own wean I was ambushed by such intense feelings that I could hardly breathe. No wonder Annie's grief had scared me, being naught but a lad at that time, with little understanding of love, or the joy that accompanies making and caring for bairns. Her vigil by the sea had seemed morbid, even pointless. Why imagine fish stripping the lads clean of flesh or waiting for their bones to float to the surface? I'd grown impatient and disdainful, barely acknowledging the reek of death, concentrating instead on an escape plan.

Annie and Mother deserved better. I told them so in a letter that also contained news about me own peddie bairn. Something akin to relief came upon me as the mailbag started its coach journey north.

I sang ancient Orkney tunes while finishing the bairn's cradle outside the cottage beneath a mountain peak that resembled a horizontal nun. Her toes pointed skywards while her hands were clasped on her chest in pray. A wimple, stiffer than a freshly starched shirt, framed her peaceful face. The sight stirred me to carve 'A great treasure lies here' on the hood of the cradle. Beuys o beuys, me life was changing.

And mine wasna the only one, as I discovered early one evening when a loud knock rattled the brass door-handle, forcing me to hide the cradle. Elsie stood on the veranda in a respectable dress, nothing like those skimpy ones she wore to pour drinks and give out cheek. William wore a grin no amount of drink could have produced.

'Come in and sit theesael' doon.'

We gabbed a bit about who'd been up to mischief, then William said, 'We're gettin' wed next week, Conran. Will you be best man?'

I shouldna have been surprised – they were well suited – but they'd beat me to the altar. I swallowed a jug full of envy and said, 'Ah will, William. That's grand news. Ah'm happy for you.' And mostly I was. 'It's a big step, mind.'

'We're ready to take it,' said Elsie.

'You're a lucky man, William. Elsie's a fine lass.'

'Well, oot with the ale, then,' said William. 'We've somethin' tae celebrate.'

Elsie ran her hand along his arm. 'My days at the hotel are over.'

'Will you miss them, Elsie?'

'Not now I've got myself a permanent dancing partner.'

William gave her a between-the-sheets sort of look. Open as could be. Soon they'd stand in front of the preacher and say their vows, exactly what I wanted with Ming Yuet.

After they left, I pictured me own wedding. If we followed the Orkney tradition, the wedding party would walk from Ming Yuet's hut to the manse, where the preacher would marry us. Then we'd walk back to the hut for the party. The fiddler would eat a tail pudden – a fatty type of mealy mixture – to counteract the effects of alcohol and allow him to keep playing. William and Elsie, Alfred and Ida, maybe Ah Sip and some other Chinamen, might celebrate with us. Perhaps Soo Tie would give the bride away. We'd sing and dance till dawn.

I wondered whether Chinamen and women had weddings with music, singing and dancing. Would they have a feast? I'd ask Ming Yuet. Maybe we could combine our traditions.

William and Elsie had a grand wedding. The two redwoods at the entrance of the Presbyterian church framed their happiness when they emerged as man and wife. We got them into a buggy – having told the driver to avoid Buckingham Street and its hotels – and sent them off to Ida and Alfred's house, where we feasted on roast mutton and vegetables, followed by apricot cream and strawberry jelly. We toasted everything, including Ida's gravy, which was less lumpy than usual. After the speeches, Alfred and William rolled back the carpet square and I played several reels and jigs. Couples careered across the floor like skittles trying to outrun a wooden ball.

During a break I went outside for a breath of cool night air. I sat on the stone wall Jack had helped build, looking up at the stars, which twinkled like bonxie in flight. Seven years old and dressed in dungarees, he'd clutched a stick and said, 'Show me how, please, Conran.' So I'd slid the trowel into the mix of sand and water and tossed it onto a board. 'Noo stir it like a cake, Jack.' He'd moved his tongue in circular motions as though it steered his hand. I resisted the urge to laugh as globs fell off the board and landed on his boots. 'Pretend you're a snail. Slide it along in a straight line. That's right, laddo. Keep it ap. We'll soon be ontae the next layer.' A smile wider than Gunnie's Hole had lit his proud wee face.

Ida ended this reverie by coming out and sitting with me. 'A worry shared, Conran.'

'You have enough o your own with Jack.'

'I've got Alfred. Maybe you need someone.'

'Well, it's a bit complicated.'

'I've all night.'

I took a deep breath. Perhaps I could give a hint. 'Well, there's this lass . . .'

These words were barely out when a flash of white appeared. Impatient hands tugged at me jacket.

'You can't say no to the bride?'

Ida tapped Elsie on the arm. 'Conran needs a breather.'

'But William wants him to arm-wrestle the baker.'

Another opportunity lost.

A late frost whitened the ground next morning, making the land and sky appear seamless, which was how I wanted to be with Ming Yuet. No stops and starts; just one long, clear run. I filled me swag with goods I'd brought earlier and settled at the kitchen table to write to Ida. Words flowed from the pen sure as the tides around Orkney tilt and surge. No doubt Stromness fishermen, the swans at Brodgar and the makers of stone dykes on the Mainland experience a similar rhythm as they head home. Ancient wisdom instructed me that morning.

I slipped the note under Ida's door afore heading in the direction of the gorge. No point sneaking through the lane. Each footstep sent splinters of ice in various directions. Land gives and it takes. Cycles are repeated. But some things never change. In Orkney, sheepmeat always tasted of sea cabbage, and flat circular stones ground wheat for bread, and full-bodied ale filled the bellies of men who performed the fish-and-barley dance. Ming Yuet's ancient land also had long-held traditions. We'd tell our bairn about both places. We'd stitch our lives together with stories.

Wild flowers would soon march again across the Arrow valley, and a hint of green would brighten the fields. We'd pack away our winter worries as though they were extra blankets and prepare to welcome our wean into the world. With no flowers yet to pick, I settled on a stone shaped like a snipe's wing, hoping it would bring a smile to Ming Yuet's sweet face and that she'd place it on Fu Ling's cairn.

I was well up the bridle path when four of the 'Macetown Apostles' appeared – King, Doc, Saint and Secretary – notorious in these parts for their drinking and gambling exploits at Montezuma, a den on a terrace overlooking Twelve Mile Creek. I was in the area building a house when they first asked me to play poker. Over the years we'd toasted wins and losses and generally played the fool into the wee small hours. Once we dug holes in the sandy soil and planted two losers up to their necks. Screamed like chiltos when they woke. We cooled their heads with snow-fed stream water.

Doc, who was magic on the concertina, once found the biggest nugget in the district. Sixteen ounces! Everyone put up with the Apostles' shenanigans because they were good men, just boisterous. Some reckoned they were the sons of aristocrats sent to the colonies and expected to stand on their own two feet. If that was the case, their fathers would have been sorely disappointed for they were often prostrate under bars or bushes.

'Good to see, Conran,' said Doc, nodding towards the fiddle poking out of me swag.

'Nivver travel withoot it.'

'Do you have work up our way?' said King.

I sidestepped his question with one of me own. 'Ah guess you have drinkin' tae do in toon?'

King chortled. 'I'll cut back when the river road opens.'

'For the day or for good?' said Doc, slapping King on the back.

We yapped about a proposal recently drawn up to gauge support for a proper road to be formed along the river route to Macetown, even though it would have meant crossing the Arrow countless times. On occasion, miners had paid fifty pounds a ton to get their goods packed into the settlement.

'Join us for a drink if you're back by Saturday.'

'Ah'll try, Doc. No promises, mind.'

'Travel well, Conran.'

They'd probably not have judged me or Ming Yuet. No doubt women troubles had hastened one or two of their departures to New Zealand.

I was still mulling over their possible reactions when Old Bob, a hatter addicted to opium who only ventured out for supplies, came along the track riding a horse and leading another. Although I tipped me cap, he kept his head down and carried on without a word. Not comfortable around people, he was willing to forgo, year in, year out, the warmth of a lass or even the handshake of another man.

Ming Yuet opened the door wearing a smile wider than a star wheel. A cacophony of trumpets, cymbals and harps filled the air.

'Ok-nee man!'

'China lass.'

Like a compass on an ancient ship, weathered by time and tides, we traversed each other, taking in the changes. She had dark smudges under her eyes and an unfamiliar pallor. I placed both me hands on the outside of her jacket. 'Is our peedie wean behavin'?'

'Move like sleepy fish.'

Fancy lying curled up like a sea creature in a skin shell.

Our usual way of loving proved impossible so I lay behind her and we did it differently. Right pleasing it was, although me beard got tangled in her queue. 'We're meant tae be taegether, Ming Yuet.'

'Gold bring me to this land. Love make me want to stay.'

'Let's talk tae Ida.'

She jumped as though I'd frightened her. But something else had caught her attention. She took me hand and placed it on her belly. Me heart did a jig. 'It's the wean's foot, Ming Yuet! She wants tae meet her Auntie Ida, too.'

'How you know is she?'

'Because she feels small and clever like her mother, na big and cuffy like her father.'

'What you like she call you?'

'Da.' It sounded so good I repeated it. 'Da. Da.'

'She quiet now.'

'She and her sweet mother are the best gold nuggets in the Arrow.'

Ming Yuet screwed up her eyes and looked puzzled. 'How can be best? Not much gold left.'

'All right, then. Ah love you both more than the sky.'

'I still talk to it.'

While she drifted back to China, I thought how different me life would have been if Fu Ling, not Ming Yuet, had come to this valley.

Eventually she said, 'Yes, please take to meet Ida.'

I hugged her with relief. Ida would know how to manage her transformation from Little Wind into Ming Yuet. Surely she'd keep it to herself until we were ready to face everyone. She could help arrange our wedding. Everything would work out.

We loved again, this time slow and tender until me pilly found her happy place, which excited me in much the same way as a velvet curtain ends a concert. I stifled the urge to clap but graciously gave an encore.

'Not long afore you bees a married woman with a husband and a bairn tae love.'

'I full with love now,' she said, poking out her stomach, making us both cheeter.

'You bring more happiness than ah deserve.'

'I give what I am given.'

The icy braes on me journey back to town were as difficult to traverse as a blunt knife going through beesmilk cheese. Land crumbled around me. Clumps of snowgrass snapped off as I brushed against them. A bitter wind had me shove a hand into me jacket pocket. Among an assortment of schist chips was the snipe-shaped stone. I'd have to give it to her next time. Thin streaky clouds raced across a crescent moon giving it the appearance of a wicker pigeon basket. We'd tell Soo Tie about the bairn when he returned.

Was his love for Lai Jau anything like mine for Ming Yuet? I was still pondering the question when a ghostly figure appeared from behind the kirkyard wall.

PART THREE

Ida

FOURTEEN

Laying Him Out with Love

I was rolling bandages in the side room when Cook called from the kitchen.

'Ida, a lunatic is about to ruin your wash.'

It was a regular and annoying occurrence, since I live on a farm that borders the hospital. Both properties, particularly over summer months, are plagued with grime as horse-drawn vehicles take the dirt road in and out of town.

I poked my head around the corner to look out the window. Dust swirled around an open dray travelling at great speed, turning a row of poplars grey.

'Must be an emergency, Cook,' I said, abandoning my chores and rushing outside into the shimmering air.

The dray sped into the hospital grounds with Peter Butel at the reins. Edsall Gruber and Elias de la Perelle were in the back. Two farm workers ran alongside, sweating and puffing. Edsall's white store apron was badly stained, giving him the appearance of a butcher rather than a chemist. He used a corner to wipe his face.

'He's in a bad way, Ida.'

They lifted out what looked more like a freshly killed side of beef than a man. Dr Robertson, who'd recently taken over from Dr Dickinson, shouted instructions while flies buzzed around his face. The distinctive V-caps on the injured man's boots caught my eye. My stomach lurched. Conran?

Bile surged into the back of my throat. I pushed my tongue hard against the roof of my mouth, a trick used to prevent vomiting in the presence of gangrene, which gives off a putrid stink. Definitely not a smell or sight for the faint-hearted. A category I wouldn't normally fit.

Dr Robertson glanced in my direction.

'Ida, please see to the men.'

I fetched mugs of water and told those who'd run beside the dray to rest and let their hearts recover. They collapsed like sponge cakes taken from a range too soon. Edsall and Peter paced, shock etched on their faces. What a time for Matron to be in Christchurch on family business. 'Edsall, what happened?'

'I don't know, Ida. A mill worker found him by the cemetery wall. He fetched Butel, who came back with the dray. They drove down Buckingham Street yelling for me to climb on board and tend to him. There's a faint pulse.'

'But what . . .?'

'Seems he's been beaten,' said Peter. 'We fear the worst.'

He grasped a side of the dray and shook it. The horses shied and skittered. Elias rushed over to settle them.

Perhaps Conran wasn't as bad as he looked. Blood mixed with dust and battered flesh can create a dramatic sight. Dr Robertson would clean him up, tend to his wounds and have him back on his feet in no time.

I paced around the grounds thinking that with Matron away Dr Robertson might let Conran convalesce under my care at the farm.

Mr Letcher, the builder, came over to the door where Cook and I waited.

'Where's Alfred, Ida?'

'He's in Dunedin with William and Elsie.'

'What are they doing, for pity's sake?'

'Elsie's shopping for furniture while the men buy tools.'

Alfred was also purchasing De Boer rose bushes for the grounds, since the cuttings I'd taken from the farm and planted outside the female ward had pleased the patients no end. Maybe I should pick a bloom for Conran. 'Garçon', with its purplish pink flowers was in abundance, while my favourite, 'Gloire de Dijon', a large double buff apricot to orange, was still in bud.

I was on my way to the garden when the door swung open. Dr Robertson leaned on the door-jamb, still in his medical apron and with his shirt sleeves rolled up. You could have heard a needle drop. I braced myself.

He cleared his throat. 'Sorry. I couldn't save him – internal injuries. Nothing could be done.'

No one moved. Even the dust settled. I waited, hoping Conran would appear and laugh at the doctor's poor joke. But our medical man's dishevelled appearance said it all. He'd never before ventured outside in a bloodied garment. I thought of Conran's music – the reels and strathspeys he played at concerts, at balls, at parties at the farm; the airs and jigs he played in the hills. I heard his voice, soft as silk, the night we'd sat on a low stone wall at Elsie's wedding, a joyous look on his handsome face. The ground swayed beneath me. Cook put one hand on the door and the other around me.

'Are you sure, Doctor?' she asked.

'I'm afraid so. He's in the good Lord's hands.'

Elias walked over to Peter, who was punching the air in despair. Peter told Alfred later that it was the first time, he had found himself, despite all his mechanical talent – genius, some called it, unable to fix what needed mending. 'My accomplishments are meaningless.

A good man's gone. He saved my business by spotting a fire when it was still at a low smoulder. But I couldn't help him.'

Edsall was hard on himself too. He walked around in circles, his blood-soaked apron gripped tightly in both hands, as though he could somehow stem the tragedy. 'There must be something I should have known about – a new reviving technique.'

'You did everything possible, Edsall. Conran was beyond saving,' said the doctor.

News of the tragedy spread quickly. Outpatients told the bedridden, who passed it on to their visitors. Cook contributed by stopping a coach and asking the driver to carry the information into town, along with his passengers.

Men soon congregated in front of the hospital, talking in low, angry tones. I felt helpless, unable to care for the living or the dead. My legs buckled again. Cook helped me to a chair and pushed my head down. 'He was such a good man,' I said into the folds of my dress. Goodness hadn't saved him, though, had it?

Half an hour later I heard Mr Letcher yell, 'Let's find who's responsible!' A loud whoop went up among the men. Conran's peaceful temperament was forgotten as they headed back to town for reinforcements.

By then I'd recovered enough to ask Dr Robertson if I could see Conran.

'He's a dreadful sight, Ida.'

'Seeing him doesn't frighten me, Doctor. It's telling Alfred and William that'll take some doing.'

'At least he hasn't left a widow and children,' said the doctor, taking my arm.

Conran's words come back to me – 'Well, there's this lass . . .' Then another image came to mind – Conran playing on a hill near Swipers Gully. I'd spotted him in the vicinity recently while tending a hatter with an arthritic hip. Later I asked why he'd walked in there. He'd said, his face bright as a new penny, 'Me notes boonce off that

190

brae in ways ah canna git them tae do in toon.' Perhaps the hills contained another attraction.

'No, but he had good friends. He was a fine musician, too.'

'Yes, I've danced to his reels and jigs and airs,' said the doctor as we reached the room in which Conran lay. 'Ida, if this proves too difficult, I'll send for someone else.'

'I can do it, Doctor.'

'Well, if you're sure,' Dr Robertson said, easing the door open. 'But call if you need assistance. I'll be on my ward rounds.'

This next bit won't be easy to tell. All my nursing experience was needed, and what Father called 'grit'. I'll begin with a general description of his facial injuries.

His right eye hung from its socket. Scarlet veins protruded from the membrane sheath. His sandy brown hair was matted with blood. A muddy boot sole had left an imprint on his forehead. His nose was broken in two places, and blood had dried in and around the nostrils. His jaw resembled a piece of crumpled sacking; his swollen mouth had set in a most unnatural way.

I clasped the side of the table and said to myself, 'Lay him out with love, Ida.' Which is exactly what I did.

First I unlaced his boots, loosened the tongues and eased both off. Next I removed the woollen socks his mother had sent from Orkney the previous winter. He had on his Sunday trousers, which surprised me since it was a weekday. I unclipped the braces and unbuttoned the fly. As I slid the trousers over his lean hips, an odd-shaped stone clattered to the floor. I picked it up, intending to place it in his hand, but both were badly mangled. Bruised tissue hung off fractured and dislocated bone. Even if he'd survived, he would have been unlikely to hold a stone, let alone his fiddle.

I sat for a moment to compose myself.

Conran had walked into the New Orleans shortly after arriving in town. Before he even had a drink in his hand he said, 'Does anyone know a surly-lookin' man workin' a claim in one o the gullies off a tributary o the Arrow?' When no one responded, he added, 'Ah think he's mistreatin' his lass. He wouldna let me in their hut when ah called by after hearin' her scream.'

According to Alfred, the butcher said, 'Don't fret, lad. I've never met a woman who wasn't improved by a firm hand.' This comment caused raucous laughter among those depraved creatures who think a woman's place is under a hobnailed boot or against a wall with her petticoat bunched tight in a closed fist, her pantaloons letting in more than air. Morals get talked about in church but are seldom practised in goldfield towns. Alfred, who, in my opinion, is the kindest man in the district, maybe the entire world, went over to Conran. While chatting, they discovered an interest in music, so Alfred asked him home for supper. Over mutton and turnip stew we discussed how to help the young woman.

Alfred thought we should wait and see what eventuated but I wasn't prepared to do that. After learning that the husband came into town for supplies each Saturday, I gathered together a group of hardy women. We set off for his hut armed with stout sticks, a stockwhip and Alfred's chain-cutter in case the monster had bolted the door.

The brute's wife was covered with purple and yellow bruises. She was chained to the stove so she could prepare her husband's meals but not get to the outhouse. We cut the chain, wrapped her in a blanket and I helped her back to the farm.

The others waited until the husband came up the track, then they leapt into action, lashing him with the stockwhip, then their tongues, until he agreed to leave the Arrow.

'He packed his belongings faster than a bush rat pierces an egg, high-tailing it down the track with a bewildered look on his slimy face,' recounted Alice, a respectable farmer's wife who'd had first-hand experience of the man's vile ways when she'd worked briefly as a seamstress in a Dunedin shop situated next to a notorious public house. 'He'd saunter in – "Oh dear, seems I've taken the wrong door" – feeling all matter of fabric, regardless of whether it was part of a bolt or on a woman standing at the counter.'

After his wife healed, which took some time, seeing it wasn't just her body that was in a sorry state, Alfred found her work as a cook on a high-country station. By all accounts she's still there and doing well.

If only we could have helped Conran.

I slipped the stone into my pocket and stood up. 'Now we'll take off your jacket.' After getting one arm out, I rolled him to the side and removed the other. His shirt and vest were already unbuttoned. Perhaps the doctor had placed his ear on Conran's chest, hoping to detect a heartbeat. I took off both pieces of clothing and covered him with a sheet still creased from the laundry-woman's iron. Only his long-johns remained. I slid my hands under the sheet and rolled them over his hipbones, down his thighs and across his right femur, which was also fractured. 'Let's straighten your limbs as best we can,' I said. I manipulated them until they settled into a more natural position, then pulled gently on his ankles to even them up. 'There, you're back to your full height.' Which was taller than Alfred but nothing like William's six foot four inches. I allowed myself a moment to consider their reaction to the news of Conran's death. Likely they'd mix anger and grief with whisky and take the law into their own hands. Tough times lay ahead.

'Let's wash you now.'

I filled a wide, low basin from the kettle in the kitchen and gathered some of the freshly washed lint cloths that lay folded in a basket, nodding to Cook as I went by, but not trusting myself to speak until I was back with Conran.

'I'll start with your head and work down to your feet.'

I soaked my cloth, wrung out the excess water and wiped his hair, repeating this action until the water ran clean. His neck was the golden brown of a man who works outdoors. I wondered if the lass he'd mentioned had ever rested her head against it. Who was she? How would I find out now?

My pulse bounded as I washed away the bloodied boot-print on his forehead. Likely it belonged to his murderer. Fancy anyone stamping on such a fine face. 'There you go, Conran, not a trace left.'

I tore a cloth into narrow strips to clean his eyes, easing the right one into its socket before placing a penny on each lid. His nose needed special care, as bone had fused with lumps of dried blood and tissue. His cheeks, despite a thorough wash, resembled raw meat. After dabbing his lips with clean lint, I held his chin in position for a few moments, focusing on his wet curls rather than the weighted eyes. Hair is capable of withstanding more than skin. Once cleaned, hair looks good as new. But damaged flesh is a different matter.

The thatch of golden hair on his chest was bloodied. I sponged it clean. Three fractured ribs had altered the contour. I placed a fresh towel under each arm, bathed and dried them, talking to him throughout. 'Look at your poor hands. And such joy they gave.' With a smaller cloth I washed between each disjointed finger, then gently cleaned his battered palm and dislocated wrist. 'Now, let's straighten them as best we can. We can't have the fingers of a fine fiddler looking like they've been through a mangle.'

I eased him onto his side to clean his back. Not unexpectedly he'd soiled – maybe during the beating, or perhaps as he died. Speaking in soothing tones, for my own benefit as much as his, I cleaned his privates. 'Years from now, men will marvel at your masonry. You've left churches, houses and barns. What haven't you built?'

His feet were last. 'These gave me no end of trouble,' I told him, 'but you danced like a swell at the New Year Ball. Pity you didn't stay – you'd have been in demand.'

Conran was considered 'a catch' because of his fine looks and steady income, although until he'd whispered those four words to me at Elsie and William's wedding I hadn't known he fancied a particular girl. He'd made time for everyone, including stray dogs and wayward souls. Always ready to listen. Wise, too, once saying in my presence, 'A man canna learn much by hearin' himsel' talk.'

Countless basins of water later I completed the task to my satisfaction. I don't remember how long afterwards but at some point I heard footsteps coming down the corridor.

'My, you've done a fine job, Ida,' said Dr Robertson. 'Come through to the kitchen for tea.'

I washed my hands in a strong carbolic solution before joining him. We didn't talk much. Some things are beyond words.

A similar feeling had engulfed me on the dock as I was about to board the *Celaeno*, not knowing if I'd see London again, let alone Arleigh, the village in Essex where I grew up. Before Father died he'd said, 'Think about the colonies, Ida. New countries like Australia and New Zealand have much to offer. You're young, with everything ahead.'

Conran was young too – not yet thirty.

'Can I take him back to the farm, Doctor?'

'Are you thinking of holding the wake there?'

That would be fitting. 'Yes, but it could start at the New Orleans. That would give me time to tell Alfred, William and Elsie.'

'When do you expect them back?'

'Thursday evening.'

'So it's the New Orleans until Friday morning, and Saturday for the funeral?'

'Yes. That would suit.'

'He'll be in good hands with you, Ida. The wardsman can fetch the carpenter to bring out a coffin. Southland beech all right? We'll take the two of you to the farm in the dray. More tea while you wait?'

'He'll need tidy clothes.'

'The wardsman can stop by his cottage.'

I didn't recognise the neatly stitched blue shirt with his name embroidered on the inside of the collar. Maybe he'd been saving it for a special occasion. The doctor helped me dress him. Then the wardsman, along with the carpenter and his assistant, laid him in the coffin and carried him out to the dray. I picked a 'Gloire de Dijon' bud and placed it on his chest. Thinking it might be significant, I took the stone from my pocket and slipped it into his.

I don't remember much about the drive home, other than the heartfelt sighs of the men who sat in the back of the dray with Conran.

They carried his coffin into the parlour and placed it on the large oval table in the centre of the room. We stood in silence for a moment. A fly buzzed against the sash window. Had Conran fought as the murderer – perhaps there were several – closed in on him?

I threw twigs into my new Richmond range, poking and blowing until they caught. If only I could have blown life into Conran. 'I'll make a strong brew,' I said to the men.

They drank their tea quickly, wanting to be on their way, which suited me, as the house needed arranging. Within twenty-four hours it would be full of hungry, grieving people.

'You'll be all right, Ida?' said Dr Robertson, reaching for his hat.

'I'll be fine once Alfred's back.'

'Would you like a woman to stay with you until then?' said the carpenter. 'My wife's most obliging.'

'Thank you, but Elsie will be here soon.'

'Well, if you're sure.'

'Come by on Saturday.'

'We'll give him a grand send-off. Bless you, Ida.'

I pulled down the blinds. They wouldn't go up until the funeral party left the house. I picked some ivy from near the back door and set seven candles among its tendrils. Their dim light helped soften Conran's injuries. Nothing eased my sadness, though. If only he'd finished that sentence . . .'

My black crêpe dress crackled and snapped when I removed it from the chest. I found my good stockings rolled in a ball in a drawer, alongside my best undergarments. After a thorough wash I dressed in my mourning costume, and squeezed my broad feet into my toe-pinching Sunday shoes. It would not have felt right to dress too plainly for the man who had brought such joy to our valley. I pinned a ruby brooch to my bodice and hung my mother's jet necklace around my neck.

During the early part of the evening I sat quietly with Conran. As the candles burned down, I sang, 'Will ye no come back again,' while the house built by Alfred and Conran wrapped its arms around me.

Sometime during my vigil I went outside for air. The sky was criss-crossed with perfectly formed silver stars that looked embroidered into a luxurious navy-blue cloth. Sweet-scented honeysuckle caught in the back of my throat. As I turned to pump a pitcher of water, a slight movement high on a ledge caught my eye. At first I thought it was a bird, then I wondered whether someone else was also watching over Conran. An odd thought rushed through me like strange wind.

FIFTEEN

We Placed Her in His Arms

I made my way in the moonlight to the bottom of the ledge, not sure what to expect. Doing this in my Sunday shoes was foolish but I didn't want to go back for my boots. Full of trepidation, I hoisted up my petticoat and dress and began to climb.

A man with a wide-brimmed hat pulled well down over his face appeared from behind a rock above me. His shadowy presence startled me, although something in his demeanour reminded me of Ah Sip. Watchful – a little hesitant maybe. I stepped from rock to rock, careful about the placement of my feet but reckless with my thoughts, wondering whether he was a harmless local or a stranger with evil intent.

On the *Celaeno*, smart thinking and wily evasion had often been required to repel unwanted advances and alarming behaviour, mostly from officers. My abhorrence of bullies is a legacy of that sea journey. Cruelness riles me. I've no time for anyone who mistreats the vulnerable. Nor do I go into any potentially dangerous situation unprepared.

I picked up a rock and spoke confidently. 'Do you need help? I'm Mrs Chynoweth, Alfred's wife and Ah Sip's friend.'

'Ah Sip?'

The man leaned further over the ledge. I quickened my pace, thus rendering myself incapable of speaking for thirty yards.

'Yes. I'm Conran the fiddler's friend too,' I eventually puffed. I don't know why I mentioned Conran – intuition, maybe. Anyway it had quite an effect. The man stepped off the ledge and headed directly for me, arms in the air, wailing as if the end of the world was imminent. He was definitely familiar. But if it was Little Wind, he'd thickened up since the party at the camp. He must have found well-paid work. Perhaps he'd been rabbiting.

'Little Wind, isn't it? What's the problem?'

Shuddery sobs ricocheted around the schist outcrops. I patted his back with my left hand while hanging on to the rock in my right, just in case. He flinched as though in pain. Maybe he'd come for medical attention, although a Chinaman seeking help from an Englishwoman was unlikely. Few of them trusted our ways. 'Rest a bit, then we'll go back to the farm.'

'Not want to be nuisance. Go own hut now. Thank you.'

'I'll make you a hot drink.'

'No thank you, I must leave. Goodbye.'

Haste, and maybe pain, caused him to stumble, resulting in further tears.

'Here, take my arm. I'll help you down to the house. No one's there except Conran.'

'Ok-nee man?'

'Yes, Conran's from Orkney.'

'He is not dead? Please say not dead.'

Why was he so upset about Conran? I peered under his hat to get a better look. Surprisingly for a Chinaman, he held my gaze. Even my good friend Ah Sip would look away. It *was* Little Wind. 'Didn't Conran play his fiddle near you?'

'Yes, on hill. Soon make music again?'

'I'm sorry, Little Wind. He died earlier today at the hospital.'

'Die. He die?' His voice quavered. Hot tears dripped onto my hand. He doubled over. I didn't comment, thinking he'd mention the cause of his pain once he felt comfortable in my presence.

'Come. See for yourself.'

After furtively dropping the rock, I tucked one arm around him and bunched up my skirt with other. No doubt we made an odd couple, shuffling down the slope. Gallbladder or appendix couldn't be ruled out. Either condition would need the doctor. 'Come inside. I'll put the kettle on.'

Big, silent tears dripped onto his jacket collar, which he'd pulled up around his face. But he bowed respectfully when I passed him a cup of tea. Nice hands, long fingers. Perhaps he was a musician. That might be the connection. Or was the rumour true? Had Conran really spent immoral time with a Chinaman? I could not bear to think about it.

'Did you know Conran well?'

'Yes, much good man. Please see?'

He shook as though attached to a thresher. I relieved him of my crockery, not wanting to be a place short. It had taken a full year of butter sales to buy that particular dinner-set.

'Con-Lan need me.'

Oh, no! The rumours were true. 'Little Wind, he's not a pretty picture.'

'What you mean?'

'He was badly beaten.'

His face folded in on itself like a crumpled paper fan.

'For what they beat?' he sobbed.

'We don't know, maybe money.'

He shook his head. 'I think not.'

Outside, the wind picked up, rattling the windows and doors. In the distance the house cow's bell jangled. I'd forgotten to milk her. And where was Jack?

'It not good Con-Lan visit me. Give him bad luck.'

Still unsure of their connection, and not wanting to cause offence or provoke further tears, I said, 'He's in the parlour. Please go in.'

'Thank you. Con-Lan say Ida most good woman. Al-Fed plenty fine man, too.'

So Conran had told him about us. But he was partial to women – surely I hadn't got that wrong?

'He was a good friend to us as well. More like a brother,' I said, nodding towards the parlour. Little Wind bowed his head. 'Please stay with him as long as you want.'

I've never heard anything more forlorn than Little Wind's desolate cry when he saw the body. He ran his fingers around Conran's face, caressing each bruise, cut and scratch.

This open display of tenderness caught me off guard. Tears welled; I couldn't hold them back. Little Wind reached over and placed a hand lightly on my shoulder. A touch that both comforted and disconcerted. My unease increased when Little Wind spoke to Conran in Chinese. I felt like an intruder in my own parlour, so I backed out of the room.

The Chinaman's melodic voice crooned through the night. Soft, soothing words, interspersed with sobs. From time to time he groaned as though in physical pain. I drank tea in the kitchen and wrote notes about what needed doing for the wake and the funeral.

At daybreak I heard what sounded like furniture being shifted in the parlour.

'What . . . ?'

'Feet must face this way, Ida. So spilits can leave.'

I was puzzled. 'Spirits, please tell me more about them?'

'Chinese believe in thlee souls, seven animal spilits. Spilits sink into soil when Con-Lan die. Souls bleak up. One stay with family, one go with Con-Lan to get payments or punishments gained in this life, and one stay with body. Feet must face opening. Or spilits cannot leave.'

His English had certainly improved since we'd met at the camp party. Noting the urgency in his voice, I said, 'That's what we'll do, then.' I could always get Alfred and William to reposition the coffin after Little Wind left.

'You good lady, Ida.'

Confused, more like. But I helped heave and push until Conran's coffin faced the door, by which time Little Wind's pains had obviously intensified, but still no explanation was forthcoming. Not comfortable asking him directly, I said, 'Is there anything else you'd like help with?'

He sighed heavily. 'Wail until Con-Lan go to next life.'

'There'll be much keening. I promise you that.'

'Con-Lan not keep plomise. He tell me not leave.'

I took a deep breath. Oh, Conran! What was going on? 'Maybe he's with you in a different way now.'

'I think old way best.'

And who could argue? 'Someone killed him, Little Wind. I'm sure he didn't want to leave you.'

'He ask me mally.'

Mother of God! What was he thinking? Men couldn't marry each other! And what about the lass he'd mentioned?

'Con-Lan say Al-Fed, Ida, William and Elsie come to wedding.'

'Did he?' Had the man lost his mind?

'No wedding now. Ok-nee man die. Leave this life.'

'Yes. We'll hold his funeral on Saturday, when Alfred and the others are back.'

'William will be much sad. Need plenty Old Tom.'

My goodness, he knew everything. 'Yes, he will.'

'We must help Con-Lan go to next life.'

Even Presbyterians like me find a comma more comforting than a full-stop. 'What should we do?' My question drifted around the room like dandelion spoor. I glanced at Little Wind, to see him pale and grip the back of a chair. Seconds later his trousers and my floor were soaked. Those pains! Goodness, what a nelly. Little Wind was a woman. Conran had loved a Chinese woman. 'Is a baby coming?'

'Yes, big ploblem.'

How had she and Conran met? How long had they been…? 'You need to lie down. Follow me. It'll be all right. I'll take care of you.'

'I do not want to leave Con-Lan.'

'His feet face the door now so his spirit will follow us.' When she still didn't move, I added, 'Think about your baby.'

'Con-Lan say will look like me.'

So he knew about the baby? Of course he did. Didn't I catch him making rockers for a cradle? 'We'll soon know whether it's a little girl or boy.'

She removed her wet trousers in Jack's bedroom while I placed clean towels on the bed-sheet. 'In you get. That's right. I'll give you a rub.'

'Thank you, Ida.'

I held her hand during contractions, and in between cooled her face with a damp cloth. Two days ago we'd hardly known each other. Now we were sharing something special and shocking and secret. I wanted to know everything.

'How did you meet Conran?'

'He save me flom flood. Take to hut. Stitch up. See?'

She raised her leg to show me the scar, which, apart from puckered tissue around the knee, took a reasonably straight line.

'We make bet. Con-Lan say, Ida's medicine best. I say Chinese is velly good.'

That would have been my boracic powder. 'Did he also give you a ribbon?'

'Yes, so can mally like in Ok-nee.'

'He told you about Orkney, then?'

'We tell evelything. I tell you, Ida. You want?'

'I would, very much.'

She recalled the night they'd danced and loved among red poppies. I was like a moth to a flame, taking in every word, eager to hear about their union. It pains me to admit it but I felt piqued. Why hadn't Conran told me from the outset? Had he not trusted me? I'll admit to gossiping on occasions but I also know when to keep my mouth shut. I carry patients' indiscretions around by the sackful. Nurses do. It goes with the job. How humiliating not to have known.

'What place you meet Al-Fed?'

'On board ship as we travelled out from England.'

'What you like about him?'

'He seemed resourceful.'

'Please what is sosh-ful?'

'Means he knew how to get what he wanted.'

'Ah, he want you, Ida!'

'Seems he did, for despite being housed in different sections – single men free to fish or play games while we had to be content with devotions and needlework – he had emerged from his hatch during a storm at exactly the same time I appeared from mine. While other passengers heaved into buckets below, and the crew trimmed the sails, we exchanged short accounts: he was a farm worker from Cornwall heading to the goldfields where he'd later buy a farm; I was looking after Jack until we reached Dunedin, where I'd place him in an orphanage and find work in a hospital. "I know a man who needs nursing," he'd said, causing me to blush and melt into his golden-syrup eyes. "Designed to match your hair, Ida," he told me after we'd walked out a few times.'

'You had no doubts, Ida?'

'Not one. What about you, Little Wind? Did you like Conran straight away?'

'I like his music. Then when save me he do many kindness. Good feeling build. But make me flighten. Him too, I think. But we cannot stop see. Soon love sound like many fiddles playing in sky.'

Between contractions Little Wind spoke quietly to their baby. Conran would have been attracted to her serenity. If only he'd confided in me earlier, we could have worked something out.

'Little Wind, when did you conceive?'

'Con-see?'

'Fall pregnant. I'm wondering how far along you are?'

'I think full time. I small though, yes?'

'Mmmmm, but your baby might be strong.' Hopefully she'd eaten nourishing food throughout her term. 'Now, tell me, has your pregnancy been straightforward?'

'No ploblem. Con-Lan bling food. But not when in hospital with chill. I not know he sick. Make sad. Baby you think big enough?'

During the next contraction Little Wind called to her mother. Memories of mine, of my dead baby sister, flooded back. Complications, Father had said. A loss that magnified over the years and had no doubt contributed to my interest in medicine. No one is ready to be motherless, regardless of their age.

'Your baby might survive. Small ones sometimes do.' Hadn't I told Conran about the one who fitted into a sock drawer?

'Many babies come to you?'

Unsure of her meaning, I addressed both possibilities. 'I'm an expert at delivering other women's babies. But I've never given birth myself.'

By now her contractions were coming in waves. Beads of sweat ran down her face.

'Can I deaden your pain with laudanum?'

'No, no. Dragon Fire steals MaMa's heart.'

This comment made no sense. Nor could I understand the next.

'Big hurt like Golden Lilies.'

I shrugged. 'Almost there. Push now, that's right – push hard.'

The iron bars on the bedstead rattled. She looked towards the window and called, 'MaMa, please help. I need you with me!'

What did her family think about her living in a goldfield town?

How many other Chinese sojourners in Arrowtown were women? Glory, what a shock.

The parlour clock chimed on the hour. Thirty minutes later a little head appeared.

'Now puff. That's right. Puff until the next big pain. Push harder this time. You're doing well. Almost there, just one more push. Ah, here she comes. Yes, you have a little girl.'

Her skin was golden as a field of buttercups but she was silent as dust.

I cut the umbilical cord, gripped the infant by the ankles and raised her up, tapping her buttocks with my free hand until she gave a frail whimper. Her body measured less than twelve inches and her ribcage resembled a scrawny chicken's. The little mite barely moved when I placed her in her mother's arms.

'You beautiful sweet be-nui. Have happy eyes same as Con-Lan. Not sad like liver baby.'

She did have his bright cornflower-blue eyes, and tufts of black hair, which I rubbed dry with a soft cloth. 'What's a river baby?'

'One not made with love.'

Such a baby was recently pulled from the Shotover. 'Do you have a name for your little daughter?'

'We call Fang Yin.' She kissed the child's forehead and little button nose. 'Name means "flag-lant melody".'

I thought of the red poppies and Conran's music. 'Perfect.'

Little Wind encircled her daughter's wrist with a finger and ran her other hand around Fang Yin's face, saying, 'Be-nui, be-nui, I love you.'

The infant's weak breaths filled me with apprehension. I checked her heartbeat. Faint. Everything about her was subdued. Her little stick legs barely moved.

'Little Wind . . .'

'We show Con-Lan. Please, hully.'

She knew.

After attending to the placenta, I folded a clean cloth and gave it to Little Wind to place between her legs. 'Now we must find you a pair of trousers,' I said, rummaging through Jack's drawer. 'These moleskins might fit. Let me help you into them.'

'Thank you, Ida. I am in debt with you.'

'No need to thank me. I'm glad I could help. Shall we wrap Fang Yin in a pretty lawn napkin? I have one in the linen cupboard.'

Little Wind tucked in the corners, arranging the lace trim so it appeared that Fang Yin wore a beautiful gown. 'Now, Ida, we go to Con-Lan.'

She carried their daughter into the parlour, saying over and over like a mantra, 'I love you, Fang Yin. Like gold. Like China. Like sky.'

When we reached the coffin, she turned and said, 'Ida, will you please hold baby?'

Her sweet little head nestled against my bosom as Little Wind lifted her shirt and unwound a red sash, sliding one end under Conran's arm and the other over his shoulder. I thought of all the babies I'd not held. Loss surged through me like an incoming tide. I swayed as though I was a flimsy piece of driftwood.

'I take her now. Thank you, Ida.'

She placed Fang Yin in the sling, where she lay like a sliver of moon in her father's arms, his soft curly beard mingling with her little black tufts.

'She looks at me, Ida.'

And it did seem as though Fang Yin stared directly at her mother.

'Now I sing Da-Da's song.'

Realising this was the only time they'd have together as a family, I left the room and went through to the bedroom, where I gathered the bloodied linen. A glimpse in the dresser mirror revealed a thirty-five-year-old woman who looked as though she'd been dipped in whitewash and hung out to dry during a violent storm. Even my hair, usually my best feature, was a shambles. Unruly strands stuck out like bristles on a broom.

So much had happened in a short space of time. Love and loss, two extremes, yet we cannot experience one without the possibility of the other, which is why Jack has always felt precious as well as precarious to me. You'd think I'd have sensed where he was, known if he was in danger, whether he needed me. But I only had questions. Had Little Wind's mother felt her daughter's pain and the fragility of a grand-daughter not meant for this world?

After Mother died, Father found a pair of white satin slippers she'd made for their last baby. 'Keep them, lass,' he'd said to me, 'for your first born.' But Alfred and I never experienced that delight. And somehow it hadn't seemed right to put them on Jack.

'Can I put these on Fang Yin, Little Wind?' I asked, taking the slippers into the parlour.

She looked at them and nodded.

They sat like small white thimbles on Conran's blue shirt. The infant's slight breaths floated into the air soft as fresh snow. I wanted to reach out and catch them, slip them back down her tiny throat to replenish her lungs. Then one last shudder and little Fang Yin was gone.

Silence settled like dust, and panic caught in the back of my throat. What if Jack or Alfred died before I did?

As though from a great distance I heard Little Wind say, 'Ida, could you please fetch two shillings? I pay soon back.'

She placed a coin each in Conran and Fang Yin's right palms, while speaking a mix of Chinese and English, her grief put aside as she ran her hands around their heads, joining them together with invisible thread. Conran and Fang Yin had entered a place that could not be reached by mortal souls. Sorrow gouged a path back to Essex, where I relived Mother's death and Father's grief.

The parlour clock's familiar chime brought me back to the present.

'What do we need to do next?' I asked Little Wind, eager to attend to her needs.

'Not good, but must keep hidden. You undee-stand?'

Regret weighed heavily as I nailed the coffin shut, sealing Fang Yin forever in her father's arms. Best tell the mourners Conran was too badly injured to view. Edsall and Peter would back me up; so would Dr Robertson. Alfred and William might ask questions but my immediate obligation was to Little Wind. A secret is not always a bad thing.

I cannot say the same about my own wicked crime.

The day after Jack's third birthday a letter arrived from England with a Lincoln postmark. By then he called me MyIda, a word so close to Mamma that it melted every bone in my body, as though I'd given him life as well as lodgings. The unopened letter tormented me. What if an aunt was claiming him? Or his grandparents had written to say they couldn't take him? Best if Jack never knew. Tossing that letter into the flames made me no better than Conran's murderer. I was denying Jack his future just as surely as Conran's killer had done his ... I was mulling over my culpability when there was a knock on the front door.

'Hide in the bedroom, Little Wind. I'll send them away.'

'Ida. My goodness, you look dreadful,' said Helen de la Perelle, stepping into the kitchen, taking over. 'Sit yourself down. I'll make tea.'

I was unable to protest, for she'd come laden with food.

'Elias thought you'd be in a state with Conran here and Alfred in Dunedin, so I'm here to help.'

'He'll be home tomorrow.' I needed to check on Little Wind. 'Excuse me, Helen. I'll fetch a handkerchief while the kettle boils.'

'Some smelling salts wouldn't go amiss. You look ready to drop, Ida. What a sad business.'

Specks of blood dotted the sill of Jack's bedroom window. She'd crept away, and I'd forgotten to give her a second pad. I was not thinking straight. Had I ever?

I tucked a clean handkerchief into my cuff and returned to the kitchen, looking into the parlour on the way. At least Conran and Fang Yin had each other. They'd not face the unknown alone. Nothing's stronger than kin. If I'd opened that letter, Jack might have been better off.

The boy had a fearsome temper. Once he threw an iron at me, hot off the hob, when I refused to let him go to a birthday party until I'd put fresh creases into his trousers. I ducked, so wasn't hurt, but the incident upset me. When Alfred reprimanded him, Jack stayed away for days.

We couldn't work him out. Life in an orphanage would surely have been a sight more vexing than living on the farm. Maybe I should have marched straight to the ship's captain and handed him over the day his mother died. Instead I'd made my way to the doctor's cabin, saying, 'This infant needs a wet nurse.'

'Only a matter of days before he joins his mother,' the doctor had said, looking directly at my bosom, thus reinforcing my poor opinion of him. His hand had strayed improperly when, shortly after boarding, he'd checked me for rashes and contagious diseases. He was indeed the dregs of his profession. 'Come inside for a warm drink,' he'd said with a smirk. Now here was Mary at the bottom of the sea and her little son alone in the world. 'Find him a wet nurse,' I said, 'or I'll have my cousin who's a newspaperman in New Zealand expose you as a predator and charlatan.' You should have seen his eyes bulge. Even though I've no such relative I stood firm, one hand on my hip, the baby clasped in the other arm. The beastly medical man turned puce. His chest heaved; the hair on his face bristled. Needless to say, I was quite relieved when he stepped back into his cabin and slammed the door.

Within an hour a married woman who'd recently lost an infant to dysentery came by with a few shillings jingling in her pocket and said, 'I'll feed him if you do everything else.' Jack, as the girls in my mess named him, since he'd popped out of nowhere like a Jack-in-

211

the-box, took to her breast like a duck to water, much to our relief, for he had a piercing cry.

Somehow I got through the day. More food arrived: some left on the doorstep, other dishes came inside with their owners. Barrels of ale from every hotelier in town lined the veranda, the contents of which would soon flow, along with tears.

After taking tea, I suggested Helen check on Elias, saying Alfred and William and Elsie would be back soon and I'd need to tell them the news.

At dusk I rinsed Little Wind's trousers in a basin and hung them on the line. Under a full moon, and with the aid of a lamp, I soaked the bloodied sheets and towels in the washtub. I also made up Jack's bed with clean linen hoping he'd be back in time to farewell Conran – then I took my kitchen rocker into the parlour and prayed beside the coffin, as much for me as for Little Wind.

She crept in well after midnight.

'I go to cemetly. Look for fiddle. Find many pieces. Note, too.'

Conran's handwriting jumped off the page as I held the letter up to the lamp. 'Have you read it, Little Wind?'

'Yes, but please I like you say aloud, Ida.' She took off her hat and sat beside me.

Dear Ida,

I'm sitting in me cottage cursing that I didn't decline Elsie's request at the wedding. Or come and see you afterwards and finish what I'd started talking about outside. Now I'm sorry. I didn't know how to put it you see, words not being me strong point. I've thought about it a lot since and have decided it's time. Me news will come as a shock but it's truly a joy. I'll tell you a bit now so you have time to digest it afore we talk.

I'm in love. With all me heart and soul. But there's a Chinese complication and I'd like some advice. Could we talk when I come back to town? I'll be with me darling for the next few nights. Then, if it's all right with you, I'd like to call by on Wednesday while Alfred's in Dunedin with William and Elsie. Will you keep me blatherings to yourself until I've fully explained? There might be trouble if it's not handled carefully.

Thank you,

Conran

'He wanted to tell me about you and the baby?'
'Yes, he thought you would know what to do.'
'If only I could have helped, Little Wind.' I put the note in my apron pocket, thinking I'd show it to Alfred later.
She stroked my fingers. 'You help much now. Thank you.'
Her hand was ice cold. Would she ever feel warm again? 'How will you get through the next few days?'
'Want to stay close to Con-Lan and Fang Yin. Cook, maybe?'
'I could say Ah Sip and the Chinamen who worked with Conran on the church will need feeding at his wake. But will you manage?'
'Yes. Make plenty food.'
'First you need a clean pad and a wash.'
'Thank you, Ida.'
Over the next few hours we roasted fowls and baked faat tie which, according to Little Wind, signify life's completeness. When Mrs Letcher called by with condolences and a mutton stew, I asked her to fetch tea from a Chinese merchant and to bring it back to the farm the following day. She stared briefly at Little Wind but left to do as I had asked.
Little Wind and I talked as we worked. I learned more about her love for Conran. She heard about the lengths I'd gone to to try to have a child.

'I studied everything written on the topic. Once I read an article about a man who rented out a "Celestial Bed" as a cure for barrenness. He said it was twelve feet wide, and the mattress was filled with hair from the tails of English stallions, all supported by forty glass pillars! After learning that this bed contained spices and essences that he said could turn stone into life, I sprinkled a similar concoction between our sheets. I left Scoles' stallion alone, though. Alfred, bless him, put up with this craziness for weeks. Years later I read that the same charlatan was experimenting with electrical therapy, rigging up his "Celestial Bed" to an electric fire and charging fifty pounds a night. Another article, also written by a man, said an active mind caused barrenness, but I've never subscribed to that view!'

I don't suppose she understood much of this tirade but she put an arm around me anyway. Our tears fell onto the roast fowls.

Little Wind said, 'Soon we must make sylup to sweeten sollow.'

In between cooking we visited the parlour, sometimes together, other times alone. I also checked the yard frequently to see if Jack had returned. But it was late morning before we heard voices on the front porch.

SIXTEEN

We Emphasised His Good Points

'Ida, what's happened?' said Alfred, bursting into the kitchen. 'Are you all right? Where's Jack?' After seeing my visitor he added, 'You have company?'

'Alfred, remember Little Wind, Ah Sip's friend? William, Elsie.'

Little Wind bowed. Alfred offered his hand, which she shook firmly. Just like a man, I thought. A puzzled expression flickered across Alfred's ruddy face, which he attempted to conceal by rubbing his forehead. William tipped his cap while Elsie gave a brief nod.

'We wis told at Lawrence that someone had been killed,' said William.

'Do you know who?' Elsie asked, eyeing Little Wind, who had turned her back and was busy flouring the bench.

'I think she might, Elsie,' said Alfred, taking in my mourning attire. 'Ida, love, what's happened? Where's Jack?'

'I don't know. I'm worried sick. I don't know where to start.'

'Start at the beginning, dear one.'

Telling them was harder than hearing the news myself, because saying it out loud made me feel as if I'd colluded in some way.

Alfred slammed a fist into the kitchen table as though the roughly hewn planks concealed Conran's murderers. 'How could a good man's life end in such a cowardly and despicable act?'

My emotions plummeted. What if it were Alfred dead in the parlour? I placed a hand on his arm. 'I know; it beggars belief,' I said.

Alfred rested his head on my hand. 'There's no logic in the Lord's ways.'

'Or law and order in this stinkin' toon,' said William, his face turning blood red. Orkney curses filled the room, sending shivers through us all. Elsie couldn't comfort him. Little Wind continued to prepare food. I brewed tea that no one drank.

'Where is he?' Alfred eventually asked, running both hands through his thick black hair.

I nodded towards the parlour.

William rushed through the door and, upon seeing the coffin, yelled, 'Ah'll kill the bastards! Kill them and burn them and curse them forever. Conran, me beuy, whit have they done tae you?' He kicked the door closed with his boot. Low, rhythmic keening seeped through the wall.

'He's taking him back to Orkney,' Elsie whispered.

Maybe with one of the spirits Little Wind talked about. By now she had finished making faat tie and was washing my best china, her hands running back and forth over the flower-sprig pattern. Was she revisiting a time spent with Conran? Perhaps a meal they'd shared? Or a moment when her heart had lifted like mine the day Alfred asked me to marry him . . .

I stroked my husband's back. A heavily built, active man, Alfred usually feels invincible, but that evening he shook like a poplar leaf in a high wind.

Elsie put her ear to the parlour door. 'William's getting up steam.'

His yelling and cursing had me fearing the windows might shatter. Little Wind told me later she thought William was calling up demons.

Alfred remained at the table with his fists clenched. Elsie walked up and down looking from me to Alfred, saying, 'What can I do? I feel useless.'

'You could help Little Wind with the food, Elsie.' Remember to say 'he' not 'she', I reminded myself. 'He's been a godsend. Look what he's made already.' Delicious food sat on plates on the bench and dresser. 'People will eat well. Who knows how many will come to pay their respects? Conran was well liked – it could be a big funeral.'

Little Wind bowed to Elsie and brought her hands together, her manners paramount even under stress.

'I can't imagine anyone wanting to harm Conran,' said Alfred. As though on cue, William let out a sound that summed up the horror. Alfred looked at me and Elsie, and our expressions sent him hurrying into the parlour. Through the open door we saw William with his hands pressed against the coffin, his tall, muscular frame shaking. Alfred went over and spoke to him in the same soothing tones he uses when I'm distressed.

Elsie pushed the door shut. 'I can't bear to see William like that.'

I wanted to tell her to leave it open so any left over spirits could depart, but I kept my new learning to myself.

An hour or so later, William took up a haunting melody on his mouth organ while Alfred sang in his deep baritone, which Conran had greatly admired. Their woeful tunes took me back to Arleigh, where copper miners coughed up blood and women struggled to make a meal. Our past lives within us, no matter how far we travel or what we accumulate.

Early next morning my women friends arrived with their husbands. Goodness knows how Little Wind had survived in this town without female company.

'How are you bearing up, Ida?' said Elias, placing yet another basket of food on the table.

No doubt he'd noticed my bloodshot eyes. 'I'm keeping busy, thank you.'

'You'll have a lot to do, but I see you've got help.' He nodded in Little Wind's direction.

Talk like a man, I told myself. Don't go into details. 'Yes.'

By midnight the farmhouse was packed with people and food and drink. Farmers brought meat and Su Sing sent a pig, which Ah Sip and Ah Lum delivered. They'd sown thin white cotton strips around their hats. A mark of respect, Little Wind told me later – like our black armbands. 'I come with a heavy heart,' said Ah Lum, who, like Little Wind, can read and write in English and Chinese and therefore is held in high esteem by his countrymen.

'Thank you for your kindness,' I said. 'Please step inside.'

'My heart is heavy too,' said Ah Sip, handing over a basket of freshly picked vegetables and removing his hat before bowing to Little Wind. 'I see you have one good cook, Mrs Ida. I make two. Yes?'

'Thank you, Ah Sip. I'd appreciate your help.' His presence might also comfort Little Wind.

'Can I offer my services?' said Ah Lum, pulling five sticks from his bag. 'I respected the fiddler. He showed kindness to my people. May I light incense for him?'

It felt right to honour Little Wind's customs. 'Yes, please do.' I said.

Grateful for their help, as my brain was barely functioning, I went to get my best table linen from the cupboard and came back with a duster. Lack of sleep, I suppose, as well as shock and grief; anxiety, too. What if whoever had killed Conran had harmed Jack as well? No, he'd be home soon. I hoped his wild mates from Skippers wouldn't appear at the wake.

The Apostles' arrival, however, was a welcome sight.

'We'll find the ruffians who took his life,' said Doc, dismounting from his horse and waving towards another rider. 'Meet Donald, a piper who knows the sacred Celtic hymn "Tha mi dol dachaidh leat".'

'What does it mean in English?' said Alfred

'I'm going home with thee.'

Every mourner hushed as Donald played – including, to my surprise, the butcher. Maybe the hymn brought back memories of places and people he'd loved and lost. Our lives had all begun in countries we'd never see again, on land that would not cover us in death. We were here to stay, unlike the Chinese sojourners.

Over at the kitchen bench Little Wind helped Ah Sip put the finishing touches to a fowl. I wondered how much he knew about her situation. A great weariness enveloped me.

'Story time,' Alfred said, putting his arm around my shoulder. 'Remember to emphasise his good points.'

Mrs Murphy recalled how Conran had brought firewood when her youngest child came down with the croup. 'And all the while his chimney went without. So there you have it. That's the measure of the man.'

'He always bought his round. Generous as the day was long. Never shirked, like some I could mention,' said Jimmy O'Grady, looking at Mr Rattingly, who, next to a certain butcher perched on a stool by a barrel of ale, glass at the ready, had the tightest fists and shortest pockets in town.

William shoved the butcher out of the way as though he was a bag of air, and refilled his own glass, tossing it down as if it was a dram rather than a pint. I looked at Alfred, who shook his head. No point asking William to pace himself. Elsie broke the tension by raising her glass. 'Let's give thanks to Conran for his music.'

I can't recall all the stories, but Jimmy O'Grady told his perennial.

'Remember when William and Conran got drunk and stumbled into the big widow's back yard?'

'We've heard it before, O'Grady, but off you go, since it's a special occasion,' said Maurice O'Leary.

'Pinched two pair of enormous bloomers off her clothesline, thinking they were sheets, and ran through town pretending to be ghosts!'

'Nothing scarier than grown men with a widow's bloomers on their head,' laughed Mr Spockett, a travelling salesman.

'Or more daft,' said Elias de la Perelle.

'Most action those bloomers had seen in a long time,' laughed the butcher, slapping his thighs and revealing an open fly.

'Button yirsel' ap – we've ladies present!' said William.

'Ach, lad, a dead bird never falls out of his nest.'

'We'll miss Conran's music – and his stonemasonry,' said Peter Butel. 'He laid stone like you plough a field, Alfred: straight and true.'

'Yes, he'll be sorely missed,' said John, Peter's brother.

'Aye, he will,' said Jacko, an old miner who'd rubbed every ointment known to man on his arthritic knees, including rancid mutton lard. 'I'll never forget his kindness when I lived in a tent with three mates on the banks of the Arrow. No gold to be had with the river frozen over for weeks.'

'Hard times,' said O'Leary.

'Icicles hung off our beards,' Jacko continued. 'We wrapped rags around our hands, hoping not to lose fingers to frostbite. No one would give us supplies.'

'You had unpaid bills all around town – don't leave out that bit,' said Robert Pritchard, a storekeeper.

'And you still settle your accounts like a clock – tick, tick, tick,' laughed Edsall.

'As I was saying,' Jacko interrupted, 'things were grim until Conran, who we didn't know from a sack of beans, came along with a panikin of flapjack mix. He made a three-sod fireplace and set a flat river stone on top. While waiting for the stone to heat, he played stirring tunes on his fiddle, stopping only to add twigs to the fire. They were the best flapjacks I've ever tasted, and he left potatoes for us to bake in the ashes.'

William filled his glass from the barrel. 'So why the hell did someone thrash him? Tell me that, will you?'

'Probably more than one,' I said. 'You wouldn't have recognised him. My knees are still trembling. Did I tell you how I nearly fainted, Alfred?'

'You did, my love, but I'm willing to hear about it again.'

Little Wind and Ah Sip moved among the mourners with plates of food. Several people looked in my direction, as if to say, fancy letting them in your kitchen. Most knew my friendship with Ah Sip was based on our interest in medicinal plants, but my connection with Little Wind would have come as a surprise. Careful to say 'he', I fielded questions from the curious. 'Yes, Little Wind came to help with the food. He's a fine cook.'

'My husband offered my services, Ida,' said Mrs O'Leary pointedly, 'but apparently you didn't need them.'

'Thank you for your concern. And how is that lovely garden of yours?' I said, steering her onto safer topics.

'Alfred, do you want a memorial card?' said the newspaper printer.

'What do you think – Ida, William, Elsie?'

'Aye,' said William. 'We'll order a card fit for a king.'

'He'd like one with musical notes around the edge,' said Elsie.

'Aye, that he would, darlin',' said William, pouring himself another drink.

If there was such a card, I'd find a way to involve Little Wind. Snatches of conversation intruded on my plans.

'All the bones in his hands were broken . . .'

'Is that right?

'Why do you think his coffin's closed?'

'Too shocking to see, they say.'

'What do you think of those Chinamen bringing their smelly sticks?'

'At least they'll mask the smell if the weather turns warm . . .'

'Who do you think killed him?'

That was the question I kept coming back to. His murderers needed stringing up and pelting with stones until there was nothing left but rope.

'A good fellow like Conran with not an enemy in the world,' said Peter Butel.

'Maybe it was a robbery gone wrong,' said James Healey.

'I tell you something for naught,' said Peter. 'I won't rest until his killers are found.'

'Same goes for the Macetown Apostles,' shouted Doc. 'We'll ride the hills once he's in the ground. But for now let's have another tune.'

Everyone took turns to sit by the coffin. When Ah Sip went in with Ah Lum and Little Wind, during the early hours of Saturday morning I heard Mrs Wallinshaw say to her husband, 'Look at those celestial heathens – walking around like they own the place.'

Mr Wallinshaw shook his spotty bald head and sucked the sweet-tasting meat off a chicken leg. I wanted to pull Sarah Wallinshaw's tongue out, throw it in the fire, listen to it sizzle and spit, watch it curl into a brittle black stump.

'They're Conran's friends,' I hissed in her ear.

She jumped and spluttered. 'Well, if you say so.'

Alfred placed his hand firmly on my arm, which is his way of saying it's not worth your worry. He was probably right, but Sarah

Wallinshaw has infuriated me ever since she turned her fourteen-year-old daughter onto the street last winter, having discovering she was with child. She never asked her if there'd been wrongdoings, which I suspect – maybe from within the family, since a brother had left town a month earlier.

I went through to the bedroom to calm myself: the woman had given me a dose of the vapours. Not a kind bone in her body; nor a decent thought in her brain.

She wasn't the only foolish woman at the wake. Margaret Kennington, being partially deaf, had once sought treatment from a travelling Canadian quack who'd sold her an ointment. He charged her so much her children went hungry that week. A week later Margaret claimed to be a medical miracle for she'd noticed what she thought was singing in her ear. 'More like a tea kettle left unattended,' said Alfred.

My apron hung over the bedpost. I picked it up to put it away and Conran's note fluttered from the pocket. How had it got from under my kitchen door to the cemetery? I suppressed a frightening thought and went back to the kitchen, where Alfred was plying Donald the piper with refreshments.

'Do you know "Whistle and I'll Come to You My Lad"? It was my father's favourite.' Father's dying words had been on my mind all day. 'We'll always be joined by love, Ida.'

I thought about Jack helping Conran to find stone for our barn. 'He tells me Orkney stories but I don't have any to share because I don't know where I came from,' Jack had said to me later. Guilt nipped at me, tart as lemon juice on an open wound. Hadn't I made up for Jack's loss by doting on him? Or had I confused his needs with my own?

As soon as the fiddler finished, Little Wind slipped outside. Once the conversation had resumed I went looking for her. She was in the barn, running a hand along stone Conran had laid. We didn't speak; just allowed the schist to soothe us.

A crowd gathered on Saturday afternoon. Everyone dressed in their Sunday best, boots and shoes polished, hats brushed and bonnets tidied. Sensible women had sown pleated bands, easily removed and cleaned independently, inside the hems of their dresses to protect them on the dusty walk to town. Ah Sip fussed over Little Wind, who looked pale and drawn.

Four men helped Alfred and William carry the coffin to our dray, which had been decorated with ivy and willow, tussock and schist – all things Conran liked. They positioned the narrow end to the back, which would have pleased Little Wind's spirits. William scattered pieces of Conran's fiddle among the tussock. Alfred clipped the reins and the horses moved forward just as the fiddler put bow to strings.

Little Wind stayed at the back of the procession, her right arm linked through Ah Sip's. Ah Lum was on her other side. We marched into town, beneath a butter-yellow sun, while the mountain Conran called the Sleeping Nun, and under which he'd soon rest, pulled us towards her. Four Chinese mourners dropped paper punched with small holes to ensure evil spirits would become confused and lose their way, leaving Conran to rest undisturbed.

The twelve Apostles formed a guard of honour at the town boundary: six either side of the road, mounted on horses with gleaming bridles. These hard but good men held their swords aloft as we passed by, bringing to mind the biblical blade that waits to fall upon the guilty. Was Conran's death my punishment for burning the letter?

Other settlers and sojourners joined us as we travelled down Buckingham Street, up the hill to Berkshire, past the church Conran helped build, and into Durham. The sorrow intensified palpably the closer we got to the cemetery.

'Conran would want to hear music, not weeping,' Elsie said, taking my arm.

She might have been rough around the edges but she had a good heart.

'Then let's make sure he does,' I said, straightening my back. I didn't want to let him or Little Wind down.

We walked up the cemetery rise to the strains of 'Sesig-bháis'. The minister waited at the gate. He took the time to greet each person in turn – mourners had come from as far away as Bannockburn. Dr Robertson stood alongside the hospital wardsman. I wondered who was looking after the patients, as Matron was still out of town.

When the tune ended the minister invited us to pray for salvation. His talk of glory in death irritated me. How could he say Conran was in a better place? Nothing could match living with Little Wind and Fang Yin in this beautiful valley.

As his coffin was lowered into the Arrow earth, far from Orkney, I imagined lying in one myself. A burial is a sober occasion. Mourners acknowledge the end of the dead person's journey and, at the same time, face their own mortality. Death stalks us like a hungry tiger. I've been in the company of many who have felt its hot breath. Some develop a glassy, fearful glint in their eyes. A trace of fear lodged in me and I slipped my hand into Alfred's.

After the service I threw two buff apricot blooms into the grave. William flung in a few schist chips, which sounded like musical notes as they landed on the coffin. Alfred and Peter each tossed in a handful of soil. Ah Lum and his friends collected pieces of Conran's broken fiddle from the dray and dropped them into the grave. Little Wind did the same with the bow, which I'd seen her pass across her lips earlier. Shortly afterwards the piper played 'Flowers of the Forest'.

People drifted back to town, calling at various hotels to celebrate their tenuous existences above ground. Little Wind came back to the farm on the pretext that she'd help tidy up. William and Elsie said they'd look in on Conran's cottage.

While Alfred tended the horses, I asked Little Wind if there was anything she wanted to take to Conran and Fang Yin's grave.

'One month pass die velly special time. Take money, food, incense.'

'Maybe we could do that together?'

'I like. Yes. Thank you, Ida. Now go to hut.'

'I'll get your trousers from the line.'

'Yes, must give back these to Jack.' She rubbed her hand down the side of the moleskins as though calling up their owner.

Where was he? Should I notify the constabulary? Dark thoughts swirled in me like bats. 'Little Wind, I'm so sorry for your loss.'

'You lose Con-Lan too. And now upset Jack not home. Too much sadness visit you.'

I'd just handed Little Wind her trousers when William and Elsie burst through the door.

'Who's having a baby?' Elsie said.

My heart skipped a beat. 'Why do you ask?'

'We found a cradle under a sack in Conran's cottage,' said Elsie.

'A grand one with an Orkney sayin' carved on its hood. So it wis a bairn he cared aboot,' said William, scratching his fair hair, which never lay flat, even when Elsie wet it and pressed it down with her palm.

'Do you know anything, Ida?' asked Elsie.

'Only that I'm weary and need my bed. Let's consider the possibilities later.'

Elsie, as if sensing a chink, said, 'Little Wind, are you going back to town?'

'My hut, I go now, thank you.'

'You can't go up the gorge at this time of night,' I said. 'Stay with us. You can sleep in Jack's bed. It doesn't look like he'll be back tonight.'

A startled look flashed across her face. How thoughtless; she couldn't sleep where she'd given birth to Fang Yin. 'Or on the couch in the back porch,' I added.

'And see the sky.'

'Yes.'

William reached out and shook Little Wind's hand.

'Thanks for helpin' Ida and Elsie with the food.'

'I do to give thanks to Con-Lan and show his value.'

Her strength and honesty spilled into the room. Like good-quality furniture wax she left behind a lustrous shine. It'll be all right, I thought. Whatever comes, we'll face it together.

SEVENTEEN

Two Women, Many Sorrows

Within days of his burial, people had divided themselves into two camps: those who grieved for Conran in peaceful ways and those who sought vengeance. A few, like Alfred and me, swung back and forth, ruminating on the possibilities. What about the surly husband we'd driven out of town – was he involved? Alfred gave his description to the magistrate. Or had Lok Yem taken umbrage to Conran crossing the river close to his claim? Settlers were often insulted by this unpredictable Mongolian miner. Most likely a gang of thieves thought Conran had gold on him.

Constabulary and volunteers, including Alfred, William and the Butel brothers, combed the hills for abandoned camps. The Apostles put the brakes on their drinking and rode over Roses Saddle to the Motatapu River and Lake Wanaka, questioning everyone they met. Ignoring household chores, I reviewed the weeks leading up to Conran's murder. How often had he visited Little Wind? Had someone seen them in a compromising position and assumed they were two men? Had they lain in wait for Conran, as my women friends had for the wife-beater?

Something had to have triggered such a vicious attack. Was it the note Conran wrote to me? Did it confirm what his attackers suspected? But how had they got hold of it? Had Conran dropped it? He wouldn't have been so careless. Who could have come across it after he'd pushed it under our door? Other than Alfred and me, there was only Jack. No, Jack wouldn't have bothered to pick it up. But what if he'd stumbled across a pack of thugs beating Conran? Maybe they murdered him too. Dear Lord, what a thought. Were those larrikins from Skippers involved? Maybe they'd been fooling around and things had turned nasty. Perhaps Jack had intervened. Was he hiding somewhere, scared we'd think badly of him?

My mood deteriorated as the days drifted by. I imagined Little Wind in her hut, overcome with grief. Ah Sip had accompanied her to Swipers, which made me wonder if he knew more than he'd let on. Thank goodness her mining partner, Soo Tie, was due back from Dunedin. Danger lurked in the hills.

Mrs Young's murder in Kyeburn was fresh in our minds. According to the attending doctor she'd fought like a vixen, dying with a handful of hair in her fist. Despite ransacking the place, the cowardly villains had missed forty sovereigns she'd hidden in her teapot. Not that money was any use to her now.

Had robbery been the reason for Conran's murder? I tossed ideas around like Jack's old knucklebones, which Conran had carved for him years ago while we picnicked late one afternoon by the river. 'Now you can play "in the stable",' he'd said to Jack.

'Sunny Boy's big and strong, Conran,' Jack had said proudly. 'Mr Scoles says he'll be the fastest galloper in the land. Soon I'll ride him all the way to England and find my real father.'

Oh, Jack. You've a fine substitute in Alfred. Best you never learn the truth. 'He was a passing fancy, Ida,' Mary, his mother, had confided, 'with a liking for quick encounters.'

Each night, murderers, miscreants and fiery executions populated my dreams. On one occasion I fought my way from a tangle of sheets, screaming, 'Jack's burning! Alfred, douse the fire!' But the flames were in me, and no amount of soothing from my husband could extinguish them.

After a particularly disturbing nightmare in which Little Wind said the murderers' names but I couldn't hear them, I rose before dawn. Careful not to disturb Alfred, who was snoring rhythmically, I set off to Swipers with fresh vegetables and fruit in my basket, having left a note on the kitchen table saying where I was going. For protection I strapped a small knife to my boot and cut a walking stick that could double as a weapon.

On the way I considered how best I could support Little Wind. She might need a poultice to relieve the tenderness if her milk was in. I also thought about Conran, who would have walked this path often. If only he'd told me sooner. I scanned the landscape for signs of Jack as well, thinking the searchers may have overlooked a clue.

No doubt my face was scarlet by the time I reached Little Wind's hut. It tends to flush with the slightest exertion. Alfred likes to watch me go pink when he teases me with bedtime suggestions, then red once he has me under his spell.

None of us is privy to the night-time activities of others, nor should we be, so I could only wonder about Conran and Little Wind's. Some say secrecy adds a certain mystique. If that's true, they paid a high price.

Little Wind was sitting on her doorstep staring at a collection of stones. Perhaps Conran had meant to give her the one that had fallen from his pocket.

'Ida,' she said, rising slowly, 'you come alone?'

I couldn't answer for I was out of breath.

'You need calming Chinese tea. Come with me inside. Mind head.'

Attractive Celadon tableware with its distinctive blue-green glaze lined a wooden shelf.

'Sit, please. You will be most done.'

I sank into one of two chairs and glanced around the room. How did she share this cramped space with Soo Tie?

'It was a hard climb,' I said, still panting. 'Yet you do it often.'

'Con-Lan say me nimble as mountain goat.'

'It's treacherous in parts.'

'Not know tet-see-us.'

'It means dangerous. You could easily fall.'

'I slip long time ago. You know Chinese saying? "He who save a man's life is accountable always to him". No? I wish I not be in flood and Con-Lan not save.'

'Perhaps that saying doesn't apply to women.'

Her eyes darkened until they resembled burnt toffee. She stopped swirling tea-leaves in the bottom of a bowl. 'Women not esteemed in China.'

'Why not, Little Wind?'

'We become wives and go to new family. Only sons stay with old family.'

'Do girls choose their husbands?'

'No. We are given away, sometimes to old men. Young gills not like stiff bones or wizened old thing but must obey husband. Not mally with love, Ida. Sad all life, like Gleat-auntie. I miss her.'

'Who else do you miss?'

'All family; I think most MaMa.'

'Did you tell Con-Lan about them?'

'Yes, so they not fade like clothes hung too long in sun. You speak of family with Al-Fed?'

'My family is dead. I'm the only one left, Little Wind.'

'Ah, this is why you love so much Jack and Al-Fed?'

'Yes, maybe, but I still have an emptiness that nothing seems to fill. It gets harder as I age. I'm getting melancholy.'

'What mel-ann-cly?'

'Means being out of sorts, like having sad feelings and thoughts.'

'Ah, I know this sickness. We talk. It might help.'

Between sips of tea we described the places we'd come from and the people we'd left behind or lost. When Little Wind told me about her sister's river babies, I asked if she'd had trouble with her milk.

'I make poultice and bind nan tight with sash.'

'If there's anything I can do . . .'

She reached for my hand. 'Enough you come, Ida.'

We sat together in companionable silence until the shadows lengthened.

'Little Wind, Alfred will worry if I'm not home soon. But I'll come back again if you want.'

'Thank you, yes, I like.'

'Will you visit us at the farm, too?'

She pressed her hands together. 'One month I go to Con-Lan and Fang Yin.'

'We said we'd visit together. Remember?'

'Yes. Make dumplings and take money. Incense, too. Now I walk with you until on path.'

I took her arm, and told her that warden Stratford, who conducted the inquest into Conran's death, was moving out of Otago to Ashburton. 'Poor man – he was too ill to attend his own farewell ceremony.'

'So he will not be in town when men who kill Con-Lan found?'

'No, but he wrote a full report, which he'll give to the next warden.'

If the decision-makers had any sense they'd appoint a tenacious character, for the trail was growing cold, although Alfred and William, along with Peter, John, Elias, Edsall and the Apostles, still rode out regularly. Looking for Jack was now as important as finding Conran's killers. Each night I prayed the two were not connected.

We said goodbye at the edge of the path, and Little Wind stood watching me until I reached the crest of the hill. Her vigil was humbling and unsettling. What if Jack had found Conran's note and unwittingly given it to the murderers as a joke? He could be a right Jack Pudding at times. The town councillors still grumble about the evening he tied walnut shells to a stray cat's tail and put the animal on the tin roof while a meeting was under way. The mayor called out the volunteer fire brigade to remove the cat because the councillors couldn't hear a word.

On another visit I asked Little Wind if she was nervous living by herself. 'Not mind if die. But MaMa be sad.'

'Have you written to her recently? Told her what has happened?'

'Only send money. Not want weigh down.'

'But she would send comfort to you in her letters. Tell you what everyone in the family was doing. You need a diversion at a time like this.'

William had thrown himself into making babies with Elsie. 'You can't transfer affections like dray wheels,' Alfred had said, but I'm hoping a baby will help. What would I do if Alfred was taken? I'd be fit for nothing.

Matron returned from Christchurch and invited me to take tea and talk about various cures and treatments but I was still distracted by Jack's absence, although I did help the wardsman tease out the mattress flock after the patients' beds became hard and knotty.

'Would you like to tell me more about you and Conran, Little Wind?'

She refilled our tea bowls. 'A fliend who listen is plecious.'

Words flowed until Little Wind's stories became mine. What if I'd raised the very person who had taken away her joy? Should I have whipped sense into Jack? Would that have made a difference?

A month to the day after Conran died, Little Wind arrived at the farm with baskets of food hanging from her shoulder pole. 'We take to Con-Lan and Fang Yin,' she said, showing me plump dumplings and succulent roast pork.

'I've cooked, too. What do you think of these chicken pieces? Ah Sip told me to place them in soy sauce and honey for two hours, then roast to make the skin crispy.'

'You good Chinese cook, Ida.'

But am I a good person?

At the graveside we filled three bowls with the best pieces of meat, and three small cups with whisky, and positioned them in front of the grave. In another bowl we placed dumplings and laid chopsticks across the rim. Then we lit three incense sticks each, which we held while making three bows with our hands together, before inserting the sticks in the earth. Trails of thin grey smoke drifted into the air as the incense burned, along with paper money, which we had also lit.

'Now tip whisky out, Ida.'

Although it seemed a waste, I did as she requested.

'What about the food, Little Wind?'

'We take home to eat.'

As dusk swallowed the sun we linked arms and made our way through town, ignoring those who whispered behind their hands.

'You'd be doing me and Alfred a favour if you stayed at the farm for a few days. We're in drooping spirits.'

'What spilit is this?'

'It's not one of those spirits; more a state of mind – glum and worried.'

She tipped her shoulders forward and made her mouth turn down at both corners. 'Same as mel-ann-cly?'

'Yes, that's it.'

'We all have sadness, Ida. Some show on outside but many hide inside. Maybe even men who kill Con-Lan have weeping shadows.'

I was in a sulk because Alfred had temporarily abandoned his search. To be fair, he'd inquired about unusual goings on and discovered who'd been in town before Conran was attacked, and he'd given the information to the warden, who had no doubt put it in his report. But I wanted him to search night and day.

'Life goes on, Ida, hard as it is,' Alfred had said that morning when I asked why he and William had arranged to inspect Scoles' new Clydesdale sire instead of scouring the hills. 'It doesn't mean we've forgotten him. We're still grieving.'

'Over ale, you mean.'

'Well, men tend to congregate in hotels and stables, women in parlours and kitchens.'

'Alfred Chynoweth, you get out and search for Jack and those murdering louts.'

He'd hurried off, muttering that his horse needed a brush, leaving me to weep onto the tablecloth. I'd wanted him to reassure me that Jack wasn't involved in Conran's death but I'd lost the ability to be direct.

I told Little Wind about my affliction. 'I'm talking in circles.'

'You becoming Chinese, Ida.'

We were still chatting when Alfred arrived home tipsy. 'That bay will need to please the ladies – he cost three hundred guineas.' He tossed his cap at a peg but missed. 'Now, speaking of ladies, what have you two been doing?' I nearly dropped dead with shock. Alfred's canny as me, often knowing more than he lets on, but he's usually careful with his tongue, even when full of ale. My foolish husband remained rooted to the spot as I took several deep breaths.

Eventually I said, 'Alfred Chynoweth, if you as much as think that in public you'll sleep in the pigsty for the rest of your days.'

'So you are a lady, Little Wind?'

I couldn't believe my ears. The man was piling straw into the sty. 'You don't have to answer, Little Wind. No doubt he's full of Scoles' ale.'

'Al-Fed is good man, Ida. Please not tell, Al-Fed. Or big tlouble may come.'

'According to William, big trouble's already arrived. They're saying Conran was an arse-shagger.'

'Alfred, mind your language!'

'What mean this us-shag-ee?'

Before Alfred could give an unsavoury description I said, 'A man who loves another man – like a husband, not a friend.'

'Ah, I know such man but not Con-Lan.'

Who did she mean? 'Conran loved Little Wind, Alfred. They wanted to marry. He was coming here to discuss his wedding plans when he was killed.'

Alfred sank into his chair and twirled both ends of his bushy moustache with his stocky fingers, a sure sign that he was agitated. 'How . . . what . . . when?'

I described Fang Yin's birth and death. Details emerged with such clarity that I felt as though I was back at the actual events. Alfred hugged me and nodded respectfully towards Little Wind, who displayed such dignity that my admiration for her trebled.

'Does William think Conran was a man-lover?' I inquired, exhausted from the effort of reliving the past.

'Elsie says he's ready to clout anyone who even insinuates the likelihood.'

So Elsie had heard the gossip. 'Why didn't she tell me? What's wrong with the woman?'

'Hush, Ida,' said Alfred, kissing my cheek. 'Maybe she thinks you've enough on your plate.'

Perhaps she did, and anyway Little Wind didn't need to see me neck deep in vapours. 'What can we do?'

'I not stay Little Wind. Become Ming Yuet, which is name MaMa give me. That stop evil tongues say Con-Lan is us-shag-ee.'

My head spun. Busybodies would feast on this development. What about those in the Chinese camp? How would they react?

What if they'd discovered Conran was seeing Little Wind and had him killed?

'Con-Lan has good name. Important it stay good,' added Little Wind.

'What do you think, Alfred?'

'Let's sleep on it, love. Little Wind, Ming Yuet – I don't know what to call you any more – stay with us tonight. We'll talk again in the morning.'

'William's blaming himself for not seeing it coming,' said Alfred, stroking my shoulder as we got into bed, for it aches in cold weather.

'Did he know something was up?'

'According to Elsie he'd been screaming in his sleep for Conran to stay out of the hills and he was drinking heavily again.'

William's need for whisky comes in bouts. The same appears true for Elias's melancholia. Give me a straightforward fracture any day.

Alfred lay on his back twisting the ends of his moustache. Honesty and openness are qualities he has in abundance; he'd be wondering where mine had gone. I hadn't felt comfortable keeping quiet about Fang Yin's birth but it wasn't my story to tell. I can be discreet when it's important. 'If only Jack would come home,' I said for the hundredth time.

'He'll appear in his own good time, Ida. He may be impulsive but he's not a fool. Now put your worries under the pillow and your arms around me.'

We always sleep like two S's on a page, even when cross; it's a comfort I can't envisage being without. But it didn't help that night.

I woke thinking about a woman who'd complained for years that something was crawling around in her stomach. To everyone's amazement one day she vomited up a lizard three inches long. Goodness knows why I dreamt about that. Perhaps it stemmed from having kept something unpalatable inside.

After I scrambled eggs for breakfast, Alfred, who ignores my 'Rules for Farmers', which I cut from a newspaper – 'Do not keep tribes of dogs or cats that eat more than they are worth in all their lifetimes' – went outside to give his animals a generous feed.

Ming Yuet and I had a second cup of tea. 'Do you want to tell William and Elsie?'

'Show, not tell,' said Ming Yuet.

When my eyebrows shot up, she said, 'Con-Lan do same to make me laugh.'

Every couple has their funny ways. I once overheard a timid woman call her husband 'my magnificent beastie' as she walked up to his sickbed, an endearment that extended his life by three weeks. No doubt about it. Alfred has different names for me, depending on the room we're in. His kitchen endearments are 'Pumpkin' and 'Peaches'.

'How will you show them?'

'Become woman. Sew new clothes. Fetch shoes Con-Lan buy me.'

'Will you mention Fang Yin?'

She nodded enthusiastically. Her determination alarmed me. Goldfields have their share of small-minded people, and Arrowtown was no different.

EIGHTEEN

Nothing's as It Seems

Ming Yuet walked with poise into the kitchen, wearing a long midnight-blue dress I'd sewed, and Conran's satin slippers on her feet. Her hair, no longer confined in a pigtail, flared down her back, gleaming like silk in the lamplight. The fringe she'd asked me to shape framed her face which, although solemn, looked soft and beautiful.

William placed his hands on his head. 'Mercy me, beuys o beuys.'

'Little Wind, Ming Yuet,' Alfred said, reaching for her hand. 'You're exceedingly pretty.'

William circled tentatively, his face constantly rearranging itself. 'How can this be?'

'I always thought something was strange about you,' Elsie said, taking William's arm, still not secure in their relationship, although he obviously adored her.

Throughout the evening William and Elsie plied Ming Yuet with questions, which she answered honestly.

'Ah can hardly believe it, Ming Yuet,' said William, 'even though ah'm lookin' at you with me ain eyes. But it explains a lot. Conran was actin' like a man in love.'

'Big love, William. Touch sky. We make Fang Yin.'

'Tell them how Conran saved you,' I said, thinking it might pay to backtrack and reveal things gradually.

'Who's Fang Yin?' said Elsie.

'Baby we make on mountain.'

Elsie's bosom bounced like jelly recently tipped from a mould. Her eyes dropped to Ming Yuet's flat stomach.

I helped Ming Yuet fill in the gaps, starting with the flood and ending with Conran's note.

'So the cradle we foond at Conran's wis for his ain wean?' William said in a voice thick with emotion.

'She was born the night following Conran's death,' I said. 'Here in this house.'

'Eyes blue as Orkney sky,' said Ming Yuet. 'Con-Lan holds beloved Fang Yin.'

'Losh seks, that's why his coffin wis shut?' William sat down with a thud. The rocker clanged against the wooden floor. 'We have to find the bastards, Alfred. We're talking two murders, not one.' Turning to Ming Yuet and lowering his voice, he said, 'You must be grievin' somethin' awful.'

'I want to find way to give Con-Lan back his good name. I not like people say he us-shag-ee. He love me and I woman.'

'We need to think carefully,' I said. 'Let's see what Ah Sip thinks.'

'Little Wind has small lor yo. When bend over in garden, make me excited. Man's lor yo not do same.'

'So you knew?'

He grinned and waggled his backside. 'Little Wind's business but we talk in camp.'

242

'You didn't say or do anything, though.'

'No one want make Soo Tie mad. He cut face in battle in China.'

'Did everyone think he was her husband?'

'Soo Tie no one's husband.'

Ming Yuet nodded thoughtfully when I told her about my conversation with Ah Sip.

'He has many baskets of kindness. I think he notice big belly but he not ask.'

'What about Soo Tie? Does he know? When does he return from Dunedin?' Alfred asked.

'Soo Tie tease me when Con-Lan play fiddle. Maybe he knows. He back soon.'

'Will you ask him to come to the farm?'

'I ask. Maybe he will come.'

'You might be safer in town for now,' I said. She turned pale as soap, so I added, 'Just until things settle.'

'You could stay in Conran's cottage,' said Alfred. 'Then you'd not be far from us.'

Elsie looked downcast. Perhaps she'd hoped to move in herself, seeing it was dry and well built, each stone well placed, unlike William's cottage down by the river, which he'd thrown together between drinks.

'Conran would want you kept safe,' I said.

'I stay in gully,' said Ming Yuet. 'Find gold. When Fang Yin old enough I go back to China.'

I puzzled over this statement, not realising until much later that she meant to take Fang Yin forward with her in time. They'd age together.

'Please, Ming Yuet, just until the fiends are caught.'

'Not beat woman.'

'They might harm you in other ways,' Alfred said firmly. 'Please do as Ida wants.'

'You wouldn't have to live there forever,' said Elsie.

'When will you let folk know you're a lass?' William said, flexing his chin, which he does when tense.

'Let's wait until Soo Tie gets back, then Ming Yuet will have his protection,' said Alfred. 'And don't forget about Ida and her women friends.'

'Where's your chain-cutter, Ida?' William teased.

'Under my pillow in case Alfred gets frisky.' What a thing to say! Sometimes – often, if I'm honest – my tongue operates faster than my brain. I can be a goose. Thankfully Ming Yuet didn't appear to understand.

After Soo Tie returned, and Ming Yuet told him everything, they came to the farm, along with William and Elsie. At first Soo Tie was wary, although he thanked us for caring for Ming Yuet, saying, 'Sad not in town when she need me.'

'You and me both,' said William. 'Conran wis a grand man.'

In the ensuing silence my thoughts swung from contemplating the most horrifying possibility to imagining Jack dead at the hands of the same ruffians. I masked my discomfort by concentrating on practical things. 'How soon can we move Ming Yuet into town? And how can we protect her once she's there?'

Soo Tie was first to offer a suggestion. 'Ming Yuet could come out like a cocoon.'

William put Elsie's shawl around his shoulders and sashayed around the parlour like a woman. His shenanigans broke the ice, and Soo Tie relaxed and accepted a cup of black tea. After much discussion we settled on a three-pronged approach using the oldest technique available – gossip.

The following evening Alfred and William announced the news in three hotels, while Elsie informed the dancing girls in another. At exactly the same moment I told half a dozen busybodies at a library meeting called to consider lowering the subscription fee in the hope that it would increase membership.

By two o'clock the next day Buckingham Street was crowded, as we'd put it about that Ming Yuet would appear that afternoon. Merchants had placed goods on tables outside their shops in an effort to encourage the distracted to spend.

'Scandal always draws a crowd,' said the draper, rubbing his hands together.

'We should be addressing the town's real disgrace,' said Mr Graham, 'not blathering on about some ill-considered liaison.'

He was referring to the forthcoming mayoralty race – between himself, Pritchard and Jenkins.

'There's a great deal of deception in this town. I was promised every vote and only got four. Why did they mislead me, Alfred?'

'Men will promise anything if you buy them drink. It's what they think away from temptation that finds its way into the ballot box. Try again next time but concentrate on the issues, not the voters' thirst.'

Alfred would have made a fine mayor, but when pressed he always threw his hands in the air and said, 'Ida, you, Jack and the farm keep me busy enough.'

I'd wanted him to be on the hospital committee as well, but he wouldn't bow to pressure, no matter how subtle.

'Ida, you'd pester me with your nursing notions and want them raised at meetings. I'd be caught between the woman I love and men I respect. Now stop feeding me chocolate pudding.'

He saw through me as though I was glass.

At three o'clock Ming Yuet walked down Buckingham Street with Ah Sip and me on one side, and Soo Tie and Elsie on the other, her head held high and that glorious hair shining brighter than a newfangled streetlamp. If only Conran could have seen her.

Initially people appeared dumbstruck, no doubt wondering how such a beautiful woman could have masqueraded for so long as a male miner. Then there were glimmers of recognition – and admiration. I hoped they felt ashamed for spreading such lies about Conran. A few nodded as though they understood. Others, including Mrs Wallinshaw, covered their children's faces, while taking a long gawp themselves. The Butel brothers brought their hands together and bowed to Ming Yuet. Many from the Chinese camp did the same. Three housewives clapped, which resulted in another saying, 'She'll never be the same as us, no matter what she wears.' But hadn't her use of 'she' already acknowledged Ming Yuet's womanhood?

'Step into her shoes,' said the new dressmaker. 'Imagine you're a slip of a girl who finds herself in a lawless mining town. How would you keep safe? Disguise yourself, of course. It was her only option!'

Sensing a sympathetic shift, I added, 'Instead of frowning upon her association with Conran we should admire her courage and quiet-living ways. Treat her with respect. She's lost her man and her child.'

'We should concentrate on finding Conran's killers,' said the miller, 'not debate his morals.'

'Who is free next Saturday to search the gullies?' said William. A sea of hands went up, including those of ten Chinese.

Encouraged by this show of support, I said, 'Ming Yuet's shifting from the gully into Conran's cottage on Wednesday. I'd be grateful for assistance in this matter as well.'

Helen and Mrs Gruber stepped forward, along with four dancing girls and the new dressmaker. Seems men are happy to ride into gullies with a lynch rope, but not lug a few sticks of furniture. 'My gratitude to those strong enough to carry a bunk on their back,' I said in my haughtiest voice, which caused Alfred to have a coughing fit. Edsall fetched an elixir to soothe the irritation. 'I should pour it on you,' Alfred whispered in my ear. Perhaps I was a bit strong, but once I'm riled there's no stopping me.

The dressmaker came over to Ming Yuet and said, 'I'll sew you a set of clothes free of charge,' and a dancing girl, vermillion rouge up to her eyebrows, said, 'If you need work come down to the Ballart. You'd be a hit.'

'Ming Yuet's a miner not a dancer. And she's a translator,' I said.

'Thank you to be kind and make suggestions,' Ming Yuet said, bowing graciously to each person in turn.

Two small boys eating candy mimicked her. Their parents quietly admonished them and smiled apologetically at Ming Yuet.

Maybe we could live harmoniously in this town.

Ming Yuet and Soo Tie stayed with Ah Sip that night, but came out to the farm the next day. We'd just taken our seats around the kitchen table when William rushed in.

'There's trouble in toon – a new group callin' themsels the Moral Crusaders are harassin' some o the ones who said they'd help Ming Yuet.'

Elsie followed, beads of sweat dotting her freckled forehead. 'Someone broke that new dressmaker's parlour window. And Nettie Witherington screamed obscenities at me in the baker's.'

'I solly, Elsie,' said Ming Yuet, her hands trembling like two frightened birds.

I pulled up chairs for William and Elsie. 'It'll pass. Give people time. It's come as a shock.'

'I suppose so,' said Elsie, helping herself to a potato scone.

I passed her the butter-dish. 'Let's concentrate on finding the killers.'

'Do you think Jack knows anything? Where is he?' William asked, looking directly at Alfred, who shook his head and opened his hands like a preacher.

That night I had another nightmare. This time Jack was covered in blood. I tried to tell Alfred but the words stuck to the roof of my mouth.

On Wednesday half of those who'd originally volunteered accompanied me along the bridle path to collect Ming Yuet's possessions, which we carried to Conran's cottage. Ming Yuet pressed her hand against the oblong window set in the door as though it was Conran's skin. Alfred stroked my cheek. Elsie sighed, while William took a sip from the glass jar he kept in his jacket pocket.

Alfred had lit the fire earlier, and I'd lined the bench with preserves and put a roast fowl in the meat safe, but the place felt somehow cold and empty. Conran's work cap hung from a peg by the door and his tin mug dangled on a hook in the lean-to-kitchen. A small cross-stitch of Stromness made by his mother was nailed to the wall. He'd never touch these things again.

Ming Yuet knelt beside the cradle, saying, 'Be-nui be-nu.' Then she pointed to a collection of stones on the mantelpiece. 'Con-Lan collect to give me.'

'We could take them to the cairn you made for your brother.'

'Thank you, Ida. I like.'

After Ming Yuet had arranged her possessions we sat and drank tea, sadness leaching from us like lime-wash off a building.

In the days after Ming Yuet moved into Conran's cottage, people who had owed him money slipped envelopes under her door. One contained three pounds and a note that said: 'For repairs to stable'. Another had five pounds and six shillings enclosed for 'a well-built wall'. A trout wrapped in newspaper was left on the wood-box with a note that read: 'Shown how to tickle by Wong Yet Song'. A week later a fine cut of pork appeared in a basket with the word 'Sorry' written on a scrap of paper.

Not everyone was as well meaning, though. On his way home one evening from the New Orleans, William found three men rifling through goods on Ming Yuet's doorstep.

Then we heard that the butcher, who turned out to be leader of the Moral Crusaders, had organised a public meeting to have Ming Yuet run out of town. William, Alfred and other friends armed themselves with batons and took turns patrolling the street at night. I marched into the butcher's and, amid legs of fatty mutton and sawdust-filled sausages, berated him in language not used by me before or since. That afternoon he delivered a letter to the chairman of the hospital trustees stating that in his opinion I should never again be employed by the institution. The chairman promised to discuss the matter at the next monthly meeting.

These vile goings on and my growing unease over Jack's disappearance meant that I was hardly sleeping. During a particularly bad night Alfred gathered me close. 'Will you tell what's going on in that head of yours?'

'It's too dreadful to utter. I'm ashamed to even think it.'

'Maybe we're troubled by the same thought, Ida.'

I reached over and lit the lamp on our bedside table. 'Jack?'

'We should declare him missing,' Alfred said. 'Have the constabulary search for him.'

'What if he was involved? How could we face Ming Yuet?'

'How could we not?'

I developed a headache that required rest and darkness for days. Alfred made pots of tea and sat on the edge of the bed, stroking my hair.

'What could I have done differently? Did I suffocate Jack with love? Is such a thing possible? Maybe I gave him everything I'd stored up for the children we never had and it was too much – he couldn't breathe under the weight. Alfred, is it my fault that he's run off – or worse?'

'You did your best. We both did, Ida.'

We reported Jack's disappearance, both dreading where it might lead. I wondered how to tell Ming Yuet, who I came across rolling a rock to Conran and Fang Yin's grave. William carved their names on it, along with a series of Chinese characters Ming Yuet wrote down for him. Then one night the Crusaders tarred a rooster, hung a sign around its neck – 'Crowing for John' – and tied it to Ming Yuet's porch.

Alfred and the others increased their patrols. William frequently guarded Conran and Fang Yin's grave, playing Orcadian laments on his mouth organ. Alfred lost weight. My interest in health matters diminished. Even Professor Huxley's claims – reported in the *Arrow Observer* – that an adult-sized heart should beat seventy-five times a minute, and that skin should throw off eighteen ounces of water, three hundred grams of solid matter and four hundred grams of carbonic acid every twenty-four hours, failed to rekindle my interest. I was pleased, however, that the hospital trustees found no reason among the butcher's ramblings to prevent me from returning to work at the institution.

Over the next month scandal sheets were pasted to buildings around town, depicting Conran and Ming Yuet participating in lewd acts. Several of us removed as many as possible but a few found their way to Conran's cottage, upsetting Ming Yuet.

Alfred employed various tactics to get her smiling again, including reading out stories from the papers. A Brooklyn woman sued a saloon-keeper for twenty-five thousand pounds for causing her husband to become a habitual drinker. 'Woe betides the Arrow hoteliers when this gets out!' Alfred said. 'Elsie could become the richest woman in town!'

Ming Yuet shook her head. 'Money not what Elsie want. She happy if William stop dlink and make baby.'

Alfred tried to cheer me up by buying me a cedar chiffonier, which I'd coveted for ages, from the Letchers when they left town. When that didn't lift the gloom he continued searching the newspapers for tantalising tales. 'Ida, listen to this one. A young woman from Chicago was asked by the preacher if she'd love, honour and obey her husband to be. She said, "Yes, if he does what he promises, financially." I didn't know you had a sister in America, Ida!'

All he got for his trouble was silence. I was desperate about Jack and there was no cajoling me. So when Alfred and William were asked to accompany the constabulary through to the West Coast after a tip-off, I urged them to go, hoping they'd capture the real culprits and prove Jack's innocence.

They were away for three weeks and returned in a solemn state. Seems the bunch of lads they'd heard about had gone to ground in the dense Coast bush. I imagined Jack living like his Australian hero, Ned Kelly, trapping, fishing and robbing.

We didn't go to the New Year ball – I hadn't the stamina or inclination. My nursing scrapbook was abandoned, despite Ah Sip's attempts to interest me in new plants. I wanted to throw myself in the fire the way I had Jack's letter. Shame overwhelmed me until I couldn't bear it any longer. I finally told Alfred what I'd burnt all those years ago.

His face dropped like a plate from the dresser, ending chipped and cracked on his chest.

'You did what? Ida!'

'I couldn't bear to lose him. But I have now, haven't I?'

'When did this happen?'

'Jack was three years old.'

Alfred took his cap off the peg, gave me a cold look and went outside. All the care I'd given others in the community would mean nothing if I didn't have my husband's respect.

It was dark by the time Alfred came back. Without a word or so much as a glance in my direction he ate a slice of bread with cheese and pickle, then retired to the bedroom. I sat at the kitchen table picking at the cuff on my dress until it frayed.

At dawn I was still sitting there when Alfred came out in his nightshirt and put a hand on my shoulder. 'I don't know how we'll get through this, Ida, but I'd like to try. It's been a shock, coming on the heels of Ming Yuet and the baby. I wonder if I know you at all.'

'I'm ashamed, Alfred. What must you think?'

'Was there a postmark?'

'Yes, Lincoln, but no return address on the envelope.'

He went over to the dresser and rummaged through papers. 'I wrote to a farm equipment firm in Lincoln years ago, asking for a catalogue. Was it a bulky letter?'

I nodded. 'I thought a ship's ticket was enclosed.'

'You nelly – it was probably the catalogue.'

Maybe, but this explanation didn't erase my guilt. I'd let Alfred and Jack down, all because I hadn't wanted my life to change. I'd been selfish and strong-willed, refusing to recognise that their needs might be different from mine.

I moped around the house for months. Even Ming Yuet's forgiving words, when I relayed my fears to her about Jack, could not lift my gloom.

'No blame comes to you,' she said, linking her arm through mine as we walked along the riverbank. 'I think lucky to have you as fliend.'

Her goodness only made me feel worse, but our walks distracted me, giving me an opportunity to learn how she'd disguised herself for so long.

'Was it difficult to behave like a man?'

'At beginning, yes, but I soon live in two skins. Man on top while woman hide below. When Soo Tie visit his friend in Dunedin I touch my nan to remember who I was, but still velly difficult to be a woman when I meet Con-Lan.'

'Because that side had been concealed for years?'

'Yes, and I know nothing of love between man and woman. So not know how to behave. When feelings come I want to flee. But leg and chest stop me. Instead I listen to Con-Lan's music and notice his kind ways. Soon I open love wings and we fly.'

'And now that he's gone?'

'He not gone flom mind. Always I keep him and Fang Yin close.'

'You are a better woman than me, Ming Yuet.'

'Not believe is so. We alike in many ways on inside, Ida, only unlike outside.'

NINETEEN

We Share the Same Stars

Lee Tow was convicted of Mrs Young's murder and Lee Guy received an acquittal. However, despite commendable efforts by the constabulary and ongoing searches, no progress was made in regard to Conran's murder. So I was surprised when the sergeant rode up on a coal-black gelding early one Saturday morning and asked to speak with my husband.

'He's taken our farm workers to the Cromwell races. They're celebrating a good harvest.' Few will come back with winnings, I felt like adding. Hangovers were far likelier.

'I'll call back later,' said the sergeant, scraping one dusty boot against the other, not a flicker of interest in my female form showing in his pale grey eyes, whereas most men give me admiring looks. I could have exploded like a furnace, sending morsels of ripe flesh around the room and he'd not have blinked. 'Happier chasing criminals than bustles,' Alfred had said after meeting him the first time.

A direct approach was needed. 'You have news?'

'I do,' he said, quivering with excitement. 'Three young ruffians are thought to have boarded a ship bound for Melbourne a week ago. One had straight black hair and green eyes so could have been your boy; another lad was described as powerfully built, quick with his fists and shabbily dressed, while the third had abundant sideburns, a sharp nose and whiny voice. Seems they robbed a coach on the coast road to Greymouth just hours before sailing – a nasty business by all accounts. The beefy one knocked around an elderly gentleman who tried to protect a female traveller. Their details have been cabled through to Melbourne but they're unlikely to wait on the dock to be arrested.'

Jack's interest in the Ned Kelly gang could have influenced his travel plans. 'Yes, he might go to Australia.'

'The constabulary in Victoria is on the lookout. We are, too, in case they didn't board that ship after all. We'd really like to know if you hear from your lad.'

What if Jack wasn't involved? Or was? How could I protect him from the gallows?

'I hope you'll question everyone who was in the district at the time.'

'That's my intention. But ruffians, like miners, move on. It's hard to catch those who don't want to be found.'

'Surely a man with your skills could locate a wayward boy.'

He puffed out a well-developed chest. 'Either I'll catch him or his conscience will.'

'Jack's not bad, just adventurous. Boys are, aren't they? He's probably working somewhere in a stable.'

Unimpressed by my suggestion, the sergeant moved swiftly to the door. A blade of burnished metal sliced the heavy air. 'Give my regards to your husband.'

'Pass mine on to those in charge.' This parsimonious comment was an unnecessary reminder that he was only a minor cog in the wheel of justice but it made me feel better for a brief moment. 'Alfred will be sorry to have missed you.'

'Thank you for the tea, Mrs Chynoweth.'

He watered his horse at the trough and galloped off without a backward glance. Dust swirled along the fenceline. I picked up a soft broom and flicked it across the window ledges, hoping physical work might erase my unease. Why had Jack glamorised the Kelly gang? After reading a newspaper story about Kelly harassing a young couple on the outskirts of a small Australian town he'd said, with misplaced admiration, 'He's never afraid. Everyone's in awe of him.'

No doubt Kelly's family have questioned their son's behaviour too. Jack's temper tantrums could last for weeks: I never worked out what was behind them. Do infants have memories? Was I wrong to take Jack to his mother's burial service?

All this stress and anxiety had physical ramifications.

'You're fading away, love,' said Alfred, lifting my nightdress one evening.

I thought time would help, having informed others often enough about its healing ability. But it was Ming Yuet's company that eventually saved me.

We fell into a pattern, without ever discussing it. Every Thursday afternoon we met on the corner of Kent and Hereford Streets and walked arm in arm around town, observing simple things such as a tree in bud or a freshly painted gate. We always called by the cemetery on the way home, to place flowers or greenery on Fang Yin and Conran's grave.

On one such visit I asked Ming Yuet about a practice that had puzzled me since I read about it in a newspaper article. 'You know how the Chinese exhume graves? Some Arrowites think opening graves brings disease, which contaminates water supplies. I don't hold such a view but I do wonder why you dig up the bones.'

'Cheong Shing Tong, the Splendid Goodness Society, want bones to go home so descendants can pay homage. They exhume, wash each bone with thoughtfulness, bind in calico and place in special lead-lined coffin. Also they pay cost of shipment back to China. No good if bones not placed in own soil.'

'Is it part of the journey to Eternal Life?'

'Yes, most important go back to own land to begin next stage.'

'I'll probably be buried here, far from Arleigh. We only send memorial cards back. I also heard you like to be buried in dry land, on a slope, with a view of flowing water.'

'You know many Chinese customs, Ida. Con-Lan and Fang Yin have a good site.'

After visiting their grave we bought a newspaper and went back to Conran's cottage, where we read stories to each other and drank tea. Printed words often felt safer than our own.

'Ida, the new Tem-pe-lance Hotel plans to sell meals for one shilling and sixpence.'

'Ming Yuet, a public auction of clothing and jewellery will be held next Saturday.'

As we became easier in each other's company we told stories about our childhoods.

'On day of the Boat Festival, I helped MaMa make jong.'

'Those balls of sticky rice filled with salted pork and wrapped in bamboo leaves that Ah Sip makes?'

'Yes, his jong is good as MaMa's.'

'My mother taught me how to embroider.'

'What em-boud-a?'

Colour drained from Ming Yuet's face as I explained.

'I do on Con-Lan's shilt.' She traced six letters in the air with her finger. His name hung in front of us.

My friendship with Ming Yuet deepened. We anticipated which days proved difficult for each other and what could bring comfort. Sometimes it was a walk, on others, silent companionship as we worked side by side in the garden or kitchen.

'Don't forget your old friends, Ida,' Alfred cautioned, which was sound advice, but while they discussed new curtains or irons or ranges, I saw burnt letters and dead babies and bloodied fists. My mind was as restless as jar of fleas.

The three boys managed to evade the greeting party waiting for them on the Melbourne dock. Alfred considered crossing the Tasman but well-meaning friends and officials advised him to leave it to the Australian constabulary, which we prayed might be more successful than ours.

I kept Jack's bedroom tidy, hoping I might wake one morning to find him tucked under the quilt I'd sewed when we moved him from his cradle into a full-length bed. Sometimes I buried my face in the soft material to recall his smell. Chores were done with one ear to the ground, as though the sound of his footsteps might reach me long before he did.

Months stretched into years. The *Arrow Observer* was replaced by the *Lake County Press* in 1882. A fire broke out the same year at the tailor's in Buckingham Street. A year later I delivered Elsie and William's twins boys. Our dear friend Elias took his own life, leaving Helen to run their blacksmith business and care for their baby. When Edsall also passed on, his wife managed their shop, causing those who propped up hotels bars to comment that widows were taking over the town. The nice dressmaker married a local bootmaker – 'a match made in haberdashery heaven,' said Elsie. These good women sometimes joined me and Ming Yuet for afternoon tea. Our conversations ranged from cures for insomnia to the state of the British Empire to a planned two-day excursion to Lake Wanaka. We rarely mentioned Jack. It was as though he'd died along with Conran.

Then Ming Yuet received a letter written on behalf of Lem Yok. She didn't mention it straight away, knowing the contents would distress me. But after I'd asked on several occasions why she had dark smudges under her eyes, she said, 'Ida, do you want to know what Lem Yok saw on night Con-Lan die?'

Although dreading what might be revealed, I braced myself and said, 'I'm ready.'

Ming Yuet, like many in camp, I know for long time you not man. But although I lonely in Arrowtown I not chase you since I have good wife in China. I did not want to be away from her even one night but we very poor so I come to New Gold Hills where my mind was not at rest. I drink to take away pain.

Many nights I walk off sorrow. See Orkneyman creep like thief through town. Twice I follow him. When he goes to your hut I worry my wife might also receive night visitors. Such thoughts torment me. I prowl like dog. Howl at the moon.

One night I drink and fall down in grass near cemetery. Only wake when hear voices laughing about note Chynoweth boy stole. One say, 'We'll stop him consorting with a Chink.' I not like his intention but do nothing when Orkneyman pass by. I let him walk into trap. Chynoweth boy sit on fence but other two knock fiddler to ground and kick like mule. I cover my eyes when they stamp on his hands, but open again when fat one from Skippers grab Orkneyman's beard and bash head against cemetery wall. Boy on wall say, 'That will teach you for mixing with Mongolian filth,' but his voice not sound angry. It shake like wind.

I feel bad for man on ground. He was always polite when cross river by my claim. But what could I do? Boys might kill me too. After they run away I go to Orkneyman and apologise for not helping. His whispered words still come in dreams: 'He's no a bad one.' Maybe he mean boy on fence, who ran away sniffing. Then Orkneyman speak of moon eyes swimming with love and fishing nets wide enough to cover wild seas.

When I hear you carry child and I nearly tell authorities what I see so boys can be punished, but then I worry that I would be arrested like Lee Yow and never see my wife again. I am big coward. Maybe you understand. Sorry for your misfortune. I had daughter this year. I cannot look at her without thinking of yours. If only I had not been a foolish man. Please take forgiveness into your heart.

Lom Yek

A waterfall of emotions washed over me. How could Jack have sat on the fence and watched? Did he somehow justify his behaviour the way I had mine after burning that letter? How would Alfred react? What could I say to Ming Yuet?

She read my thoughts.

'Ida, nothing can give me Con-Lan and Fang Yin back. But Jack is still alive. He will come home one day. Soon I send note to Lem Yok and also I have one to give Jack. I not want his life always spoiled. When Jack young he sweet like Day-Day.'

'Your youngest brother will be grown up now.'

'Yes, I miss his life, like you miss Jack. Come, Ida, let's walk off sadness.'

That summer, even though my sleep patterns remained erratic, and Alfred's hair turned snow-white, I regained my interest in medical matters after Matron persuaded me to start back at the hospital on the pretext that another typhoid outbreak was imminent. 'Pays to ensure typhoid patients rest the bowel, Ida, so only beef tea or milk. Solids would perforate ulcers in the region and cause a hamorrhage. Adequate sleep is essential, too.' Her views matched those currently published in medical articles, which I once again devoured in great quantities.

I spent my days telling patients amusing tales and tempting those who were low with bowls of broth. If a mother fretted, I visited her children and returned with news. I wasn't above embellishing the truth if I thought it would aid her recovery.

The following autumn Matron asked if I knew anyone who could take over the hospital laundry, as her current woman was leaving the district. I recommended Ming Yuet, who had suffered financial hardship after Su Sing left the district, although she still mined out at Swipers. She'd saved thirty pounds to send to her mother, this time entrusting it to a respected Chinese friend to whom she paid ten per cent commission. Three trustees argued that Ming Yuet would spread disease and patients would end up with oriental bugs on their sheets, but Matron and the others stood firm and Ming Yuet got the job.

Fear's a queer thing. I worried about Jack with good reason, whereas those who feared Ming Yuet did so out of ignorance. If only I'd disciplined Jack firmly, but I'd been scared he'd stop loving me. Sometimes in bed, after Alfred had fallen asleep, one arm thrown across his face as though shielding it from night terrors, I played out what I could have said.

'Jack, when you call Ah Sip a Chink or a Chow or a heathen it makes him feel inferior.'

I swear I heard him reply, 'Like I felt when children at school said I was a pack-saddler's son.' It was a term given to those sired by men who used their packsaddle for a pillow and left before morning. Even though it was my own thought, it felt like a breakthrough. I woke Alfred.

'You could be right, Ida. Jack did what was done to him.'

'He was bullied . . .'

'Remember how he came home from school with bruises?'

'He said they were from games. Do you think it was because I mollycoddled him?'

'I've been thinking about something else.'

'What, Alfred?'

'Remember that afternoon when Jack was nine or ten and he was late home? Bad weather was forecast and we were busy cutting hay. We lost track of time.'

'Yes.' I folded my pillow in half and leant on my elbow.

'Jack ran into the field screaming that a Chinaman walking by the farm gate had waggled at him and yelled, "Come see, little boy," and we laughed, told him not to be a baby and went on working.'

'Go on.'

'He got really angry after that. What if it wasn't a fist but something else?'

'Oh, dear God, you don't think ...'

'No. But maybe just the sight of it made him wary of all Chinese.'

'That would explain why he started called them names. His lack of respect had to come from somewhere. We certainly didn't teach him to behave like that. But why do you think he became involved with Conran's attackers?'

'He probably got caught up in the moment, felt important when he found the note.'

'He is impulsive.'

'What's your worst fear, Ida?'

'That he's somewhere in Australia sobbing his heart out.'

'Maybe he's making something of himself.'

'What if we never see him again or hear his side of the story?'

'Until we know his whereabouts we can't help him. But we can contribute to the prosperity of this town.'

'You're finally going to run for mayor?'

'Oh, Ida, I have no intention of standing for public office and arguing over how many streetlamps to purchase. Now let's get up and you can help me feed the animals.'

When Ah Sip became naturalised and purchased a freehold property for fifty pounds to establish a market garden we held a party at the farm. Ah Sip convinced Ming Yuet to join us, saying, 'I tell her no hanky panky, just listen to music and be with friends.'

'That Ah Sip could convince horses to fly,' said William with a chuckle.

'But what will I wear?' said Elsie. 'I don't suit those dull imported costumes or silk skirts. Buxom women need something brighter and less fussy.'

'A London physician recently said that only one fashionably dressed woman in five hundred can draw a full breath with her clothes on,' I said. 'Perhaps we should take his study into account when making our party dresses.'

'Alfred, what do you think of the pains our ladies go through?' said William, swirling around as though he wore a fancy dress.

Ming Yuet laughed, along with Elsie and me, but our lighthearted mood didn't last. A week later she received a letter from China saying her father and eldest brother had gone missing on the river. 'MaMa does not say, but she needs me, Ida. And I want to feel MaMa's skin, talk as women, tell Chinese stolies, smell peach blossom. Day-Day has wife now. I will love his babies like good auntie. Give them what I did not give him. It is time to buy coach and boat tickets. Be dutiful. Do not look sad, Ida. I am happy. China is my home. Too long I not walk on Pearl River delta. But I will miss you.'

'What about Conran and Fang Yin? You can't leave them. Oh, you wouldn't exhume her bones, would you?'

'Fang Yin has fifteen autumns, same age as me when I come to New Gold Hills. She and Con-Lan will have made good bones. Nice shade of golden yellow. But, no, I not take them. Con-Lan want to stay in this land. It is his home. And he needs Fang Yin always to be with him. Benevolence extends beyond this life.'

'Sometime I wonder how you can bear to be in my company. I raised Jack.'

'One day he will look back on his foolishness and lament. His high opinion of you and Al-Fed will again come to mind. He will want to see you both.'

'How can you be so charitable?'

'We give what we hope will come to self.'

'No wonder Conran loved you. He'd be so proud, Ming Yuet. If only things could have been different.'

She took my hands in hers, looked directly into my brimming eyes and said, 'I find love and fliendship in this place, so have much happiness to pack. Be gentle with self, Ida,' then before I could speak again she disappeared through the door of Conran's cottage. Perhaps it didn't matter, because everything worthwhile had already been said.

Epilogue

My sojourn is almost over. All the stories have been told, although this does not mean they cannot be retold. Other people may give different accounts or include aspects not considered worthy in this telling. Such is the nature of story.

Shortly I will travel by coach to Dunedin to say goodbye to Soo Tie and Lai Jau before I sail home to China. Ah Sip plans to stay in Arrowtown. Ah Lum also wants to remain.

Ida will visit Fang Yin and Con-Lan each Thursday. She still carries great sorrow but Jack will return. Al-Fed will advertise in Australian papers and one day he will receive news.

I pray that Con-Lan and Fang Yin will listen with goodwill if Jack visits their fung mu. I wish him an honourable future. Not one plagued by past foolishness, but one ripe with possibilities.

Tomorrow Elsie, William, their twin boys and youngest son move into Con-Lan's cottage. Soon there will another child, maybe a daughter who will sleep in Fang Yin's cradle and bring them great joy.

Although later today I must leave Fang Yin, my beautiful fragrant melody, each night I will ask a star to shine upon her. And every morning a silver flash will appear in the river below this well-positioned site.

Today I also give thanks for Con-Lan's music, which will travel with me through my years. William started a fund so I could return to Pong Woo with much wealth, but I asked that a music society be set up instead. Al-Fed has agreed to hire musicians from all denominations to play for Con-Lan each Saturday. When their music floats like whispers into town, people might stop what they are doing, remember the troubled times, and vow to do better. That is my hope for this town and its settlers.

I sit now content at Con-Lan and Fang Yin's fung mu. Even though my time with them was brief, it still holds great significance. Love cannot be weighed on scales like gold. Nor can it be measured against what others share. Each love has its own colour and shape and size. Ours will forever be in harmony.

And always Con-Lan and Fang Yin will rest in my heart, and each night when the mynah bird opens her wings, I will come to them on the wind.

ACKNOWLEDGEMENTS

Various people assisted me during the writing of this novel, generously providing time, knowledge and expertise. In particular, I owe grateful thanks to: Eva Wong Ng who checked Chinese aspects; Jim Ng for his meticulously researched volumes entitled *Windows to a Chinese Past*; Neville Ritchie for his informative PhD thesis, 'Archaeology and History of the Chinese in Southern New Zealand during the 19th Century: A Study of Acculturation, Adaptation and Change'; Ray Clarkson, who shared his wealth of historical knowledge about Arrowtown and the surrounding district; Pamela Wood and Jude Roddick for verifying medical practices of the era; ex-Orkney sojourner Maggie Atkinson for introducing me to the works of Orcadian poets and writers such as George Mackay Brown; and Iain Clark, who, along with his daughter Lauren and colleague Sheena, attended to Orcadian nuances, language and characteristics. I would also like to thank the following Orkney residents: Lesley Macleod, Jean Leonard, Innes Kennedy, Harvey Johnston, Donna

Heddle and Steven Heddle, who kindly responded to my emails and sent me helpful information.

Several friends, including those in my Wednesday night group, commented on early drafts and made insightful suggestions for which I am truly indebted. Thanks also to Noel, who supported me in numerous ways during the writing process.

Throughout my life Alterio and Ferns family members have accompanied me on walks and climbs in the Arrow area, including numerous tramps to Macetown and beyond. These shared experiences enhanced my appreciation of the landscape and contributed to my affection for the area. Thanks to everyone, especially to my father, John, who took me on my first trip up the gorge, and to my brother Mike, who came on my last climb over Big Hill. Additional thanks go to my mother, Lorna, who discovered which roses grew in Arrowtown during the period I wrote about, to my sister Denise, for helping me check the proofs, and to my children – Nic, Jo and Kate, who continue to enrich my understanding of love and companionship.

I have also enjoyed a long friendship with Verona Cournane, who once owned a stone cottage in Arrowtown built by two Orcadian brothers. *Ribbons of Grace* was started in this cottage in 1999 and completed in Verona's new home, also in Arrowtown, in 2006. Thanks, Verona.

My heartfelt thanks also go to the Penguin Books team for believing in this novel from the outset. I particularly want to acknowledge the generous support given to me by Geoff Walker and Rebecca Lal. Rachel Scott deserves a special mention, too. Her thoughtful and astute editorial comments provided me with yet another lens through which to view my work and to revise sections as a consequence. Thanks also to Sara Bellamy for her superb cover design, and to Jeremy Sherlock, who managed the final publication stages.

Parts of this book were written with the help of a Creative New Zealand grant. I am extremely grateful for this assistance, as I am to past and current Lakes District Museum staff, who attended to my requests for archival documents and audio material. Hocken Library staff also helped with my research and sourced photographs for various presentations, particularly in relation to the Arrow District Hospital. Thank you for your excellent service.

To aid this novel's historical authenticity I have given several original settlers and sojourners cameo roles. Primary characters, however, such as Ming Yuet, Conran and Ida, are entirely fictitious. In various storylines I have blended historical evidence with historical imagination, a concept currently being researched by nurse historian Pamela Wood who, along with Lynne Cunningham and John Stephenson, Kay, Chris, Woody and Duncan Stables, Sally Brown and Phil Race, and Annie and Chris Price, accompanied me on parts of an unforgettable personal journey while I was overseas in 2006. Finally, I am immensely grateful to Dan Nguyen, who also played a significant role during this period. Lifelong thanks to you all.

Maxine Alterio
Arrowtown, 2007